Neil Olson is the author of *The Icon*, a novel of art theft and family intrigue, and the play *Dealers*. He lives in New York City with his wife and works in the publishing industry.

The Black Painting

Neil Olson

ONE PLACE. MANY STORIES

This novel is entirely a work of fiction. The names, characters
and incidents portrayed in it are the work of the author's
imagination. Any resemblance to actual persons, living or
dead, events or localities is entirely coincidental.

HQ
An imprint of HarperCollins*Publishers* Ltd
1 London Bridge Street
London SE1 9GF

This paperback edition 2018

1

First published in Great Britain by
HQ, an imprint of HarperCollins*Publishers* Ltd 2018

Copyright © Neil Olson 2018

Neil Olson asserts the moral right to be
identified as the author of this work.
A catalogue record for this book is
available from the British Library.

ISBN: 978-1-84845-713-3

MIX
Paper from
responsible sources
FSC˚ C007454

This book is produced from independently certified FSC™ paper
to ensure responsible forest management.

For more information visit: www.harpercollins.co.uk/green

Printed and bound by CPI Group (UK) Ltd, Croydon, CR0 4YY

All rights reserved. No part of this publication may be reproduced,
stored in a retrieval system, or transmitted, in any form or by any means,
electronic, mechanical, photocopying, recording or otherwise,
without the prior permission of the publishers.

This book is sold subject to the condition that it shall not, by way of trade
or otherwise, be lent, re-sold, hired out or otherwise circulated without
the publisher's prior consent in any form of binding or cover other than
that in which it is published and without a similar condition including this
condition being imposed on the subsequent purchaser.

For my mother, Rose

1

Last night she dreamed of the house on Owl's Point. Waning sunlight bathed the old brick face, and waves pounded the rocks below. Her cousins were there. James, whom she loved, and his sister Audrey, whom she despised. James tried to warn her of some threat hidden in the pines, but his sister only laughed. Audrey was grown-up, looking as she had at her wedding. Disheveled and slightly mad. James was the child he always was in her dreams, never older than eleven. As if his life had stopped there. Though the dream disturbed Teresa, there was nothing odd in the fact of it. At her grandfather's request she was returning to Owl's Point for the first time in fifteen years.

The train car swayed gently. Connecticut coast swept past the window. Rocky woods gave way to broad swaths of gray water and the dark smudge of Long Island. Streams ran through acres of marsh grass, and an egret took flight, white wings pumping. Sometimes it felt like Teresa had spent her life on this train. Going back and forth to school. Later to visit friends and professors still in New Haven. Before that, long before, were the trips to her grandparents in Langford. The house and grounds were a vast and beguiling world where she and her cousins burned countless hours, outside the normal flow of time. They built a tree fort in the big oak. They explored the inlet by the bridge in their canoes. They played epic games of hide-and-seek. There was no beach, but Audrey—against all warnings— would leap from the black rocks into the surf. Just as she would climb the tallest trees, or slip out an attic window to crawl around on the slate roof of the mansion. No punishment or injury deterred her, and that recklessness continued into adulthood.

It was Teresa and James who discovered the indoor secrets. The dumbwaiter that ran from the cold cellar to the master bedroom—by way of the kitchen, where you could fling open the door and scare Jenny, the cook. The hidden closet under the stairs, where they fell asleep one afternoon and threw the house into a panic. The unfinished room in the attic, the crawl space in the wine cellar, more places that she had since forgotten. Only Grandpa's study was off-limits. Teresa looked forward to the trips to Owl's Point for weeks beforehand. They were the highlight of summer, or any season. Until they abruptly stopped.

No one else left the train at Langford. The platform was short and broken. Only eight cars were in the lot, none of them her grandfather's green Jaguar. Teresa remembered that he no longer drove, so she looked for Ilsa. Had they forgotten she was coming? That seemed unlikely, but ten minutes passed without any sign of a ride. She reached for her phone, then stopped. If she had ever known the Owl's Point number, it was lost to memory. She could call her mother, of course, but she would rather drink paint thinner. It was two miles to the house, more or less. On a narrow and twisty lane. Teresa sighed. Then she slung her bag, walked past the coffee shop, bank, jewelers, and up the slope of Long Hill Road.

"There is absolutely no need to go there," she heard her mother say, an echo of last night's argument.

"He's asked all the grandchildren," Teresa had replied, though Miranda knew that. "Kenny and Audrey and James have agreed."

"That's their choice. You can make a different one."

"Mother."

"Whatever he wants to say he can put in a letter or a telephone call."

"Do you know what he wants to say?"

"For goodness' sake, how would I know that?"

"Because he's your father."

Miranda treated the fact as an accusation, and the conversation went downhill fast. Trudging up the steep and tree-shrouded lane, Teresa pictured her mother in the West Village apartment, bought when there was still family money. Tending her exotic roses or painting in her studio. Flitting about in those bright Indian shawls with her artsy friends. Clueless about the real world.

"Stop," Teresa said aloud. Only the trees as witnesses. Just stop. Stop being angry with your mother, with everyone.

A car was rushing up the hill behind her. She could hear the high performance motor straining through the steep turn. They all drove too fast around here, and of course there was no sidewalk. Who would walk anywhere in Langford? She stepped off the road into a mass of saplings and early fallen leaves. Praying not to be hit. Or that at least it should be a quick death from a very expensive car.

It was a red Lexus convertible, which missed her by several feet. She saw a blur of blond hair and sunglasses, then the car slowed immediately, pulling onto the scant margin forty yards ahead. The driver jumped up in the seat and turned, calling out merrily.

"Tay-ray!"

Dear God in Heaven. Audrey.

"Well, don't just stand there," her cousin shouted.

At least she would not have to walk the rest of the way. Dutifully, Teresa marched toward the vehicle. Like a condemned man. To her horror, Audrey leaped out and swept her into a hug. She smelled musky. Some combination including sandalwood, vodka and sweat. She carried a few extra pounds, though in all the right places. Audrey stepped back to survey her younger, skinny, dark-haired cousin.

"Look at you all grown-up," she gushed.

"I was twenty years old at your wedding," said Teresa.

"Yeah," Audrey conceded. "But there were, like, four hundred people there. And I was completely wasted." Teresa had to laugh at the admission, and Audrey flashed a peroxide smile. "Get in. I guess we're going the same way."

Teresa climbed in and buckled up as Audrey gunned the engine. With hardly a glance either way, she shot back onto the road.

"When did you get this car?" Teresa shouted over the wind and motor.

"In the divorce," said Audrey, matter-of-fact. "Piece of

crap, but I'm broke right now, so I'm stuck with it. What do you drive?"

"Nothing."

"Seriously?"

"New York has excellent public transportation."

"Socialist," Audrey jeered. "This ain't New York. Why were you walking?"

"Because you were late?" Teresa guessed. Audrey did a double take.

"Wait, what? Nobody told me to pick you up. I didn't even know you were coming."

Teresa's anxiety, briefly quelled, rose up again.

"There was no one at the station. I figured Ilsa would get me. We spoke two days ago."

"Ilsa," Audrey scoffed. "She must be like a hundred years old now."

"I don't think she's more than seventy. Maybe not even."

"Whatever, at least you were wearing the right shoes."

Teresa's boots were low-heeled and comfortable. She never wore anything that was not good for walking. For her grandfather's interview, she had put on a tasteful gray suit. Audrey was driving barefoot, but a pair of red pumps was jammed half under the seat. She wore tight black jeans and a white V-neck tee to show off her big tanned boobs. Because you never knew when you might meet a hot guy at your decrepit grandfather's house.

"So *qué pasa*, Tay-ray? What's going on in your life?"

The nickname came from her father Ramón's pronunciation. Not the Anglicized *Ta-ree-sa*, but the Spanish *Tay-ray-sa*. For the Saint. James started calling her Tay-ray when they were four years old. She liked the name on his lips. With Audrey, it always sounded like a taunt.

"I'm back in school," Teresa replied. "Graduate school."

"I heard. Art appreciation or something?"

"It's called art history," she said impatiently. "Art appreciation is what your mother does at the country club."

"*My* mother just got plowed there." Audrey slid the sunglasses down and smirked. "A little defensive, are we?"

"No."

"Are you painting? Isn't that what you really wanted to do?"

"Watch the road."

They had swung up on the rear of a gray Volvo. Its cautious speed annoyed Audrey beyond reason.

"This is ridiculous. Speed up or move over, granny."

"Don't," Teresa said, sensing her cousin's intention. "Do not try to pass her on this narrow— Audrey!"

The Lexus was already moving around the slower car, simultaneously shaping a very tight—and blind—curve. Teresa closed her eyes and prayed to the God in whom she no longer believed. When she opened them again they were accelerating along what must be the only straightaway in Langford. Audrey was hooting.

"Oh, Tay, you should see your face. Am I going to have to clean that seat?"

"I would punch you in the head if you weren't driving."

Audrey laughed even harder.

"I like this feisty you," she declared. "You were such a drip as a kid. With your pasty skin and your books and your *condition*. Who knew you would grow up to be such a tough girl? All ninety pounds of you."

It was a hundred and three, by why argue? Teresa had as much trouble keeping weight on as other women did losing it. It was actually a problem, but not one for which she would get any sympathy, so she learned not to discuss it.

"Is James at the house?" she asked, as much to change the subject as from real curiosity.

"Nope," Audrey answered. "James and Kenny were yesterday. You and me today."

"Oh." Teresa tried to hide her disappointment, though her cousin surely noticed. She used to tease that James and Teresa would get married someday. "Why?"

"Why do you think?" Audrey said, smile gone sour. But her disgust was not with Teresa. "Boys first, then girls. Men have serious stuff to talk about, right? Careers, obligations, all that. Women, we're just frivolous creatures."

It probably doesn't help that you act like a frivolous creature, Teresa wanted to say, but did not.

"I don't think Grandpa feels that way. I don't remember—"

"Exactly," Audrey cut her off. "You don't remember. You were how old the last time you saw him? Nine, ten?"

"I'm the same age as your brother."

"So eleven. Both of you off in your own little world. Kenny and me were older, we saw what was going on. This family has always been about the boys."

"Did James tell you why we've been summoned?"

"No," Audrey said. "Little prick hasn't returned my call. I'm guessing it's to pass on some precious wisdom before the old geezer kicks it."

Teresa recognized the brick pillars wreathed in ivy even as Audrey slowed for the turn. Sixty-Six Long Hill Road. Owl's Point. The drive dipped down into a marsh with a narrow bridge, barely wide enough for the car. This was where they swam and canoed. Where Kenny caught the sand shark. Where he nearly drowned Audrey after she teased him once too often. It was as Teresa remembered, but also different. Smaller. They ascended again, through a grove of cedars and a huge bank of rhododendron. And there was the house. Three stories of red brick and slate. The blue shutters and door were faded. The steel cross on the lawn—the work of some second-tier sculptor—was rusted and had a branch wedged in the crossbar. There were no cars in sight. Audrey killed the engine, and silence fell over them.

"Huh," Audrey said, beginning to share Teresa's unease.

"You think they might be out?"

"Ilsa maybe." Audrey stepped from the car and slapped her door closed, startling a crow from a pine tree. "The old guy never goes anywhere."

"Have you seen him?" Teresa asked, getting out and following. "I mean, have you been here since…"

"Since the theft? Maybe twice, but not for years. You?"

"No," Teresa said. "Never. I've spoken to him on the phone. I thought I might see him at your wedding."

"He was invited," Audrey said. "I think someone told him not to come. Wow, this place has really gone to hell."

They stood before the door, which was badly chipped. The whole house had a mournful air about it, though that may have been Teresa's imagination. And the late September light. Audrey was about to hit the bell when Teresa noticed the door was a few inches ajar.

"Look. It's open."

They exchanged a quick glance. Then Audrey pushed the heavy door and marched in.

"Hello? The girls are here—anyone around?"

Teresa followed her into the front hall, papered in a fading green of leafy vines. A wide, carpeted stairway ascended on the right. The look and even the smell of the place—wood polish and dust—was instantly familiar. Yet like the property outside, it was diminished by time and wear. That magical house of Teresa's childhood no longer existed. Near the stairs, Audrey was looking at the control panel of what must be a fairly new house alarm. The display read: Disarmed.

"They must be home or they would have set the alarm," Audrey said, tightness creeping into her voice. "You look around here, I'll check upstairs."

Teresa started to protest, but could think of no reason why. Then she realized that she did not want to be left alone. Her face flushed with embarrassment, but Audrey was already bounding up the stairs. Get a grip, Teresa said to herself. It's an old house. Full of sadness and memories, but nothing to be afraid of. You haven't believed in evil paintings since you were a little girl, and anyway it was stolen. It's not here anymore.

It took only a glance into the sitting and dining rooms to confirm they were empty. She went slowly down the hall, glancing at old vases and portraits without seeing them. Dread gripped her. She had shed childish superstitions in college. She took pride in her scientific view of art, of the world. Yet some habits stuck. Such as the belief in her own instinct, which was correct more often than she could explain. And which was telling her right now that there was nothing alive in this house.

The billiard room was also empty, the table covered in a white tarp. Teresa enjoyed the game, but she was a poor player. Audrey was the pool shark. Hustling Kenny for his summer allowance while James and Teresa played chess in the corner. For a moment, she saw the ghosts of their younger selves scattered around the room. There and gone.

The corridor to the kitchen beckoned, but she was stopped short by something she had never seen before. The door to her grandfather's study stood open. In all of Teresa's time here that door had been a virtual wall. Locked when the old man was not inside, closed even when he was. Always closed. Now, just the glimpse of afternoon light falling across an ornate desk and a blue-and-red oriental carpet, thrilled her with fear and wonder. She took a deep breath and forced herself to walk through the door.

It was a smaller room than expected, but otherwise exactly as she had envisioned it. Bookcases lined the walls, though there was space enough for one painting directly behind the desk. Did she only imagine the faint square where the cream paint seemed brighter? It had hung there a long time before some brave soul seized it. She looked away, as if even this outline might retain a lethal potency. A set of casement windows let in the mellow autumn light. The fireplace stood like an open black maw. Was that the same iron poker the thieves had used to clout Ilsa, or did Grandpa replace the set?

On the near wall was a cracked leather sofa, and on it sat a man.

Not sat, but sprawled, in a position that must surely be uncomfortable. One slipper dangled off the pale left foot. His dressing gown—dusky gold with red Chinese dragons—was badly rumpled. Teresa knew that dressing gown. Indeed, she would have said the man was her grandfather, except for his awful stillness. And the expression of abject terror which twisted his features. The dead blues eyes were fixed on the empty space across the room.

"Teresa?"

Audrey's voice from the back stairs broke the spell. Teresa shuddered with an animal revulsion, then backpedaled. Until she struck a bookcase and fell to her knees. There had been a noise. A deep, guttural moan whose source she could not identify. The man? Had he groaned? Then she understood that she herself had made the noise. She tried to speak, but no words would come.

"Was that you?" Audrey asked, rushing into the room. "Did you hurt yourself? What is the… Oh. Oh, man."

Teresa could not even look at her cousin. As much as she wished to, she could not take her eyes from the hideous gray face.

"Okay," said Audrey between deep breaths. "Okay, Teresa? Look at me. Don't look at him, look at me."

She tried to obey, but could not move her head. She could not even close her eyes. She would be looking at that face for the rest of her life. Then something intervened. Audrey's white T-shirt. Then her face. Those blue eyes. Like their grandfather's, though bright and full of life.

"Audie," Teresa whispered. A frightened four-year-old girl again.

"I know, sweetheart. It's all right, let's get you out of this room. No, *don't*." The voice went from compassion to anger in a moment, or maybe it was only panic. "Don't you dare have one of your fits right now. Stay with me, Teresa."

It was no use. The hard edges of the world fractured into prismatic color. Her senses closed down, and she saw into the heart of the universe. For a bare moment she understood everything. Then a blinding light absorbed her. She felt her body go slack, go liquid, vanish. She gave herself up to the light.

"Teresa. *Teresa.*"

2

For madness, no one could top Goya. Drunks, murderers, victims of violence. Lunatics beset by demons or witches summoning them. Gods destroying their children. The Spaniard had seen it all, in the war-torn landscape of his country or in his own troubled mind, and captured it on canvas. Including at least one thing he should not have caught.

Francisco José de Goya. Teresa had known the name always. It was synonymous with fear. She was as easily scared as any sensitive girl who read too much, and the scariest things were those left to your imagination. Her grandfather, usually kind, was stern and absolute in one matter. Stay out of the study. Never go in for any reason. The fear could not be explained away as Teresa grew older because it was so obviously shared by her mother and uncles. They had also known of the painting all their lives, although only the eldest, Philip, had actually seen it. And he never spoke to his brother or sister about what he saw. Of course the old man saw it every day, and he was neither struck dead nor driven mad. There was a trick to it, or there was a type of person able to withstand the portrait's awful gaze. More than withstand it, but learn and prosper from the contact. This was explained to Teresa by her father, Ramón, who counted himself among those so gifted. For he had seen the painting many times. Whether and how it had damaged him was anyone's guess.

There were many reasons Teresa could invent for her obsession with art. Because it was something she shared with her father and grandfather, who took her to all the best museums in New York and Boston. Because her impulse toward the mystical and curiosity about her Spanish heritage found their perfect union and expression in the artists she adored: El Greco, Zurbarán, Goya. Because she was so bad at the hard sciences that a humanities degree was her only choice. But she knew very well that the obsession had its roots in that first terror and fascination of childhood. The haunted self-portrait by Goya from his solitary days in the Quinta del Sordo. A painting that had left one man dead in Teresa's lifetime, and carried the rumor of death and insanity in a long train behind it. A painting she had never seen, and never would.

The ambulance made its slow way around the drive and out of sight. No lights or siren. There was no need. A police cruiser escorted it, but the nondescript brown sedan that arrived later was still parked out there. The detective must be somewhere talking to Audrey, yet the house was quiet. Teresa was in the sitting room. She had been lying down, recovering from her migraine. But the settee was too hard, made for perching, not reclining. She was sitting up now, sipping from a glass of water Audrey had left for her. Everything that had happened since finding the dead man was vague and disjointed.

She was ashamed of her uselessness. She should be calling people, starting with her mother. She should be speaking to the sad-faced detective—it was she who had found the body, after all. Mostly she should not be falling to pieces like a fragile girl, leaving Audrey to handle everything. Audrey, who had been praising Teresa's toughness only an hour ago. Who had kept her cool in the presence of death. Whatever her faults, the woman clearly had strengths which Teresa had been slow to perceive. Slow or unwilling. Her sense of Audrey as a person was trapped in the past, in a wounded child's perceptions.

Voices approached down the hall, and Teresa stood. She was unsteady, but did not want to seem meek or ill. Audrey's voice rose sharply just outside of the room, then fell silent. One set of footsteps retreated, and a moment later the detective appeared in the door.

He was tall and lean, though his face was puffy. Dark hair retreated from his forehead, and his hound dog eyes made you want to comfort him. It was a face you trusted, which must be useful for a detective.

"Miss Marías. How are you?"

"Fine," she said, pleased by the firmness of her voice. "Call me Teresa."

"I'm Detective Waldron."

"You introduced yourself before," she remembered.

"Right, I wasn't sure if you, ah…"

"Was in my right mind?" she supplied, forcing a smile. "I really am okay now. Won't you sit down?"

Won't you sit down! Who was she, a society hostess? This wasn't even her house. But he did sit, and she did, too, which was a relief.

"This shouldn't take long," he said, flipping through a small notepad. "Ms. Morse has filled me in pretty thoroughly. I wonder if you could run through your arrival here, and the um, the discovery of your grandfather's body?"

Your grandfather's body, thought Teresa, reality hitting home. Not "the body" or "the dead man" but Alfred Arthur Morse. Arrogant, secretive collector of and dealer in European art, with a big house, a bad heart and three estranged children. A man to whom Teresa had once felt close, and for whom she harbored a lingering affection. She had suppressed how deeply she was looking forward to seeing him, and tears welled up in her eyes.

"I'm sorry," Waldron said, closing the notepad and beginning to stand. "Your cousin said it was too soon."

"Is this normal?" Teresa asked tightly. Humiliated by his sympathy.

He slumped back into the chair.

"Your shock? It's absolutely normal, most people never have to—"

"I mean you being here," she corrected. "He obviously had a heart attack or a stroke or something. Why would they send a detective? Is it because he's rich or, or what?"

He nodded several times.

"His prominence has something to do with it," Waldron

conceded. "That's off the record, please. Also, there's the matter of the housekeeper."

"Ilsa." She had forgotten all about the woman.

"Yes, um, Ilsa Graff. I understand that she lives in the house. For the last—" he consulted his notes "—thirty years or so?"

"I guess that's right," Teresa said.

"Do you have any idea where she is?"

"No, none. She was supposed to meet me at the train. Or I think she was. I don't remember anymore what we agreed."

"But you didn't see her at the station?" he prompted.

"No," Teresa replied, clutching the water glass nervously. Why was she nervous? "So I started walking. And I got about half a mile before Audrey pulled up."

"There was no understanding between you two before-hand? She simply appeared?"

"There's only one road," Teresa said, annoyance creep-ing into her tone. "Whether you walk or drive."

"Nothing implied," Waldron said, holding up a for-bearing palm. "These are routine questions. I hope you understand."

"I don't, to tell you the truth." The headache was puls-ing behind her eyes again. "You think Ilsa did something to my grandfather?"

He puffed up his cheeks and exhaled.

"I think her not being here when you two were expected is odd. But I have no theories at this time, and every ex-pectation that it'll turn out as you say. Older man, weak heart. We just have to be as thorough as possible."

"All right."

"So you were walking *to* the house when your cousin drove up?"

"Excuse me?"

"Ms. Morse said you were standing off to the side of the road. She couldn't say with certainty which direction you had been going before she came around the turn. I just want to confirm you were coming from the station."

As opposed to where? Teresa's hands were shaking, and there was a buzzing in her ears. She could not tell whether she was stunned or furious or both.

"Is this about my father?" she blurted.

He sat back and gazed at her curiously.

"I don't know. Is there some reason it should be?"

Idiot, Teresa scolded herself. That's exactly what he wanted you to say. This is not a friendly talk, it's a grilling. He thinks you did something.

"I already said that I was coming from the station," she replied slowly.

"Apologies, my notes are a little messy. You mentioned your father."

"I don't think I have anything more to say to you, Mr. Waldron."

"If we could cover one or two other points," he said patiently, "then we're done."

"Get out."

Teresa had not seen Audrey enter the room. She was standing very close to the detective, a murderous look in her eyes. Waldron stood and nodded politely at her, as if she had not spoken.

"Get out," Audrey said again, louder.

"Your cousin and I were discussing the—"

"I heard what you were discussing. I told you to leave her alone."

"I believe," Waldron answered, "that Miss Marías is best equipped to make that decision herself."

"Then you obviously know nothing about trauma," Audrey said. "So listen to me. Our uncle, who will be here any minute, is a big-time attorney. And I will sue you personally *and* your entire podunk department for harassment, coercion, mental cruelty and anything else I can think of, if you do not get out of this house right now."

The detective shook his head like a man wronged, but not overly concerned about it. He tucked the notebook into the pocket of his baggy trousers and shuffled out of the room. Audrey followed him closely, a barely restrained violence in her posture. Waldron did not seem to notice.

"I'm sorry again for your loss," he said by the front door. "And I apologize for causing any distress during this difficult time."

"Save it for the judge," Audrey growled.

"It's all right," said Teresa, coming to her senses. They were both overreacting badly; the man was only doing his job.

"There's no tape on that door," Waldron mentioned, speaking of the study. "But please do keep it closed and locked. I'll be in touch if there's any need to follow up. Oh, and please let me know right away if you see or hear from Ms. Graff."

"We'll do that," Teresa said, a moment before Audrey slammed the door. And they were alone. Audrey turned to her with such vehemence that Teresa stepped back. She could feel her cousin wanting to lash out, and Teresa was now the only available target. Yet the angry eyes seemed blind to her presence.

"You okay?" Teresa asked.

"He was trying to twist my words."

"I don't know what—"

"He was trying to make it sound like I thought you were coming from the house. I never said that. I never *implied* it."

"Of course not," said Teresa. Was that what upset her so much? Or was it shock finally kicking in? That seemed more likely. Teresa looked steadily into those blue eyes until the other woman met her gaze. A phrase popped into her head. "Mental cruelty?"

Her cousin blinked rapidly. Then giggled, and just like that the old Audrey was back.

"Okay, maybe I had a divorce proceedings flashback."

"It sounded good," Teresa said, relieved. "I think you scared him."

"Nah, only embarrassed him a little. I've yelled at cops before. They don't listen to most of what you say."

"Maybe just as well. But it's weird, right? Him coming here?"

"Not really," Audrey replied, wandering into the sitting room and throwing herself down on the blue settee. "Ouch, how did you sleep on this?"

"I didn't."

"Are you all right now? You scared the shit out of me."

"Yeah, fine."

"Aren't you supposed to be taking medication?"

"I do," Teresa lied. In fact, she did, but not lately. "It doesn't always work. So why do you think he was here?" she persisted.

"Ilsa's disappearing act, for one thing. And, you know. The history."

Her father's face appeared to Teresa. Or her memory of it, she could no longer attest to the accuracy. Long nose, black hair to his shoulders, black eyes. An expression which said that he had seen things others could not see. That he knew things which he would impart, if you only had the means of understanding. Maybe when you were older.

"That was a long time ago."

"A long time to you," Audrey said. "You were just a kid. I doubt enough happens in this boring town that they're going to forget something like that."

"They convicted Jenny's brother."

"His name is Pete."

"I know his name," Teresa said, though in truth she had forgotten. He was always simply Jenny's brother, with his shaggy beard and crazy eyes, who helped out with the yard work. And helped himself to whatever was lying around. Silver serving utensils that no one used, fine china collecting dust in the cellar. The occasional brooch or cigarette case. He had never touched any of the artwork before that day of the funeral. "He went to prison. What would that have to do with this?"

"He's been out of prison awhile," said Audrey, letting the fact hang there a moment. "And a lot of people don't believe he took the painting."

"I know what they believe," Teresa snapped.

"I didn't mean that," Audrey groaned. "God, you and your mother, so defensive."

"He was my father."

"So what? You can say what you like about my father, I don't care. He bailed out on the two of you."

"He had problems," said Teresa, barely above a whisper. Her throat was almost too tight to speak. "I don't want to talk about this."

"Anyway, it isn't only the theft. There was that appraiser keeling over a few years before. You probably don't even remember that."

"I remember," said Teresa.

"Right in front of the painting. On that same leather sofa! You don't think that might seem odd to the cops?"

"That an obese art historian and a sick old man had heart attacks on the same sofa twenty years apart?" she replied. Incredulous. "What should that mean? I really hope the police are smarter than that."

"Well," said Audrey in a reasonable tone. "Maybe it's just me that finds it odd."

"Even if you believe in fairy tales," Teresa went on, wondering why she did, "like a portrait killing the appraiser, it still makes no sense. Grandpa looked at that painting for decades. And it's not even here anymore."

"You don't believe in the painting?" Audrey asked, eyeing her closely. "You used to."

"Like you said, I was a kid."

Teresa retrieved her water glass and sat in the chair the detective had used. She was twice as tired after her outburst. The chair was hard. The room was hard. You were supposed to look at it, not actually use it. One of those stupid customs of the rich.

"I spoke to my dad," Audrey said. "And Philip. I didn't

call your mom, I figured it would be weird me calling since you're here. She may have heard from one of them by now."

"I'll call her," Teresa said, wondering where her phone was. "Thanks for doing all that. For taking care of everything."

"That's what I do."

"Yeah?" Teresa said, her mind elsewhere.

"You thought I just made messes that my father had to clean up," Audrey replied, a hard edge beneath her light tone.

"I didn't mean anything."

"I admit that's been true too often," Audrey went on. "But I also watch out for everyone. Don't you be surprised if—"

She was interrupted by the front door opening.

"What now?" Audrey complained, jumping up. "Did he forget his plastic badge?"

It was not Waldron but their uncle Philip. The very man who was to terrorize the Langford police force, in Audrey's overblown threat. The attorney's face was more lined, and his hair grayer than when Teresa last saw him. He wore a suit, though it was Sunday. No tie, loafers without socks, and a deeper tan than his niece, though he never took a vacation. Through the lenses of his designer glasses, his eyes looked startled.

"Audrey," he said softly. "You poor thing."

The words rang false. Perhaps because Teresa had never heard gentleness from her uncle's lips. Or perhaps because she was a fault-finding bitch who had swallowed her mother's hatred for her family whole. And yet she did not mistake the distaste with which her cousin recoiled from their uncle's embrace.

"Hey, Philip," Audrey said. "Sorry about Grandpa."

"Yes," he said distractedly. "Yes, it's... Teresa, look at you."

Not wanting to embarrass the man twice, Teresa gave him a quick hug. He was tall, like all the Morse men. Philip patted her back perfunctorily, then took her by the shoulders.

"Are you all right?" he asked. How many times would she have to answer that today? Not this time, anyway, since he went on immediately. "Have you called your mother?"

"Not yet."

"I've spoken to her already, but you should call. She's worried about you. Audrey, where is your father?"

"Don't know," she said with shrug.

"You don't know? You told me you talked."

"He was in an airport. In the States, I think. Said he would get here as soon as he could."

Philip shook his head in annoyance. Audrey's father did some kind of international finance, or maybe it was mergers and acquisitions. Teresa could not keep it straight. But he was always flying around the world. Making and losing fortunes, but mostly losing them. Philip turned back to Teresa.

"You found his body?"

"Yes," she said.

"That must have been terrible. Terrible. I'm so sorry. Where are the police?" he asked Audrey accusingly. As if she had made up their presence. Or as if she had chased them away, which was in fact the case.

"The detective just left," Audrey replied. "I told him he would be hearing from you."

"Damn right he will," the attorney said, though what he meant was unclear. True to form, Philip seemed supercharged with purpose. Yet in these circumstances, uncertain where to direct it. "He was in the study?"

"We're not supposed to go in there," Teresa said automatically.

"Girl Scout," Audrey snarked.

"Why not?" asked Philip. "Did they say there was an investigation?"

"No, but they're worried about Ilsa."

"As we all are," he said, moving swiftly down the hall. "I don't see what that has to do with sealing off rooms. The study is where Father keeps his papers."

"Action Man is here," Audrey announced, as they listened to Philip rattle the handle to the study door.

"What in God's name," he called. "They locked it? Where is the key?"

Audrey reached into her pocket and pulled out a key, dangling it before her cousin and putting a finger to her lips. Audrey was always stealing keys when they were young. She even claimed to have been in the forbidden study. Teresa shook her head in puzzlement.

"You're Waldron's watchdog now?"

"Nah, I just enjoy pissing off Philip. But it's funny," Audrey mused. "I don't remember telling him that Grandpa was in the study."

3

Miranda surprised her. Teresa's mother had done nothing but disparage her father for years, and was all business when Teresa finally called. Caring only that her daughter was well. But her arrival at Owl's Point that evening told a different story. Her eyes were red and damp, her face haggard. She clutched Teresa fiercely and would not let go for a long time. They were not a warm family. Neither Grandpa Morse nor Ramón Marías were physically demonstrative. Yet there had once been this kind of strong affection between mother and daughter, so long ago that Teresa had nearly forgotten. When did it stop? And which of them had been the one to pull away?

"He loved you very much," Miranda said as she drew back. "I'm sorry he didn't get to tell you. I'm sorry I kept the two of you apart all these years."

Her tone was matter-of-fact. No hair-pulling theatrics

from Miranda; that was not her style. But Teresa heard the depth of grief in those few words.

"He told me," she said. Had he? In one of those occasional phone calls? If he had not used the word, he had surely conveyed love in the ways of which he was capable. In his curiosity about Teresa's life, her studies, her desires and fears. "I could have gone to see him anytime. I spent four years half an hour away from here."

"You knew it would upset me," her mother countered. Which was true, but not the whole truth.

"It doesn't matter now. I'm sorry for you. You must have been close to him once."

"No." Miranda dabbed her face with an overworked tissue. "I don't know, maybe when I was small. Mostly he was this faraway figure. Always traveling, or locked in the study. Then he would come crashing over us like a storm. Poor Phil got the worst of it."

"Never heard you sound sorry for Philip," Teresa said.

"Yes, well. These last few hours some things have come back to me. Memories."

After briefly enjoying her uncle's torment, Audrey "found" the study key and gave it to Philip. He searched the room at length, not finding whatever he sought. Later he was on the telephone, barking at lawyers and law enforcement types, talking to the newspapers. Now he sat at the dining room table, speaking quietly with his sister. Audrey's father—Alfred Arthur Morse III, called Fred—was flying in the following day, and James and Kenny were both on the train from New York. Audrey was phoning friends and family, and pouring drinks. Mostly for herself. Teresa kept falling asleep. All it took was sitting down and she went right out. Shock, the others kept telling her. Rest, we have it all covered. But she would not be under more than a few minutes before that dead gray face came swirling out of the void. Jolting her awake. It was going to be a bad night.

A good smell drew her to the kitchen, where she was treated to the sight of Audrey in a frayed pink apron. Stirring the contents of a large pot.

"Don't laugh," Audrey warned.

"I wasn't going to," said Teresa. "Okay, I was."

"Rick used to say I could burn water."

"Is that why you divorced him?"

"Try this."

"What is it?"

"Ilsa's famous beef stew. There's a vat of it in the fridge."

Teresa did not remember the famous stew, nor did she usually touch beef. But she had eaten nothing since an apple on the train, and slurped the spoon greedily.

"Delicious, count me in."

"Find some bowls."

Teresa served while Audrey got a bottle from the cellar. A dark, complex French red. Teresa did not know wine, but it seemed too fancy for a grieving family eating leftovers. Then again, maybe there was no better occasion.

"This hasn't had time to breathe," Philip complained.

"Neither have I," Audrey shot back. There were a few minutes of peace while they ate, but Audrey could not endure peace for long. "I wonder if this is poisoned. Like if that's how Ilsa knocked off Grandpa?"

Everyone stopped eating but Miranda. Teresa felt her stomach turn over.

"Ilsa did not poison your grandfather," Philip said. "She was devoted to him."

"Sure she was," Audrey agreed. "But who knows what all those years of abuse can do. How it can twist a person. You know what I mean?"

Philip would not meet her gaze.

"Stop it," Miranda said, dropping the spoon into her empty bowl. "Father didn't abuse Ilsa. She was the one person he always treated with respect." Then she began to laugh. "Sorry, I'm imagining poor Freddie coming in and finding us slumped over our bowls."

"Oh yeah, that's really funny, Mom," Teresa said, but Audrey was also laughing. Look at you two, Teresa thought, not for the first time. There was no love lost between them. Audrey thought Miranda was pretentious, and Miranda found Audrey a bad influence on her cousins. Yet they were similar in so many ways. Same dirty blond hair, bleached gold. Same round face and high cheekbones, same curvy build. Same sense of humor and raucous laugh. If you had to guess the mother and daughter at this table, Teresa would not be in the equation. As a teenager she used to ask, who is my real mother? Of course Miranda was not reckless like Audrey. Or not anymore, but Teresa had heard stories of her youth. Crashing her mother's car on Long Hill Road. Calling home from a Mexican jail during spring break. Sleeping with her professors, including the one she married: the handsome, penniless, half-mad philosopher from Madrid. What a disappointment it must have been when her father ended up loving Ramón. Teresa herself had heard Grandpa Morse say, "He is more of a son to me than my sons."

"Dead soldier," Audrey announced, tipping the last of the bottle into her glass. "Tay-ray, help me pick out another."

"You're still calling her that ridiculous nickname?" Philip said in dismay. "She's a grown woman."

"At least I know how to *pronounce* her real name," Audrey replied, sauntering off.

"I'm useless about wine," Teresa said, but she got up and followed.

The door to the wine cellar was between the kitchen and study. She got shaky even approaching the latter room, but made it down the wooden steps without incident. The cellar was dimly lit, yet brighter and cleaner than Teresa remembered. The cracked stone walls had been smoothed over and it appeared that some racks had been replaced, as well. She had once known this chamber intimately—it was James' favorite hiding place—but now it felt alien.

Rather than examine bottles, Audrey leaned against the wall and slipped something out of her pocket.

"Sorry," she said, unwrapping a baggy and removing a bent joint. "Had to get away from the grown-ups."

"Aren't we grown-ups?"

"Speak for yourself." She patted her pockets, looking for a lighter, no doubt. "I'm holding out 'til my forties."

"Good plan."

"You've always been an old lady."

"I guess," Teresa said, leaning against the wall beside her. "Or just a weird one."

"You and James," Audrey scoffed, finding a tiny blue lighter. It had to be tiny to fit into those jeans. "You're so *invested* in being different."

"More like resigned."

"I love my brother to death." Audrey lit the joint and inhaled. "He's a good kid," she squeaked, holding in the smoke. Then exhaled forcefully. "But nobody could dispute that he's a little off, you know? You're not like that. You get other people. You see the world straight on. I always feel like you're faking the weird girl act."

"I'm not faking anything," Teresa said. She knew better than to let Audrey rile her, but she was feeling vulnerable. "I promise you, I spent years trying to be like everybody else. To like the clothes or the music or the movies they liked. To have friends. To fit in."

"Poor little Tay."

"Fuck you. You call me a fake and I don't get to answer?"

"Hey, we're just talking."

"It's not just talk," Teresa insisted. "Words can do damage. You don't say whatever you like to someone."

"Why not?" Audrey replied evenly. "You can say whatever you like to me."

"Can I? So if I called you a talentless, overweight drunk with a mean streak, that would be okay?"

The flicker of shock moved over her cousin's face so swiftly that Teresa nearly missed it.

"Whoa," said Audrey, fixing her cracked smile back in place. She took another hit off the joint and immediately began coughing.

"I'm sorry," Teresa sighed.

"No, no," Audrey said between coughs. "I asked for it. Forgot how well you read people's weakness. Know exactly where to stick the knife."

"It's not a skill I cultivate."

"Guess you're a natural, then."

Teresa slid down until she was sitting on the cold concrete floor. A few moments later, Audrey slid down alongside her and passed the joint. Teresa held it for too long, sniffing the pungent smoke. Tempted. Then she handed it back.

"I can't, my brain's too messed up."

"This will smooth you out," Audrey replied. "But suit yourself."

"I'm sorry I said that."

"Let it go. It's all… Do I really look overweight?"

Teresa laughed.

"What?" Audrey asked, but she wore a sly smirk.

"That would be the one word you focused on," said Teresa. She had remembered how Audrey always hurt her feelings, but forgotten how she could make you laugh at anything. Not a bad talent to possess in the current circumstances. "You look gorgeous. You always look gorgeous, I'm just jealous."

"I don't believe that for a minute," Audrey quipped.

"Go ahead, let me have it," said Teresa. "I'm too short, I'm too skinny. I'm either too shy or all snotty and superior. I have a blank expression on my face because I'm always stuck in my own brain. What else?"

"That's pretty good. I think that about covers it."

"Oh, come on."

"Well." Audrey considered. "You have kind of a martyr complex. And your clothes are pretty awful. You do have a nice face. Your dad's face."

"Certainly not my mom's."

"Your dad was hot."

"Please, Audrey."

"What? He was. You can't help being short, and being skinny isn't against the law." She took another hit on the almost vanished joint. "It should be, but it's not."

"I'm glad we got that straight," Teresa said, feeling calmer. "We should go back up."

"Nah, let's hide down here. You and James used to do that, remember?"

"I do. There was a crawl space. Like an alcove they walled up partway and forgot. It was a tight squeeze."

"Too tight for me," Audrey recalled. "James showed me once, but my hips wouldn't fit. You're shocked, I know."

"It was bigger inside. Not much." Enough for two nine-year-olds to sit side by side, Teresa thought. Holding hands, whispering. All the space we needed.

"Where was it?"

"I think," Teresa said, starting to crawl on her hands and knees, "back along this wall somewhere."

"Back here?" Audrey came shuffling after her. "There's a rack in the way."

"I know, but that's new. They've moved things around. It was near a corner, I'm pretty sure it was this one."

They both peered through wooden slats and over dusty bottles. There was nothing to see but wall.

"Wrong place," Audrey decided.

"No, it was here. They've plastered it over."

"What?" Audrey seemed outraged. "Your kiddie hide-away—how could they do that?"

"Might have even filled it in." Teresa stood, bracing herself against a momentary dizziness. "It was strange that it was there at all."

"Huh." Audrey remained crouched by the rack, biting

her thumbnail. Then she stood also. "Let's drink more of Grandpa's wine. Though I guess it's not really his anymore."

"Whose is it?"

"That's what we all want to know, right?" Audrey said with a wicked laugh. "First we have to get through the fake expressions of grief. Then stick him in the ground."

"Jesus, Audie, do you have to be so…"

"What? Okay, you were shocked, that was a rough thing to see. But are you really upset that he's dead? Couldn't you use a few bucks for school, or whatever?"

"I didn't think there was any money," Teresa said, which was the wrong response. Yes, I am upset that he is dead. I seem to be the only one who is. But Audrey would not believe her, nor believe that Teresa didn't care about the money one way or another. "He couldn't even pay his help, and the house is a wreck."

"Dad thinks he was just cheap. He's sure the old guy was sitting on a pile of cash."

"He told you that?"

"Of course not," Audrey snorted. "I hear things. But I'm with you. He never paid the help enough, that's why Jenny and Pete stole from him. But he wouldn't be selling paintings or letting the place fall down if he had the money to fix it."

"He was selling paintings?"

"You don't keep track of any family stuff, do you?" Audrey seemed half appalled and half impressed. "Don't worry, there are plenty left, and the property is worth millions. He was cash poor, but there's money in the estate. Question is, who gets it?"

That was not Teresa's question.

"What do you think happened to him?"

"Heart attack," Audrey guessed, wandering down a dim aisle between racks. "These are the Rhônes."

"Then why did you mention the Goya, and the appraiser?"

"I was trying to see it like the cops would, that's all. Did you like that Châteauneuf we just drank?"

"You saw his face," Teresa said pointedly.

The other woman was quiet for a moment. "Yes."

"Something scared him to death."

Sounds came through the ceiling. Heavy footsteps followed by voices raised in greeting.

"The boys are here," said Audrey, her voice brightening. "Better grab an extra bottle."

Audrey was always cheered by the arrival of men. Apparently even her brother and cousin did the trick. Teresa was also pleased. She was eager to see James, and their presence would liven up the gloomy house. Yet she was uneasy. Why? Because too many Morses in one place meant trouble? Perhaps it was only the echo of those last words she had spoken, and the memory they conjured.

While Audrey slid bottles out, blowing off dust and mumbling to herself, Teresa went to the stairs. She was halfway up when the door at the top opened and a figure loomed. She took a panicked step back down, trying to make out who or what it was.

"Hello," a voice said uncertainly.

"James?"

They had stayed in touch by phone and email, but not often. Despite mutual affection, they were both hopeless introverts, afraid of intruding. She had seen him at Audrey's wedding, and once since, but they had been with other people. He hunched his shoulders and avoided eye contact. Teresa was surprised when her mother mentioned how tall James was now. In her mind he was still a floppy-haired boy.

"Did I frighten you?" he asked.

"No," she stammered. "Yes. I frightened myself."

Teresa rushed up the stairs and threw her arms around him. It was out of character, but what the hell. He had an unfamiliar smell. Like a man. Yet underneath was the warm bready scent she remembered. After a short hesitation he wrapped his long arms around her. The very awkwardness with which he did it was comforting.

"I'm so glad you're here," Teresa said.

"Your mother told me. I'm sorry."

"Be sorry for all of us," she said, stepping back to look into those curious brown eyes. His expression had not changed.

"I'm sorry it was you who found him."

"Might as well be me as anyone."

"No," James said earnestly. "You're more sensitive. It should have been Uncle Philip or Audrey. It wouldn't have bothered them."

You didn't see his face, Teresa thought. She had not told her mother or uncle about the expression their dead father wore. It seemed cruel and unnecessary. Yet Audrey was sure to say something. If not immediately, then eventually.

"Audrey was there. She took care of me."

"She takes care of everyone," he said. Repeating his sister's mantra, without conviction.

"Yeah, I heard that."

"I need to talk to you," James murmured.

"Of course," she replied, stepping closer. But a voice nearby intruded.

"Where else would she be?" Kenny shouted back to his father as he approached. Loud, confident Kenny. "Probably grabbing all the best bottles for herself."

"Later," James said, staring at his shoes. "When we're alone. I need your help."

"Whatever I can do."

"You know what's going to happen." His voice grew hard, as did his eyes when he looked at her again. "Don't you? They're going to blame this on me."

4

In a fever dream she rose and fell. Surfacing, she was in the bedroom at Owl's Point. It was day, but the light through the curtains was weak. Rain spattered the window. Her skin was hot and damp. James stood next to the bed, watching her with a clinical concern. He was a boy again, or still, or always.

Is she going to die?

She better not, said another voice. Or we'll get the blame.

We didn't make her sick.

We're in charge of her until they get back from burying Grandma.

Why isn't Ilsa in charge?

Don't be stupid, Audrey said. Ilsa's the help. We're family.

James leaned in and touched her burning neck with his cool finger. His touch was soothing.

I don't want her to die.

Then get your hands off her, Audrey said.

Why? he asked, pulling away.

Because you're the Angel of Death. Everyone you touch dies.

I am not, he screamed. James rarely raised his voice, and the pained cry was awful to hear. That's not true. That's not true.

All right, Audrey groaned. Shut up, I'm sorry. She slumped down in the window seat. God, this is boring. Tell me if she stops breathing.

James leaned close again, careful not to touch her. There were angry tears in his eyes. Don't die, Tay. Please. I'm going to help you, Tay.

She was pulled under, into a black and suffocating silence. She struggled, not seeing, not breathing, a red flashing behind her eyes. Suddenly the darkness released her, and she shot upward.

The same room. But empty and nighttime. Teresa was sitting up in a small bed. The same that she had slept in when visiting this house as a child. The same bed in which she had thrashed in a fever on the day of her grandmother's funeral. Miranda had not understood how sick her daughter was, and in any case it was her mother they were burying. She had to be there. Audrey was assigned to watch Teresa, and James stayed with them. Which meant they were all in the house when the theft occurred.

Teresa reached for the water glass and took a sip. It was a different dream than usual. She knew dreams were not memory, and that even memory lied. But the standard nightmare featured James' faraway scream of terror. Audrey waking from her nap in the window seat to rush out and find him. Teresa desperately trying to rise from the bed, only to collapse again. Something like those things had happened. This new dream took place earlier that day, and must be an anxiety-fueled construction of her unconscious. Surely Audrey never said those cruel things. Surely James' words to Teresa the previous evening—that he would be blamed—had simply worked their way into her sleep.

She drank more water and put the glass down. Where had he gotten the idea? How could he be blamed? She had learned no more; they were not left alone the rest of the evening. James receded into himself while everyone else talked manically and to no purpose. Teresa fell asleep in her chair, then finally dragged herself to bed. She waited for James to tap on her door, but if he ever did she was long gone to dreamland.

As the room slowly brightened she realized there would be no more sleep. She rolled out of bed and unzipped the travel bag her mother had brought, with spare clothes. The ugly green corduroys and extra-large Yale sweatshirt. Good old Mom. Teresa dressed, pulled on her sensible boots and went down the back stairs to the kitchen. Then out the mudroom door. A heavy mist rolled in from the sea. The pines were shadows and the ocean invisible. The house might have been sitting in the clouds. It was cold. She needed a jacket, but was not willing to go back for it. She drew her hands into the sleeves of the sweatshirt and wrapped her arms around herself, then made her way toward the sound of surf. The gazebo materialized out of the mist. It needed paint, and the floorboards were rotting. How long since anyone had sat here, drinking a cocktail and watching the sunset over the Sound? What a bleak and barren place this had become in her time away. She could not have imagined it. Maybe she would come out here this evening. Wrapped in blankets, with a whisky.

The lawn ended abruptly and there was the ocean. Or a murky stretch of it. Just beyond where she stood, a rocky slope fell thirty feet to the phosphorescing water. Teresa looked for a spot where Audrey might have leaped into the waves without killing herself. It did not seem possible. Maybe it had been farther along the ledge, or maybe the tide was higher. Maybe Audrey was indestructible. For the first time in days, Teresa missed Marc. He would try to comfort her if she called him now, but she would not do that.

She stared down at the dark seaweed swaying in the white foam. Afraid of losing her balance, she crouched. Her fingers twitched, seeking a pencil. How would she capture this on paper? The monstrous shape of that rock, the black water. Would she shade in the mist or represent it as an absence, the white of the page? And why was she thinking about this when she had not sketched in months? A shred of memory or an image from a dream flitted around her brain, and she tried to get hold of it. Before she could, a strong emotion seized her. Indistinct at first, it coalesced into a kind of dread. Which shifted quickly to fear as Teresa sensed someone rushing at her from behind. She stood up fast and turned.

No one. Only the mist, beginning to dissipate. She had been certain of a presence, about to place a hand on her shoulder. An involuntary shudder went through her. Cold and damp were penetrating the sweatshirt. She started back to the house and immediately saw a figure in the pines. It was a man in a gray coat, his head bent in thought. He had cleared the trees and was crossing the lawn before she realized it was James.

"Good morning," she called.

He stopped and looked at her, making no reply. He seemed distracted, possibly anxious. Damp hair hung in his face.

"I didn't think anyone else was awake," Teresa said as she reached him.

"Me, neither," James replied. "I couldn't sleep."

"And I'm all slept out." She nearly mentioned the dream, then did not.

"Kenny snores."

"What, Mister Perfect?" she laughed. "Don't tell me you were in the same room."

Kenny and James had shared a bunk bed those summers when the house was full.

"No, but I could hear him through the wall."

"He had a lot of wine," Teresa remembered. "I guess we all did."

"Not me."

"You still don't drink?"

"A little," he conceded. "People make a big deal if you refuse. But I don't like the feeling it gives me."

"I didn't used to," she said. A fallen woman. "Now I like it too much."

"You seem the same." The words surprised her. "I thought you would have changed, but you seem the same to me."

"Is that good?"

"Yes." He smiled bashfully. His smiles were so rare that it felt like a gift to get one. "I think it is."

"We've all changed, but I'm glad that I seem familiar. You also seem the same, except for being too freaking tall."

"Sorry," he said. "Couldn't help it."

James had never cared for small talk, and Teresa waited for him to seize this chance to speak of what troubled him. Yet he showed no inclination. Last night's urgency had vanished, or been suppressed.

"You're brave to walk the woods on a morning like this," she said, taking his arm and starting them forward again. "Must be spooky."

"They're just trees," he said with a shrug. "I was looking for our old tree house."

"My God, is it still there?"

"Sort of. The roof and one wall are gone, but the rest is intact."

"I don't remember how we got up. There was a ladder?"

"Wooden rungs nailed into the trunk."

"Right," she said, the memory coming back.

"They looked kind of rotted. I didn't try to climb."

"That was wise. Audrey would have," she said, at the same precise moment that he did. They both laughed. Even his laugh was awkward, a high-pitched gurgle that pulled on her heart. She squeezed his arm. "How is school?"

James was in medical school in Boston. Doing well, Teresa had heard, which was no surprise. He tested off the charts in IQ and everything else. But he did not do well with other people, and needed five years and three colleges for his undergraduate degree. Then he left law school after one year, hating it. No one in the family had gone into medicine before.

"Good," he said firmly. "I like it, especially the labs. I like doing things instead of talking about them."

"Have you dealt with cadavers yet?"

"It doesn't bother me. Everyone is afraid of them, but you can't hurt the dead."

"That doesn't make them fun to spend time with," she said, fighting another shiver.

"There's no better way to understand the human body than to open it up and look inside. I want to help people. No one knows that about me. Nobody believes it."

"I believe it," Teresa said.

"They think I'm crazy and can't take care of myself. But I want to help people. You have to be willing to do the hard things."

They were near the mudroom door, and James shuffled to a stop. As if he could not bear going inside. Teresa tugged him the other way, toward the front of the house.

"What did you want to talk about last night?"

He looked away, then shook his head quickly.

"I shouldn't have said anything."

"I'm not going to call you crazy. Trust me." But he would not speak. The yew hedges beside the garage had grown rangy and brown. The sun was beginning to cut through the mist. She tried a different tack. "What happened yesterday, with Grandpa?"

James tensed up instantly.

"Do you mean the day before?" he asked.

"Yes," she sighed. "Sorry, I've lost track." It seemed one long and shapeless day since she had stepped onto the platform at Langford Station. It also seemed like a week.

"It was bad," said James, biting off the words. "We argued."

"About what?"

"My erratic behavior. I think that's the word he used. One of them."

"Such as?"

"You know," he said impatiently. Assuming that Teresa had heard the family gossip. "Temper tantrums, as if no one else has those. As if Audrey's aren't ten times worse than mine."

"What else?" she asked.

"Pointing a knife at her. At Audrey. I wasn't going to hurt her, but you know the things she says. Threatening a professor."

"Really? How did you threaten him?"

"This was years ago," he insisted, as if she was missing the point. "At Amherst. The guy was a condescending jerk. I don't remember what I said, but I didn't do anything. I wasn't going to do anything."

"Okay." Teresa squeezed his arm again. "It's okay, I believe you."

"I guess Grandpa was writing it all down," he said bitterly. "Keeping track of everything I ever did wrong. And not only me, all of us."

"So we're all behaving erratically?" she asked, trying to lighten the mood. The things he said should have disturbed her, but she had witnessed such behavior when they were children. She knew what Grandpa Morse was getting at, but she also knew James. He did not understand people, didn't get their jokes, became easily frustrated. Instead of taking that into account, friends and family taunted him.

For their amusement, maybe, or simply because it's what people did. James' own father, Fred, was a terrible tease. Miranda, too. And of course Audrey was the worst. She knew how to send James into a fit with just a few words. He would cry and yell and break things. Hurt himself, perhaps. But never hurt anyone else. She had never heard of his doing so, and could not imagine it.

"Kenny argued with him, too." James spit the words out, as if ashamed of speaking.

"He told you that?"

"Yes. He left before I got here, but after my talk with Grandpa I went to the city to find him. He was staying with a friend, in the place he rented when he used to live there."

Which answered a question that Teresa had been meaning to ask. Why had James arrived with Kenny from New York instead of coming from Boston?

"I couldn't remember where it was," he went on, "so I wandered around for a long time. It's a big city."

"It is," Teresa agreed, imagining James wandering Manhattan's late-night streets. He was lucky he didn't get mugged.

"I slept on a bench. When I woke up I remembered the address, so I went there."

"In the middle of the night?" she laughed. "I bet he was thrilled to see you."

"It was morning, but yeah, he wasn't happy. He had someone with him."

"I bet she wasn't too happy either."

"It was awkward," James concurred. "Once we started talking, I could see he was upset, too. That his conversation had been as bad as mine."

"What was Grandpa's problem with him?" she asked. Curious to know what flaws Kenny could possibly possess.

"The thing is, he had a problem with all of us. He was calling us in one by one to tell us our faults. What we had to fix. The old jerk."

"Jerk" was about as harsh as James got. But she heard more hurt in his voice than anger. They cleared the last corner of the house and the sun struck them full in the face.

"Why?" Teresa brought them to halt short of the circular drive. "Why was he doing it?"

"Because he didn't think his heart was going to last much longer."

"So?" she said, exasperated. "He had to tell us the errors of our ways before sailing off into eternity?"

"I like how you put things," he said. "I should read more."

"It rots the mind."

"It's about money, Tay." James shifted uncomfortably. "We had to change these things about ourselves if we wanted to get any money. In his will."

She looked to see if he was joking, but of course he would never make such a joke.

"You've got to be kidding. That's what it was about?"

Could he be lying? Not lying, James would not consciously lie, but telling a story he believed? Why would he come up with this? No, it was a sad revelation, but all too credible. And yet more proof that she had never really known her grandfather. What would her own flaw have been? She could think of many, but what would have seemed important to the old man? And what about Audrey? Drinking, drugs, sleeping around? A list too long to consider. It did not matter now; they would never know.

A hundred feet to their right, the front door opened. And there she was, as if Teresa's thoughts had conjured her from the mist. Audrey. She wore the same clothes from yesterday, but with an old green coat over her T-shirt. They waited for her to look in their direction, but she skipped down the steps and toward her car without a glance left or right.

"What's she doing up at this hour?" Teresa wondered.

James shrugged, but he watched his sister carefully.

Audrey jumped into the Lexus and gunned the engine to life. Without waiting for it to warm up, she spun around the drive and out through the opening in the rhododendrons and was gone. It was only then that Teresa realized Philip's car was also missing. Philip had gotten Miranda from the train yesterday, and James and Kenny had taken a taxi, so the drive was now empty of vehicles. Despite James standing beside her, Teresa had a panicky sensation of being abandoned on this foggy point of land. In this house of the dead.

"Where is she going?"

"It's no use trying to figure out Audrey," James said in resignation. "Be happy she's gone for a while."

His words raised questions about the sibling relationship, but a more urgent question nagged Teresa.

"How does that stuff about Grandpa make you to blame for his death?"

"I didn't say I was to blame."

"You said you *would* be blamed. Why?"

"Because," he said, then said no more. A crow shambled from one pine tree to the next, a blue jay shrieking after it. She waited him out. "Because I was there," James finally continued. "Every time something bad happens, I'm around. Grandma falling on the terrace. The painting vanishing. Now Grandpa dies right after I argue with him."

"Oh, James," Teresa said, grabbing the lapels of his coat and shaking him. "No one thinks you're responsible for any of that."

"Maybe you don't," he mumbled.

You're the Angel of Death. Everyone you touch dies. Who had said that? Where had Teresa just heard it?

"Has anyone accused you of something?" she asked.

"They don't have to. I can see it in their faces."

"Grandma fell because she had a stroke," Teresa said patiently. "It was, like, her fourth. One of them was going to kill her. Audrey was there, too. And she and I were both there when the theft happened. As for Grandpa, well, it sounds like he started the fight. With Kenny also. It's not your fault."

It was like talking to stone. He was still as a stone, too, his whole body gone rigid. He stared at the ocean with absolutely no expression. Teresa was good at reading people, but could read nothing in that blank visage. Despite the sun, the damp had penetrated her clothes and she began to shiver.

"I'm sorry, I have to go inside."

"I saw someone," James said then. "Or I thought I did. In the pines."

"Just now, when you were walking?" Philip and Audrey had clearly been awake, but what would either have been doing out there? "Anybody you recognized?"

"No. I couldn't tell. He, um, he had..." James' voice shrunk to a whisper. "He had something covering his face."

What did it mean? Did it mean anything?

"But you're not sure you saw him?" she asked, confused.

"Afterward, it didn't seem to make sense. I've been told to question the things I see. That I think I see."

"Who told you that?" Teresa demanded to know.

He shook his head firmly. Doors opened and closed within him swiftly, and hammering on them never seemed to do any good. James looked down and noticed her shaking.

"You're cold," he said in surprise. "You should go in."

"Will you come with me?" she asked.

"In a while. I don't like it in that house."

"Please? I don't like it either. I'll make you an omelet."

It was one of the few things she could make, and she hoped there were eggs.

"I want to hear about your school," James said. "I've been reading a lot about art lately, and I have some questions."

"You're full of surprises," said Teresa. "Come inside, then, and we'll talk."

She moved toward the front door, willing him to follow. Reluctantly, he did.

5

It was the right house, but no one was home. How he could know that without leaving the car was a fair question, yet Dave felt certain. There were obvious tells. No vehicles in the drive, no lights, no gently parted curtain. It was more than that, though. There was something about houses, about the way they sat. They announced their occupancy. This one was empty. No spirits within, living or dead. He drank his coffee and read the *New York Times*.

He was early. He was always early, a habit picked up during the years when meetings carried potential threat. Arrive first, check out the location, see who else is watching. Dave supposed there might be threats today. The guy was a lawyer, after all, and had reason to dislike him. They would not be of the lethal kind, however, and he was not worried. More curious, which he had not been for some time. Which was the reason he was here at all. That and needing money.

At 8:55 a.m. he decided to survey the property. It was a nice house. Yellow clapboard with white trim, a porch running along two sides. Big, but no mansion. A top attorney from a wealthy family could do better. It certainly could not compare to the old man's pile of brick by the sea. Then again, maybe the son would inherit that, the father having keeled over yesterday. Dave had read the obituary in the car. The collector got two columns with a photo. The tone was decidedly negative, which was sad. Dave had known the man a little, and it was hard to like Alfred Morse, but he felt a grudging respect.

Tennis court, luridly green lawn, bushes all around the house—laurel, azalea? He wasn't good with shrubs. Primitive security system. Dave was ready to give hidden cameras a friendly wave, as if he were not casing the joint, but he saw none. He was back in the car sipping coffee when Philip Morse drove up, fifteen minutes late. Older model Mercedes, well maintained. The man was also well maintained, yet stress showed around his cold blue eyes. The eyes always give you away, thought Dave, stepping out of his car.

"Thanks for your patience," said the attorney. No doubt he had read some asshole's success-in-business guide that said never apologize. He did not shake hands but headed straight for the house. Dave followed, not hurrying. The side door opened into the kitchen, which was large and white and appointed with the latest gadgets. For the wife, Dave guessed. He would bet twenty bucks that Philip Morse could not boil an egg.

"I've been at my father's," the attorney said, lighting the gas jet under the steel kettle. He knew how to do that much. "I need to get back as soon as possible."

"I'm sorry about your father," Dave replied. "I liked him."

"You were among the few," Morse said sourly.

"I would have been happy to go to his house, under the circumstances."

"I wanted this to be private. Would you like some tea or coffee?"

Dave declined, and Morse turned off the kettle, making nothing for himself. They sat at the kitchen table, and the attorney played with his glasses before speaking.

"My wife is in Paris," he said pointlessly. Maybe to explain the empty house. "With friends. She'll be back for the funeral, of course."

"Of course. Your children are around?"

"My son, Ken. He's at the house. You know why I asked you here, I suppose?"

The question had an accusatory edge, but Dave was not playing.

"I try not to presume anything. I would guess it's related to your father's death, except you called me before he died."

"I did," Morse agreed. "You'll remember I tried to speak to you after your investigation."

"I remember," said Dave. "I wasn't free to talk."

"You invoked client confidentiality. But your client is now deceased."

"Well, you would know better than me," Dave replied carefully, "but I'm pretty sure that confidentiality continues after death."

"Client-attorney privilege does," Morse said, "but you're not a lawyer. And even lawyers are allowed exceptions when settling estates."

"Are you the executor?"

"I assume," Morse huffed, tossing his glasses on the table and looking uneasy. "I haven't seen the will yet. I'm meeting his attorney later, at the house."

"That case was a long time ago," Dave noted. "I'm no longer employed by that firm."

"I am aware of that," said the lawyer snidely.

"I was required to leave my notes with them." A half-truth. That he was *required* to do so did not mean that he did. In fact, Dave had been reviewing them last night. "And my memory isn't what it used to be. I mean, fifteen years…"

"So you don't intend to tell me anything."

"About?"

"About your conclusions. In your report to my father."

"I see." Dave leaned back in his chair. It was what he expected, though the timing was odd. Why all these years later, twenty-four hours before the old man's death? If the attorney knew the death was imminent, then it was estate-related. Money. It was always money. "I'm not sure what I could say that would be useful."

"Then why are you here, Mr. Webster?"

Yes, why? A rainy afternoon in Madrid. Dim rooms on the second floor of the Prado. Luisa had dragged him in to see something else, but he was taken hostage by those nightmare images by Goya. If they were Goya, no one knew for sure. Maybe his son, or the son painting over the father. Maybe the Devil himself. That was easy to believe when you stood before the works. Fourteen of them. Mad pilgrims with white eyes, screaming a song. Saturn's dark maw devouring a bloody corpse. Witches floating in the air, the black shadow of the He-Goat before his coven. Fourteen, and one missing. A ghost painting, a rumor. For Dave, an obsession. Three years later Alfred Morse called Luisa's father, Dave's boss. There had been a theft. An indescribably precious work. He had no faith in the police. Luisa's father gave the job to Dave, and his life unraveled. Not at that moment, but inexorably over the months and years that followed. And you ask why I'm here.

"You don't even know why," Morse said contemptuously.

"Let's say out of respect for your father. And your loss."

"I don't need your respect," said the attorney. "I need your assistance. I would not ask if it wasn't necessary, but it's you who created this mess."

"Me?" said Dave, amused. "Do you think I took the painting, Mr. Morse?"

"No, but you apparently thought *I* did," the attorney raged, straining forward in his chair. Dave wondered if the man was about to attack him. "You destroyed my father's trust in me. Ruined our relationship. And now you can sit in my house and smirk at me like that, you pathetic fraud."

That didn't take long, thought Dave.

"Even if any of that is true," he answered, "it's a couple of days too late to fix it."

That was cruel, he thought, surprised at himself. Why was he provoking the man? Did he want a fight? Did he want to roll around on the spotless tile floor with the lawyer, trading punches? Dave did not like Philip Morse. Fine. But the man had just lost his father, and there was some truth in his words.

Used to being provoked, or maybe embarrassed by his

outburst, the attorney grew calm. He smoothed his hair and put his glasses back on. Like Superman becoming Clark Kent.

"Sadly, that is the case," he said. "I can't express my hurt at the idea my father died believing me guilty. Another man might feel shame, but I can see you aren't such a man."

"You have it wrong, Philip."

"Then set me straight," the attorney insisted. "How does your silence serve anyone?"

How indeed? He should beg the man's pardon and leave. But he knew that he was not going to do that.

"Why now?" he asked. "Why after all this time did you call me two days ago?"

"Why should I answer that?"

"You don't have to," Dave said. The attorney eyed him closely, sensing an unspoken deal. He rose from his chair and went to the sink, gazing out the window there.

"My father had no use for his children," Morse said. "The feeling was more or less mutual. So his coldness toward me in the last decade didn't really register. It was only a few days ago that I learned he suspected me of stealing the painting."

"You had no suspicion before?"

"Why would I?" the attorney demanded, wheeling around on him. "He was upset with all of us when it happened. Like it was some group failure. But I didn't feel it was directed specifically at me."

"You think I put that idea in his head."

"You're free to deny it."

And who will you blame, then, Dave wondered.

"How did you hear? Who waited until the last couple of days to tell you?"

"That person only just heard it, as well," the attorney replied. "I'm not free to say who."

The man desperately wanted Dave to talk. If he would not reveal his source under that inducement, it was pointless to push.

"I can only speak about the investigation as it related to you," Dave said. "No one else."

The attorney moved back to the table and sat.

"Understood."

His expression was so eager that Dave hesitated. But it was too late to hold back.

"I didn't come to any conclusions," he said. "For that matter, I didn't submit a report. There was nothing on paper, it was all verbal."

"What, on the telephone?"

"Never," Dave replied. "In person. In his study. I think we met three times." The big mahogany desk, the blue eyes even colder than his son's, a crown of white hair swept back from his forehead. And that empty space above where the demon portrait so recently hung. "That's how he wanted it done. I reported on my progress and he asked questions."

"About me," Morse said.

"All the children," Dave admitted. "Spouses, the help, the caterers for the wake, dealers and collectors. It was a long list, and I didn't get through half of them."

"Why not?"

"I can only conjecture. We didn't trade theories. Your father kept his own council."

"Tell me about it," said Morse, massaging the bridge of his nose. "Conjecture away."

"He didn't believe the groundskeeper was the thief. Or if he was, he acted on someone else's behalf."

"We all suspected that," the attorney said dismissively. "But whose?"

"There was a collector who wanted the work very badly," Dave replied, violating his own conditions. "A man named Charles DeGross."

"That's right. He made my father at least two offers. Generous offers, I understood."

"You encouraged your father to sell to him," Dave stated, rather than asked.

"And that makes me suspect? My mother, my brother and his own lawyer encouraged the exact same thing."

"Yes, but they didn't meet secretly with Mr. DeGross. You did. Twice."

Morse took a deep breath. Far from looking angry, he seemed relieved to have arrived at the heart of the matter.

"It wasn't secret. For heaven's sake, we were in a restaurant."

"You were in a private room. Alone except for the waiter. And on at least one of those occasions you lied to others about where you would be."

Morse sighed again and shook his head.

"Your memory is better than you claim," he said ruefully. "Fibbing to my secretary is not a crime. It was essential that it be kept private. I was, in fact, acting in my father's interest."

"Just without his knowledge or permission," Dave replied.

"You have no idea," the attorney said sharply. "Or maybe you do."

"About what?"

"His finances. My father didn't understand money, and he ran through it at an alarming rate. He paid high prices for works he wanted, and hardly sold a thing. It wasn't sustainable. Ten million dollars would have gone a long way toward curing his problems."

"He felt the painting was worth many times that," said Dave.

"To whom?" Morse asked, tossing his hands up. "You're not a dealer, but you must understand the market a little. That kind of money was a delusion. No one has ever paid that for a Goya, and certainly no one would without a clean provenance."

"You think your father acquired it illegally?"

"I don't know, nor do I care. That painting..." The attorney became glassy-eyed for a moment. As if he went away from the conversation, away from the bright room to some other, darker place. "That painting was never going to a museum," he rasped, his gaze slowly finding Dave again. "Anyone who would take it for a good price and keep it hidden was doing our family and the world a service."

Dave held his tongue. They had come to what he cared about, but the questions he wanted to ask would take them away from the lawyer's concerns, and expose his own. He mastered himself.

"What was your purpose in meeting DeGross?"

Morse nodded, as if he, too, had forgotten the point and was grateful to be brought back to it.

"The first time was after his initial offer. Seven million.

I convinced him that my father swearing not to sell was a bluff, that he should go higher. *I'm* the one who got him to ten million. Not that Dad would have thanked me for it."

"Which of course he couldn't," Dave pointed out, "because he didn't know. Why the second meeting?"

"DeGross asked for that. After my father rejected the higher offer. He wanted to know if there was any point in continuing. If there was anything left to try."

"Like stealing, for instance," Dave baited him.

"DeGross may have been behind the theft," Morse answered evenly. "But he didn't share his plans with me. I did not have anything to do with that, Mr. Webster. And I still don't understand why you stopped the investigation."

He sounded sincere, Dave had to admit. He might be a good liar, or he might have talked himself into his own innocence. People did that. Or, Dave conceded grudgingly, he might be telling the truth.

"Your father suspected DeGross. I could tell from his questions. But I couldn't find a link to the groundskeeper or any of the other help. I didn't investigate the caterers closely, that was another thing I was going to get to. The suspicious behavior I did uncover involved members of the family. Especially you."

"You mean those meetings with DeGross."

"That was the worst of it," Dave confirmed. "Your father was determined to solve the case. He put all his energy into it. When I told him about those meetings, well, the steam went out of him. He didn't even want to hear about my other findings. He just asked me to leave. The next day he called to say he was ending the investigation."

They were both quiet for a time. The attorney was so

deeply wrapped in thought that the sound of a car pulling into the driveway did not rouse him.

"I understand this is painful for you," Dave said, risking the other man's wrath. "And I'm not accusing you of anything. But one way to look at this is that your father was trying to protect you. As important as that painting was, it was more important to him not to implicate his son in any wrongdoing."

Morse stared at him with a curious expression, and Dave considered the possibility that for once in his life he had said the right thing. A car door slamming erased any response the attorney might have made. He rose quickly and went to the window.

"What the hell does she want?"

Three seconds later the kitchen door banged open and a woman in tight jeans and a baggy coat swept in. Curvy, blond and flushed. And obviously a Morse. She barely paused to throw a contemptuous glance at Philip, but she stopped short when she saw Dave. He stood up fast, banging his knee on the table.

"Sorry, did I interrupt something?" she asked, not sounding sorry. More annoyed that the presence of a guest required a halfhearted courtesy. "Who are you?"

"What are you doing here, Audrey?" Philip snapped. The girl made him nervous, though Dave could not guess why.

"Clothes," she said.

"Clothes?"

"For the funeral and, like, the next few days. It's four hours round-trip to my apartment, without traffic. And the cops want us to hang around."

"I wasn't aware," said Philip suspiciously, "that you had left clothes at my house."

"Don't be silly," she said, making *silly* sound like a humiliating condition. "Cynthia and I wear exactly the same size. Nice to meet you…"

"Dave," he said, taking her offered hand. Her blue eyes had a warmth missing from her uncle's, and her smile seemed genuine, if not exactly kind. She had a firm handshake.

"I'm Audrey," she replied, brushing against him as she passed. More closely than the space required. "Maybe I'll see you around."

"Wait, have you spoken to Cynthia?" Philip called after her.

"She won't mind," Audrey declared, already in the hall and headed for the stairs. Philip went as far as the kitchen door in pursuit. Then stopped, shoulders sagging.

"My niece," he said in resignation.

"I remember," Dave replied. She was a mouthy teen when he last saw her. The children had been off-limits for questioning. Which was appropriate, yet frustrating, as three had been in the house during the theft. One of them had actually been in the room. A boy, in therapy for some trauma. Dave could guess the source of that trauma, but none of the adults would speak of it. He'd met Audrey because she sought him out during her father's interview. Flirting, he guessed. Or wanting to know what was up, the way teenagers did. She was cute, but fifteen-year-olds were not his thing, and he hadn't given her a second thought. She was all grown-up now.

Morse shuffled back to the table. Audrey's entrance had

severed the brief bond between the men, and Dave sensed a dismissal. But the attorney sat down again.

"Thank you for telling me those things."

"I can't imagine they were what you wanted to hear," Dave answered, sitting down also.

"No, but not as bad as I guessed. Tell me something else, please. Did you believe I was the thief? Is that what you would have reported to my father?"

"That's a tough question, Philip."

"The truth will do. You won't offend me."

"I hadn't made up my mind. I needed more time, and more freedom. You looked suspicious, but so did other people."

"Like my brother-in-law," the attorney said. "Ramón."

"I can't answer that."

"You don't need to." Morse reached into his jacket and slipped out a checkbook. They had not discussed a fee for Dave's time, but without asking, the attorney began to write. "What I would like to do is ask you to pick up where you left off fifteen years ago," he said, tearing the check from the book. "I don't know how realistic that is."

"It's a cold trail," Dave managed, covering his surprise. Was he serious? "I would have to track down a lot of people. They would have to be willing to talk."

"Many hurdles," the lawyer agreed. "Don't answer now, but consider the possibility. Last question. Or request. Would you be willing to repeat everything you've just said to my brother and sister?"

There it was. The old man was gone but not the siblings. Did one of them control the purse strings? Or was this just an emotional thing? Did it matter?

"If they're willing to listen," said Dave, "I'm willing to talk."

Morse nodded and handed over the check. It was for a thousand dollars, far too much. Dave thought of handing it back, then thought better.

"Consider yourself on retainer," the attorney said. "We'll be speaking more."

6

The diner was a mile from Morse's house, at the first inter-section going east. Anyone returning to Owl's Point would pass this way. There was also a gas station, post office and antiques shop, but little activity this Monday morning. Little to attract Dave's eye while he ate a late breakfast of scrambled eggs and toast. He could not have said what he was watching for until the red Lexus sped by the window.

Philip had shaken his hand when they parted. As if they were pals now, or at least co-conspirators. Dave did not know why it bothered him. He had worked for worse men, and very little had been asked of him so far. He had no inflated sense of his own honor, but there was something tainted about the attorney. About the whole family. They were people to avoid; Dave felt it on an instinctive level. Yet he'd accepted the check, and gave Morse his mobile number. Going to his car, he had stolen a glance back and caught a figure in a second-floor window. Near the back of the house, the master bedroom probably. It was her, Audrey. She examined a blouse in the window's natural light, and it took a moment to realize she wore nothing but a white bra. She didn't look up, but Dave had no doubt the show was for him. Before he averted his gaze, she turned around quickly. As if someone in the room behind had startled her. Yet she made no effort to cover herself.

He had been trying to sort it all out—what the attorney really wanted, why Audrey had made an appearance, what was going on between the two of them—when her car shot by. She drove too fast. Any careless pedestrian would have been instant roadkill. In the minimum time it would take to find a place to turn around and come back, the Lexus reappeared and swung in next to his blue Taurus. She got out slowly and scanned the long window until she spotted him. Then waved. Dave did not wave back, but she bounded up the stairs and entered the little diner nevertheless.

The same black jeans, but now she sported a pink blouse with the sleeves rolled, along with a turquoise bracelet and silver chain around her neck. Also fresh lipstick and eye shadow, which did not quite distract from the dark crescents of sleeplessness. She had the weathered look of a woman a few years older, a look Dave found appealing. Indeed, he was quite attracted to her, and the sooner he admitted that to himself the better he could resist.

"Hey," she said, sliding in across the table from him. "Mind if I join you?"

"You already have. But I was just finishing."

"Doesn't look like you enjoyed it." She grabbed his coffee cup and took a swig, leaving a red smear on the white ceramic. "That is terrible," she announced.

"It is," he agreed. "You didn't give me time to warn you."

"I know you," Audrey said, drilling him with those blue eyes. It struck him that she had a slightly crazed look, and Dave could not decide if it was natural or a put-on. "I could feel it right away, but it took a little while to figure out. You won't remember me."

"I do."

"Really?" She seemed far too pleased. "They wouldn't even let me talk to you."

"You managed to barge in anyway."

"For like thirty seconds before they hustled me out."

"You were too young," Dave said. "It wasn't allowed."

"I was fifteen. I made a statement to the police."

"And I got a copy of that."

"Maybe I didn't tell them everything," she said, letting that sit. He would not take the bait, and he could see that she had no patience. "So what's the story, Dave? Did my uncle hire you to investigate something?"

"I can't say."

"That means he did," said Audrey, narrowing her eyes. "What?"

"Why are you so desperate to know?"

"Desperate? Nah, I'm just curious."

"Curious enough to hunt me down."

"I didn't *hunt* you," she laughed, enjoying his choice of words. "I was just driving by and saw your car."

He deliberately chose nondescript vehicles. She must have taken careful note and been looking out for it not to have passed right by the diner. The diner, he now remembered, that her uncle had recommended. She also managed to pack several days' worth of clothes from another woman's wardrobe in twenty minutes.

"It's not a big deal," Dave said. "He wants me to make a statement."

"He's paying you to say he didn't swipe the painting, right?" Her smirk annoyed him, but he tried not to show it. "Too late now, isn't it?"

"I need to get going."

"You were looking for me," she said. "The same as I was looking for you."

"I was having breakfast."

"You were pushing around lousy food while you waited."

"Why would I do that?" he asked, his tone too sharp.

"Do I really have to explain?" she said in a low voice. He had an impulse to throw the bad coffee in her face, but understood that he was angry at himself.

"What do you want, Audrey?"

She sat back and blew the hair from her face. From playful to sullen in an eye blink.

"I'm bored. We're stuck in that house until the funeral. You're the most interesting thing that's happened so far."

"When's the funeral?"

"Tomorrow," she said. "No, Wednesday. They have to wait for the autopsy results."

"Autopsy, really?" Now he was intrigued, but she only smirked again. More secrets she might share, if he would… what? He still could not guess what she wanted, and would not flatter himself that it was his company. "I thought it was a heart attack."

"Most likely."

"Was there anything suspicious?"

"Depends on who you ask," Audrey replied, sliding the coffee mug between her hands.

"Who found the body?"

She opened her mouth, then paused.

"I did," she said, and a disturbed expression flickered over her face.

Dave touched her hand. A simple gesture of sympathy, performed without thought. She froze. It might have been fear he saw, or something else, but it was not pleasure. He withdrew his hand. Audrey blinked rapidly.

"Wait," she said, as if he had confused her. "That was okay. You can touch my hand if you want to."

"It didn't seem okay."

"I'm kind of jumpy. Nothing," she barked at the waitress who had not even reached their booth. The woman turned away without comment. "This has all been kind of strange."

"Of course," he said. The tough-girl act was just an act, as he should have known. She made him uneasy in ways that messed with his perception.

"You ever see a dead body, Dave? I mean, before it gets cleaned up and mummified."

"Yeah. Once."

"Was it…" She licked her lips. "Was it bad?"

"It was pretty bad," he conceded. Audrey leaned across the Formica table, her eyes big.

"Wait, was it someone you killed?" she asked breathlessly.

Dave leaned away and laughed.

"Why would you say that?"

"I don't know," she replied, looking a little disappointed.

"Do I seem like a killer?"

"What does a killer seem like?" she asked, reasonably. "Anybody can take life, under the right circumstances. Don't you believe that?"

"I don't know about anybody. But most of us, yes."

"You have a temper," Audrey said, scrutinizing his pale, unshaven face. "Yeah, I could see you doing someone in."

Well, this is going brilliantly, thought Dave. It was time to leave.

"Do you like that idea?" he asked instead. "That I might be a killer?"

"You're asking if I like dangerous men?" She considered the question seriously, without flirtatiousness. "I guess. Except they usually don't turn out to be dangerous. Just mean. There's a difference."

"No doubt. What did your uncle tell you about me?"

"Why would he have told me anything?"

"That's a great question, I've been working on it. You do seem awfully close."

"What?" She was so instantly furious that she could barely speak. "I despise my uncle," she said, with all the venom four words could hold.

"That makes two of us," Dave replied, unmoved by her rage. There was something calmingly familiar about a woman being angry with him. "It doesn't rule out him telling you things."

"I suppose not," she agreed. "Why do *you* despise him?"

"That's too strong. I dislike his self-importance. I've met too many guys like him."

"His self-importance," said Audrey coldly, "is the least of it. He doesn't like you either, by the way. Thinks you can't be trusted."

"And that's based on what?" Dave asked.

"Oh, maybe that your own father-in-law fired you?"

"I quit."

"That you work with criminals on illegal deals," she persisted. "That you steal."

Don't defend yourself, he thought. She's having fun, let her. What he really wanted to know is how much of it the attorney actually said, and how much she was making up.

"He told you all that?"

Audrey shrugged, taking another swig of bad coffee.

"Some he told me, some I overheard. He's been on his phone like twenty-four hours straight."

"And you've been spying on him."

"He has a loud voice," she replied. "But, yeah, I keep my ears open. Never know what you'll hear, especially with my insane family."

"Are they all insane?"

"Pretty much. Oh, did you mean me?" She leaned toward him again and lowered her voice. "That would be yes, Dave. But it's all relative. Hah, you get it?"

"Funny."

"I'm the sanest one among them. I'm the one you need to come to for answers."

"What answers would those be?"

"How are you going to prove that Philip is innocent unless you find out who is guilty?"

Where was she going with this? Trying to undermine her uncle in some way? Was she simply as bored as she claimed?

"Do you know who's guilty?" he asked.

"If I knew that," she answered with a crooked grin, "there wouldn't be anything for you to solve, would there?"

"Does everyone in your family think Philip was part of the theft?"

"As far as I know, nobody thinks that. I mean, beyond everyone suspecting everyone else for a while."

"Despite the fact that someone was actually convicted of stealing."

"Poor Pete. Stealing, yes, but they couldn't nail him on the painting. They only threw the book at him because he wouldn't squeal on that collector. What was his name?"

"So you think Pete was innocent, or just too harshly punished?"

"I'm not the investigator," Audrey replied. "Pete was a thief for sure, but I don't think he took the painting."

"Do you think it was someone in the family?"

"Who else?" she said, as if the question was stupid.

The cook, the housekeeper, the caterers. Someone nobody had thought of yet. But his own theories were less interesting to him at the moment than hers.

"Why do you want the painting found?" he asked instead.

"Isn't it valuable?" she said automatically.

"A few million, maybe. If you could find a buyer who didn't mind its sketchy history."

"Not to mention that it might kill you." She tried to sound flippant, but the words caught in her throat. Dave wondered if she could truly be afraid of the painting. Then he remembered Philip Morse's face when he spoke of it. A family fear, bred in deep. The old man had done a number on all of them.

"Maybe it would be better if it wasn't found," Dave offered.

"Yeah, I've thought of that," she said. "The thing is, that painting did a lot of harm to people who never even looked at it. It messed up our whole family. And it's still going on."

"What are you afraid of, Audrey?"

Because it was clear she was afraid. Among the many shifting emotions on her face—anger, curiosity, contempt—quick flashes of fear kept appearing.

"I'm not sure," she said, looking him up and down. As if for some clue hidden in his hands, his face, the folds of his jacket. Some proof that she could trust him.

"He was bludgeoned and strangled," Dave said, surprising them both. "The dead man that I discovered. He was a thief and a bully, a truly bad guy. But no one deserved to die like that. It's funny, until that moment I fully believed an old saying of my former boss. I repeated it again and again to nervous clients. 'Nobody kills over art.' But I was wrong."

She nodded slowly, as if they had agreed on something.

"My grandfather," she said cautiously. "Something bad happened to him. His face was all… I'm sure it was his heart. I don't expect the autopsy to turn up anything. But something terrified him. Something or someone."

"And you think that someone is a threat to you."

"I don't trust any of them," she whispered. "I worry about my brother. He's fragile. Anything can set him off. Whatever happened in that room during the theft, he's never been right since. I worry about my cousins, too. I feel like I have to watch out for them, but I don't even know what I'm watching out for."

She wanted protection, Dave understood. Yet neither of them knew from what threat.

"Look, I'm flattered that you felt you could tell me this," he said gently. "But I'm not sure what I can do to help."

She nodded again, understanding. The hopelessness in the gesture made him want to reach over and take her hand, to tell her to forget what he had just said. She could count on him. Don't get played, Dave, he cautioned himself. How many times have you fallen for this?

"Well," Audrey said, standing up. "Thanks for the terrible coffee. I should let you get going."

A minute later they stood outside the diner. An old man walked his ancient beagle, grunting some complaint as the dog looked at him adoringly. They both gazed fixedly at the touching scene, lost in their separate thoughts. She flexed her fingers in a familiar way, and Dave waited for her to light up. Then recalled that she had not smelled of smoke even faintly.

"When did you quit?" he asked. She glanced sidelong at him. "Smoking," he clarified.

"Three weeks ago," she said. "Three weeks and a day, to be precise. That's good, Dave. Are you showing off for me?"

That's exactly what he was doing. Like a teenager trying to impress a girl.

"Busted," he confessed.

"That's sweet," she said, punching his shoulder playfully, but a little too hard. "Thanks for talking to me. There was no one else I could share that with."

Dave dug into his wallet and pulled out a card.

"Here," he said, handing it to her without making eye contact. "Give a call if you really need something."

"But only if I *really* need it, huh?"

"I'm on retainer to your uncle. He might consider my talking to you a conflict of interest."

"And you need this gig," she said. "I get it." She strode to the Lexus, hips swinging in a way that made an ache form in his chest. "Don't worry," Audrey said, flashing a white smile before she swung into the car. "I won't screw things up for you."

No, Dave thought. I'll find a way to do that myself.

7

"What do you see?" Kenny called to her.

Teresa braced herself against the tree fort's rickety wall, which came only to her sternum. Even with the oak continuing to grow all these years, she was no more than a dozen feet off the ground. Through a narrow space between pines she spied sunlight on water.

"The Sound," she answered. "The Lost Kingdom of Long Island."

"It should stay lost."

"And if I stand on tippy-toes I can just see Portugal."

She did not expect him to get the reference, but when she glanced down he was beaming. Kenny, with his perfect hair and teeth. A lawyer in San Francisco now, with a big apartment and a succession of cute girlfriends. What was it like to be that successful, that confident?

"I'd forgotten," he said. "That was Audrey."

"No, Audrey said France."

"Yeah, geography wasn't her thing."

"You said Portugal," Teresa continued. "I couldn't wait to be old enough to climb trees so I could see Europe, too. I believed whatever you told me."

"Well," he replied good-naturedly, "I guess it was a good lesson about men."

"About cousins. My God, the bullshit you guys made up. Then I would go and say it to my friends or my teachers."

"Like what?"

"Like the Civil War was fought over the right to wear mustaches. Or that women got pregnant from swallowing seawater. Or damn, what else? There were others."

But it did not matter, because Kenny was laughing too hard to hear.

"You didn't believe those things?" he gasped.

"Of course I did, I was five years old!" She might have been six or seven. She probably would have believed them at ten. She was a gullible child. Lost in fantasies and ignorant of the world. "Are you coming up?"

"Not a chance," he replied. "You come down before that thing collapses."

Teresa did not believe their old fort would tumble under her weight, but she stepped over to the hole in the floor and carefully descended the makeshift ladder. The rungs were spongy, as James had warned, but sufficient to hold her. There was a gap at the bottom, and Kenny took her by the hips to lift her down. An intimate act, which he performed without fuss. It was not until she was on the ground that Teresa spotted the big hole in the trunk that used to scare her as a kid. Just out of arm's reach from the ladder. A good house for a family of squirrels, she thought now, but nothing to be frightened of.

"Thanks," she said to Kenny. "You want to go a little farther?"

"Not in these shoes."

His loafers already had tree mulch stuck to them. Why didn't people ever wear the right shoes?

"You want to go back?"

"Not really," he said, gazing through trees to where the looming house sat. "Although we should be taking advantage of the quiet while Audrey's gone."

"Where did she go?"

"No idea," Kenny replied. "I tell her stuff. She never tells me anything."

"Why do you tell her?" Teresa asked.

Kenny shook his head, perplexed.

"I don't mean to, but somehow she wheedles it out of me. Most of the time she already knows what I'm going to say. She seems to know everything."

"Yes," Teresa said. They sounded like two picked-on children discussing the playground bully. "You think she's up to something?"

He looked at her oddly. "What would she be up to?"

"I don't know. She's acting kind of… It almost seems like she's enjoying this."

"She thrives on chaos. And she's not too happy with her life right now."

"Ah, so she tells you some things," Teresa replied.

"We talk. She's in White Plains selling insurance. Nothing wrong with that," he added quickly, "but she doesn't love it. Broke up with a boyfriend in the last few weeks, I think. Then there was the divorce."

"That's a couple of years ago."

"So?"

"She didn't even like him," Teresa said defensively.

"You think? I guess she always says that."

"You don't believe her?"

"I don't know. She changes stories according to her mood. But I have the impression she was crazy about Rick, and the divorce totally upended her."

"I heard they fought all the time."

"Well, yeah," Kenny said. "We are talking about Audrey. And about marriage, which seldom runs smooth. Which of our parents didn't fight all the time?"

"God, is that supposed to be our model? How badly our parents did?"

"I bet you've read more psychology than me. That's how it goes. We repeat the same mistakes, generation to generation."

"Is that why you're not married?" she asked him.

He gave her a sour look and kicked the damp earth with his pretty loafer.

"I'm only thirty. Don't rush me."

Too handsome, she thought. Too many choices. Men didn't pass up their chances at his age. And how would you know, she scolded herself. You know almost nothing about Kenny. He could be the sweetest man on earth. He could be a serial killer.

"What about you?" he asked.

"Me?" she mumbled. "I'm back in school."

"I know that, Teresa. Don't be coy."

"I also broke up with someone a couple of weeks ago." Which ought to have made her feel some kinship with Audrey, or at least a little compassion.

"Was it serious?"

"For me it was," she said, imagining Marc's smiling face. *That's Marc with a c.* It was the first time Teresa had been able to picture him doing anything but sulk since they split up. "I guess for him, too."

"Sorry," Kenny said. "It's never easy."

"I liked that girl I met at Audrey's wedding. What was her name?"

"Trudy," he replied, grinning. "She's a good kid, we're friends."

"She was beautiful," Teresa mused. "I've never been able to do that. Stay pals with ex-boyfriends. Not that there have been that many."

"You're, um, not very good at casual. You're a pretty intense girl."

"Am I? I am. Is that bad?"

"It's what it is. I'm guessing you don't date a lot, don't let guys get too close. Yes? But when you find the right guy, boom, you're all in. So when it blows up, you take it that much harder."

She wanted to ask who he thought he was, pretending to know her so well. But she was too distracted holding back tears. Damn it, what was this about? She was not a crier, but tears were waiting every time she let her guard down in the past twenty-four hours. She reached out and touched Kenny's arm, tipping her face away.

"That's right," she said thickly. "That's exactly right."

"Come on, let's head back."

"Wait," Teresa said. "What did Grandpa say to you?"

He looked at her and looked away. And she saw instantly that she had it wrong. Again. She could not stop seeing them all through the lens of her childish insecurity. Kenny's smile was a mask. He was as troubled as any of them. At this moment, maybe a little more.

"I don't want to talk about that."

"You talked to James," she countered. "When he showed up on your friend's doorstep that night."

He wheeled on her, and Teresa saw a flash of his adolescent temper.

"If he already told you, then why are you asking me?" Kenny snarled.

"He didn't tell me anything about you," Teresa replied, looking him in the eye for three or four long moments. He had James' eyes, without that lost quality. A little haunted, perhaps. He looked away first.

"It's nobody's business," Kenny said. "I only let him in because he surprised me. And he was so messed up from talking with the old guy. We agreed not to speak to anyone else."

"What could be so terrible?" Teresa demanded. "I'm not going to judge, I just want to know what—"

"You want to know what he was going to say to you." He cut her off. She started to protest, then stopped. She was curious about the others, but ultimately that *was* what she wanted to know. "I can't help you," he said. "Whatever my issues with Grandpa, he had his rules. He didn't mention anyone else when he spoke to me. Each lecture was for that person alone."

"Shape up, kid, or no cash for you."

"Yeah," he said. "That was bottom line."

"But how was he going to enforce it? Was he monitoring all of our lives? And now he's dead, so..."

"So we're basically screwed. Whatever's in the will right now is what we get."

She glanced at his profile. The strong nose like his father's, eyelashes she would kill for.

"Do you care that much about the money?"

"No," he said. "Not that."

"Then what?"

He began marching away from her, turning back only as he reached the edge of the trees.

"Are you coming?"

"I'm going to walk," she replied. "I'll see you in a bit."

"You have a good imagination, Teresa. Use it. Go to the place that's most private to you. Most humiliating. You know what I mean? That tender spot. That's right where he would have put his finger. I'm glad you didn't have to go through it. No one deserved a heart attack more than that old bastard."

He turned away again and moved through the last trees toward the house.

The wooded part of the property was not large. No more than a few hundred square yards, but it was the only part of Owl's Point Teresa did not know. As a girl, the big pines had frightened her. The way they shrank the view and swallowed all sound. Every time Kenny or Audrey ventured in, she was certain they would never emerge again. Now she found that same silence calming, and she wandered aimlessly. In very little time she arrived at the iron fence marking the property line.

Clearly it had once been an imposing wall of black spikes. It was rusted now, more orange than black, and fallen down in many places. No animal or man would find it difficult to pass through. She wondered if this was where Pete had slipped out with his stolen goods. He had been spotted more than once heading into the pines at day's end. Including the day of the theft, when he had a large black bag slung across his shoulder. Someone on the catering crew had seen him. Pete denied it at first, then eventually confessed to taking a silver platter and a few other items. But not the Goya. He swore up and down that he had never touched the painting. For all the good it did him.

She walked along the fence until she found what looked like a trail through the trees. There was a narrow strip where the ferns did not grow, and the earth was slightly furrowed. Had there been more leaves down, she never would have seen it. Teresa followed the trail back in the general direction of the house. It passed over marshy ground and through a grove of red maples. Twenty yards away she spotted a cove, the existence of which she had never known. Just big enough for a small boat. Maybe that's how Pete got the goods out? She smiled at her runaway imagination, but the smile froze on her face.

There were only a handful of pines between her and the lawn, but standing among them was a figure. Forty feet ahead. Dark pants and a long greenish jacket. She could not make out the head at all, let alone the face. It stood so still that Teresa tried to convince herself it was not real, but there was no mistaking the form. She would pass within a few yards if she kept to the trail. She could cut into the trees, but would lose sight of the figure and risk losing her bearings. Instead she began to walk backward slowly. Within five steps the figure started forward. Toward her. Teresa turned and ran.

Stop, she told herself. Why are you running? There's someone else in the woods, big deal. Turn and confront him. But she could not do it. The panic was too strong. In a minute she was back at the iron fence, where she crouched down and risked a peek at the trail. Nothing. Yet she heard something in the underbrush. A thrashing or snapping. Squirrels? Had she heard that earlier? She could not re-member, she could not think straight. She looked for the path by which she had originally come, but there had been no path, just idle wandering. Where was the house? There, more or less. She moved back into the trees.

Beneath pines, a brown carpet of needles silenced her steps. But when Teresa reached the big oak, leaves and sap-lings gave her away. She might as well have been blowing a horn and shouting I'm over here! She increased her pace, rushing under the crumbling tree fort. The black hole in the trunk made her flinch, as if an arm might reach out and grab her. From the corner of her eye she saw a figure. On the right, closing quickly. She ran faster.

And burst onto the lawn, stumbling for several steps, then falling headlong in the grass. She rolled onto her back and scanned the trees. A pine branch swung madly where she had just emerged, but otherwise there was no movement. Nothing visible. Knowing she should rise, Te-resa nevertheless lay there a minute or two, collecting her breath and wits.

"Who's there?" she asked. Meaning to shout, but it emerged a whisper. "Who's in there?" she said more loudly.

At last she dragged herself to her feet and walked backward toward the house. Then turned and walked normally. Determined not to look back, she twice did so anyway. No one was following. The afternoon sun had become surprisingly low, the day slipping away.

She rounded a marble statue of an angel and sensed movement. Where? Had the mudroom door just shut, or did she imagine that? Teresa circled the house to the front door. Philip's and Audrey's cars were back in the drive, along with others. It took her a moment to identify the brown sedan as Detective Waldron's. Her hand hesitated on the doorknob. He was only going to be in touch if anything odd turned up. And here he was. She had been holding her breath for the last day, it felt like. Anticipating some new threat, and the moment had arrived. Teresa opened the door and went in. They were waiting for her.

8

They had been speaking in low voices, but when Teresa entered the dining room they all stopped and looked up. Philip, Audrey, Miranda, Uncle Fred and his latest wife. And an old man in a gray suit, who looked vaguely familiar.

"Where have you been?" asked Philip curtly.

Several pointed replies occurred to her, but Teresa could not get them from her brain to her mouth.

"Are you okay?" her mother asked. "We were worried."

"You've got pine needles in your hair," said Audrey.

Fred nodded and the wife—Laura, Lauren?—rushed around the table to hug her. As if they were close, though they had met only once. She was brunette and in her forties, a strong contrast to her younger, blonder predecessors. Like James and Audrey's mother, who'd died of an aneurysm. Or a drug-induced stroke, depending on whom you believed. The second wife had been her physical duplicate, and taken most of Fred's brief fortune in their divorce. You could see why he might have tired of blondes.

"Aw, honey," said...Laurena, that was it. She wore an abundance of sparkly green eye shadow and had a slight Southern twang. "So good to see you. How are you holding up?"

"What's going on?" Teresa asked. "Where's Kenny and James?"

"My idiot son," Philip said, "is making a statement to the police."

"What did he do?"

"He hasn't done anything," her uncle snapped. "They want statements from all of you."

"I'll explain," said Audrey. She was transformed since this morning. A coral-colored blouse had replaced the T-shirt, plus a fine silver chain. And she had made herself up carefully. She took Teresa's arm and led her across the hall to the sitting room. Teresa did not like being dragged, but had to admit that she felt calmer away from the others' scrutiny.

"Here's the deal," said Audrey in a breathy voice, standing close. Every conversation was a seduction. "They found Ilsa."

"Is she okay?"

"Apparently. She was at her sister's in Pennsylvania, but she's pretty badly spooked. Something happened here to frighten her."

"Like, beyond Grandpa dead in the study?"

"Yeah, something more than that," Audrey confirmed. "I don't know what, but I plan to find out."

Teresa had no doubt that she would.

"Who's the dude in the suit?"

"Mitchell, Grandpa's lawyer. Older than dust, but he knows stuff. Turns out he's got the only copies of the will, and Phil's pissed off because he won't show it to him."

"Where's James?"

"I thought he was with you," Audrey said. Insinuation in her tone.

"I haven't seen him since this morning."

"Then he's hiding. Doing his scared-little-boy act, like he always does when shit gets serious."

Teresa let that go. Sisters were allowed to say things.

"I'll find him," she answered, starting away. Audrey caught her arm.

"Are you going to talk to Waldron?"

"I guess. Are you?"

"After how he tried to twist my words? Anyway, Philip doesn't think we should."

"And you always do what Philip says," Teresa scoffed.

"He *is* a lawyer."

"So why is Kenny talking?"

"Interesting, right?" Audrey flashed a nasty smile. "First he ignores his father's advice. Then he won't even let him be in the room. You know, as counsel. Some tension in the perfect family, seems like."

Which was clearly cause for glee. There was a rivalry between Philip and Fred that had extended to Kenny and Audrey. Not that it was a real competition. Fred made money, but lost it all. Audrey was a mess. Meanwhile Philip was the successful lawyer his father intended he be, and Kenny had followed in his footsteps. Teresa never felt part of the competition, but her own family—dilettante mother, mad father, her sickly and indecisive self—surely numbered among the losers. Yet she did not hate Kenny for that, or even Philip. She pulled her arm away.

"I'm going to find James."

She turned in time to see Kenny striding toward her. He threw Teresa a shy glance and went straight out the front door. Coming slowly up the hall behind was Detective Waldron, who locked eyes with Teresa.

"Miss Marías, hello. There have been some developments."

"I heard."

"I was hoping to speak to your cousin first, but since he's not available…"

"Yeah, yeah," she said. "Let's get this over with."

Rain mottled the window. Teresa watched gusts shake the dusk-black pines until darkness replaced them with her face in the glass. It was the four of them, in their accustomed spots. James and Teresa over the chessboard, Audrey and Kenny circling the billiard table. Sliding out of each other's way or hip-checking, depending upon their mood and who was winning. The door to the hall was open, but there might as well have been a sign saying No Grown-ups. They were left to themselves.

"Six ball, side pocket," Kenny said, pushing up the sleeves of his silky blue shirt.

"No way," Audrey retorted, but a moment later the green sphere dropped lightly into the worn leather pocket. "Lucky shot."

"You're too generous," he quipped, moving around her to size up the seven.

"Teresa," James said gently. She swung around to face

him. "Your move," he added, for what was surely not the first time.

"I'm sorry," she said, surveying the board. She had no idea how the handsomely carved ivory pieces had achieved their current positions, no memory at all of her last move.

"I put my bishop there," James said, pointing to the black figure threatening her knight. The white pieces looked fretful, as if wondering how she was going to get them out of this mess. Good luck with that, guys. She reached for the knight and James spoke again.

"You don't want to do that."

But I do, she thought. She had lost her feel for the game, as well as her ability to concentrate.

"You're not supposed to coach me."

"All right," he agreed. "Did I tell you that I found a sketch you did of me?"

"Really? It must be very old."

"I think we were ten or eleven. It's good. You had so much talent even then. I can only imagine how much better you are now." His faith was heartbreaking, and Teresa could not find the words to tell him that she had given up. "You should sketch me again," he added.

"Miss, miss, miss," Audrey chanted, but it was no use. The eight ball rocketed into the corner pocket, and Kenny raised his cue triumphantly. "You suck," Audrey pouted. "I never win with stripes."

"Stripes or solids make no difference in the probability of victory," James said.

"Shut up," Audrey replied, swatting his head as she passed. "New game. Girls against boys. Come on, Tay-ray, let's kick some butt."

Teresa was worse at pool than she was at chess, but had to admit that smacking balls with a stick seemed more appealing right now than trying to outthink her cousin. She tipped over her king and James nodded his understanding.

"What are we playing for?" Kenny asked. "Gender pride?"

"Money," said Audrey.

"No," said Teresa, the idea coming to her that moment. "Secrets."

Audrey smiled wickedly and James looked glum, but no one objected. Teresa racked the balls while Kenny and Audrey did rock-paper-scissors. Kenny won, but James' attempt at a break sent the cue ball skittering off the table. Audrey broke forcefully, scattering balls everywhere without pocketing any.

"So how does this work?" Kenny asked, lining up a shot.

"Sink a ball, ask a question," Teresa said. Everyone was hiding something, and she wanted answers. Though she had given little thought to the questions that would elicit them.

Kenny missed and it was Teresa's turn. She lined up the two, not because it was her best shot but because blue was her favorite color. "Side pocket," she said, striking with insufficient force. The cue ball tapped the two's edge, and it rolled ever so slowly toward the pocket. Teetered a moment, then dropped in.

"Yeah," said Audrey. "Solids, baby." She gave Teresa a high five.

"Where did you go this morning?" Teresa asked, bringing Audrey up short.

"Wait, you can't ask me, I'm on your team. Then it's just everyone for himself."

Teresa conceded the logic.

"Why did you agree to talk to the police?" she redirected to Kenny. Unlike her cousin, Teresa allowed Philip to play her attorney. Waldron's questions were straightforward—nothing about her father or the long-ago theft—and she had answered them all. She did not mention the figure in the woods. She had become less and less sure of what she had seen. True to her word, Audrey refused to speak to the detective, and James had not even been asked.

"Same reason as you," Kenny replied. "I've got nothing to hide." He looked pointedly at Audrey, and then they all did.

"Then why did you keep your father out of the room?" Audrey demanded, but Kenny waved a finger at her.

"One ball, one question."

Teresa missed her next shot. Then James missed badly, almost tearing the green baize with the tip of his cue. Kenny shook his head in disbelief.

"I'll trade two questions for a new partner. Just kidding, Jimbo." He slapped the younger man's shoulder.

Audrey sank the four. She sized up her next shot before speaking.

"Why has your father hired an investigator?"

Kenny looked at her blankly.

"What are you talking about?"

"He hired somebody this morning. I'm asking you why."

"I don't know anything about that."

"Well, this is a pointless game," she said, bending over the table. "If I'm the only one who knows anything." The shot was lined up perfectly, but she struck too hard. The one ball rattled around the corner pocket before bouncing out.

Kenny swiftly sunk the fifteen.

"So where *did* you go this morning?" he asked.

"Your parents' house," Audrey answered, flipping hair out of her face in annoyance. "To borrow clothes. It was too far to go to my apartment. Big woo."

"I thought that looked like my mother's shirt," Kenny said. "She's going to be pissed when she sees you wearing it." He sank another ball. "How do you know my father hired an investigator?"

"I met him," Audrey replied. "At your dad's."

"Why didn't you ask him what he was up to?"

"One ball, one question."

Kenny tried a bank shot, which missed. Teresa lined up the five, but her mind was on Philip hiring an investigator. A strange development, yet one that proved she was not simply bored or paranoid. Something was up. She missed the orange ball completely.

James stepped up and shot without aiming. Balls rattled around the table, and the nine—a stripe—dropped into a side pocket.

"No good," Audrey declared. "Didn't call it."

"Oh, come on," said Kenny. "He'll probably never sink another one in his life."

"Give it to him," Teresa agreed. Expecting a fight from Audrey, but all she got was that withering look of pity mixed with contempt.

"Play to win, sweetheart, or don't play."

James ignored them, staring at the table as if trying to decipher some message there.

"How did the demon get into the painting in the first place?" he finally asked.

"Whoa," Kenny laughed. "Where did that come from?"

"That's my bro," said Audrey. "No lightweight stuff for him. I don't know who is supposed to answer that."

"The idea," said Teresa, "is that Goya was beset by a demon. That he spent those months in the Quinta del Sordo purging himself of it, by painting all of those horrific images." She was waiting for someone to interrupt, to tell her to stop repeating creepy family tales and get on with the game. No one spoke; they only looked at her. James urged her on with his eyes. "You've all heard this."

"I haven't," said Kenny. "I know Goya made it and we weren't supposed to look at it, but beyond that..."

"Fill us in, professor," Audrey added, spinning her cue stick like a baton.

"He painted right on the plaster walls of his house. Possibly over earlier works, some of them look that way. They were transferred to canvas after he died. Long after, in the 1880s, I think. I don't know who called them the Black Paintings, but that name stuck. A few have become famous. *Saturn Devouring His Son. The Witches' Sabbath.*"

"One went missing," James prompted her.

"There are fourteen at the Prado Museum," Teresa said, laying her stick down on the table. Her palms were clammy. "Some conjecture a fifteenth. There's a painting in a private collection in New York which a few historians think is that lost one."

"But we know it's not," James insisted, "because Grandpa had it."

"Maybe they're both real," Teresa replied, not liking his

agitation. "Maybe neither. I never saw the portrait. The point is…" What was the point, she wondered?

"You haven't answered his question," Audrey pressed. "How did this demon get from Goya into the painting."

"You're being too literal. The demon is a metaphor for the trouble in his life." Why did she have to explain this? "He was old and sick. Deaf. He was too friendly with Napoleon's gang when they occupied the country, so the Spanish nobility had no use for him anymore. The next step was exile in France, which is where he died. That little house by the river was a kind of internal exile. A place to work the darkness out of his soul."

"But he left the darkness behind," James said accusingly. "In the paintings."

"He certainly left a powerful record of what he was struggling with."

"He left the demon in that portrait."

"James," she said softly. She could see he was on the verge of some kind of outburst and did not want to push him over.

"Where is all this coming from?" Kenny asked.

"There's been plenty written about the Black Paintings," Teresa replied. "You can look it up online."

"But nothing about the demon," James interjected. "I've read it all. It's never mentioned."

Teresa was surprised, then realized she should not be. He was obsessive about topics that interested him. He read everything, interrogated anyone. Much like herself. She shrugged.

"Then that part is Morse family legend, I guess. The stories we were told."

"Not me," said Kenny. "I mean, I might have heard some things, but not this kind of detail. Who told you?"

"Her father," Audrey said, with smug certainty.

"Maybe," Teresa conceded. She had been hearing Ramón's voice in her head a lot the last two days. It seemed obvious that he was the one to speak of the portrait; everyone else was too frightened. Fear would not have been his lesson, just the reverse. He believed in the work's power, but not in a negative way. He believed there were things to learn from it.

"Accepting that it's just a metaphor," Kenny went on, taking up James' cause. "How do the stories say the demon got into the painting?"

"I don't know any story that speaks to that," Teresa replied. "Maybe it was a matter of his talent for depicting emotional states in—"

"What do you know about the curse?" James interrupted.

"Curse?" she asked. "I don't know anything about a curse."

"I need a drink," said Audrey, slapping one ball off of another. Game over.

"Let's hear it, Jimbo," sighed Kenny.

James glanced at the doorway. As if an angry adult might rush in to silence him. Audrey went over and pushed the door almost closed.

"The demon doesn't want to stay in the portrait," James said quietly. "Right? It's like a prison. It wants out."

"I guess that fits traditional demon lore," Kenny allowed.

"The demon offers each owner of the portrait a deal,"

James continued. "He'll advise them about their, um, worldly pursuits. You know, business or war or whatever."

"You're saying the portrait literally spoke to the owners?" Teresa asked in alarm.

"It's a *story*," Kenny complained. Though he looked as anxious as Teresa felt. As did Audrey, who was saying little. "Let him finish."

"The advice is always good, and the owner becomes successful at whatever he tries. Influential. Rich. But part of the bargain is they have to free the demon after some agreed time. And when the time comes, they're not willing. They try to cheat it."

"Never a good idea," Audrey said. "But there's a problem with your story. Grandpa Morse sucked as a collector. He lost a ton of money."

"Not always," Teresa corrected. "He made some shrewd deals. Anyway, collecting isn't about making money."

"What's it about?" Audrey asked.

"Most often it's about indulging your tastes."

"If you're going to lay down tens of millions indulging yourself, you better have the bank to back it."

"Teresa's right, though," Kenny said. "The old man used to be pretty good at the game. He knew how to push the price on second-rate work. He'd create some story around it, pretend he didn't want to sell." Kenny shook his head in admiration at this subterfuge. "My dad used to help him. Then he lost his touch, or lost his marbles. Wouldn't sell anything."

"The demon withdrew his assistance," James explained, "and things went wrong. That's what always happens. It

wants to find a new owner, one who might keep the bargain."

"And how exactly do you keep it?" Audrey asked.

"I was just going to ask that," Kenny chimed in.

"It's obvious," James replied, gazing at the dark window.
"By destroying the portrait."

"Where did you get all of this?" Teresa demanded. Her
voice jumped from the shudder rippling through her body.
James looked at her fixedly. The first time he had made eye
contact with any of them since beginning his weird tale.

"I don't remember. I've just always known. I thought
all of us did."

What had each of them been told, Teresa wondered.
What had they forgotten, and what had their imaginations
created over the years? And how would they ever know
now which was which? As a group, their eyes went to the
door. And saw Philip standing there. He studied them with
a curious or perhaps suspicious expression. Or was Teresa
inventing that? How long had he been there, listening?

"Sorry to barge in," Philip said, though he stood just
outside the door. "Dinner in about ten minutes."

"Thanks, Phil," said Audrey, leaning far over the table
to give him an eyeful down her shirt. "I hope you have
a good bottle of wine *breathing* somewhere." In one fluid
stroke she launched the eight ball into the corner pocket.
"Bang. I am so good at this game."

9

All good motels are alike. Each bad motel is bad in its own way. Dave had awakened in many strange rooms and was not particular. The Wildflower was cheap and near the highway, and the blue house encircled by apple trees exuded charm. But behind the house was the typical concrete block of rooms. In number 12 the lamp was broken, the mattress was—somehow—both misshapen and hard as stone, and the bedspread stank of the cleaning woman's Marlboros. Dave fixed the lamp, spread his notes on the spare bed and waited for Philip Morse to call.

His phone rang at two in the morning. He hated mobiles, and shoved the device in his sock drawer between jobs. But while working a case he always answered, day or night. Especially at night. Darkness got to people in a way that daylight could not match. Paranoia, drunkenness, despair had them dialing friends and strangers to confess all sorts of things, true and false.

"Hello," he mumbled, still partway in a dream. He had been trying to find Luisa in a deserted European city. Dave dreamed of his ex-wife often.

"Did I wake you?" asked a woman.

"Who is this?"

"I imagined you as an insomniac."

"Audrey," he said, becoming alert. He only half recognized the voice, but had no doubt it was her. "Are you all right?"

"Fine," she replied. "Do you have someone there?"

"You were only supposed to call if it was an emergency."

"If I really needed something, is what you said." What could she need that badly at this time of night? "Are you in the city?"

"No," said Dave. "A motel."

"Which one? I know the motels around here pretty well."

"Guess I should have called you first."

"They all suck. And I don't see you at some schmancy B and B. With homemade jam jars on the table and the owner's dog sleeping on your feet."

"The dog part sounds good."

"You like sleeping with dogs, huh?"

"Why don't we talk in the morning?"

"We have to meet," she said. "I need your help with something."

"Not tonight."

"Okay, in the morning. Although I was hoping to get a jump on things. You're not in one of those New Haven dumps, are you?"

"No," he said, "and I'm hanging up now. Call me to-morrow if you have to."

"It's raining here," she said softly. "Is it raining where you are?"

He listened to the light spray on the window. Listened to her breathing.

"Yes. Go to sleep, Audrey."

In the morning he slept until the rain stopped, then went out for coffee and a bagel. Back in the room, his phone rang. Her again. This was becoming a problem. Dave let it go to voice mail, determined to speak to her in his own good time. Then he settled into the hard chair and paged through old notes, newspaper clippings, depositions, photographs. Synthesizing as best he could on a yellow legal pad.

Early 1960s Alfred Arthur Morse acquires the Goya portrait. Seller unknown.

1982 Miranda Morse brings home professor boyfriend, Ramón Marías, who becomes fast friend and confidant of AAM. Supplanting Philip Morse in that role. Two years later MM and RM marry. (Daughter Teresa born 1985.)

RM shows obsessive attachment to portrait. Philip and AAM's wife (Dorothy) encourage sale. (According to both AAM and PM.) PM meets twice with DeGross during this time.

October 1996, Dorothy Morse dies from stroke. Buried two days later at Cedar Hill Cemetery. Most of family in attendance except:

Teresa Marías (11), stricken with an illness that morning.

James (11) and Audrey Morse (15)—children of Alfred Arthur III, aka Fred—left as companions for TM. Other reasons? James distraught over grandmother's death, known for episodes of hysteria (source?). Audrey troublemaker. One or both not wanted at ceremony? Punishment for some behavior?

Dave sipped coffee and flexed his fingers. His mind returned to Audrey. Not Audrey the smart aleck or manipulator, but the strong, troubled woman who occasionally showed through. If he could only speak to that person. He shook off the thought and took up his pen again.

Also at Owl's Point that day:

Jenny Mulhane (mid 40s), cook.

Peter Mulhane (31), Jenny's half brother, employed at her behest (AAM). Handyman, ex-Marine and Gulf War veteran, casual thief.

Ilsa Graff (56), longtime housekeeper and sometime companion of AAM (according to Fred's second wife, Joyce—credible?). Overseeing prep for wake and keeping eye on the children. Very little memory of day's events due to head blow.

Old Langford Catering Co., four employees (two men, two women; names?), setting tables outdoors. Did not enter house farther than kitchen, according to JM. (Jenny in pantry/cellar at times, so alibi not ironclad.)

RM leaves service early "to check on Teresa" (multiple sources). Arrives Owl's Point an hour later, longer than drive should take. Alibi to police unknown, but never seriously investigated. Before his arrival:

James Morse wanders to study while cousin and sister sleep. Why? Never questioned. Presumably he finds door open and witnesses theft in progress.

Approximately 3:20 p.m. IG, AM, TM, all hear JM scream. TM too ill to rise, sees AM rush from room. IG (last memory is going to check on Teresa) arrives at study first to be struck in head by thief. Audrey arrives next to find Ilsa unconscious, James in fetal position, painting gone. Runs to Jenny, who calls police.

About same time (?) two on catering crew see Peter Mulhane entering woods with a large black bag.

This was possibly critical, and frustratingly uncertain. In her first statement, one caterer reported seeing Pete a little after three o'clock. Questioned again, she conceded that it could have been later, even twenty minutes later. Was she led to change her story by the prosecutor? Did Pete's lawyer challenge it? And who was the other—

His thoughts were interrupted by a shadow moving across the beige curtains. They were still closed from last night. The figure shifted around at the spot they met, trying to see into the room. Dave rolled out of the chair and padded to the door in his socks. Not wanting to give whomever it was time to run off. He turned the bolt slowly, pulled the door inward and leaned out.

A black Dodge pickup sat in the lot, blocking Dave's Taurus. A large man in jeans and a leather jacket was moving away. Toward the next window, where he again tried to peer through the curtains. So he knew what car he was looking for, but not which room. Dave thought of going back inside and bolting the door, but he was too curious. In any case, the man glanced in his direction. Dave stepped all the way out, socks on the damp concrete, and leaned against the doorjamb. The big man strode back toward him. Rangy build, black hair cropped short, beard. Handsome in a brutal sort of way. The kind of man Audrey would like, no doubt. Audrey. Of course.

"Where is she?" the man asked.

"Who are you?"

The big man sighed, drooping his shoulders.

"I'm not doing this again. I speak to her, no one else."

"Tell me who you're looking for," Dave said. "Maybe I can help."

He saw the arm move and ducked away. Instead of striking, though, the man seized a fistful of his shirt and flung him aside. He was strong, and Dave stumbled a few yards before catching himself on the hood of the Taurus. Before he turned around, the man had disappeared into his room. Dave rushed after him. Embarrassed and angry, but also aware of the need for caution.

The big goon moved swiftly through the room, checking the bathroom and the closet. He slammed the closet door and looked at Dave expectantly.

"You want to look under the beds?"

"Where is she?"

"This is where we started. *Who* is she and why do you think she's in my room?"

"She told me to meet her here."

"Well, nobody told me about a meeting." Then he thought of Audrey's call this morning, the voice mail still sitting there. "Can you give me a second?"

The man crossed his arms and waited, but before Dave could do anything they heard the rumble of a car pulling into the lot. Dave caught a glimpse of the red Lexus before the other man shoved him aside, heading for the door. It might have been protective feelings toward Audrey that clouded Dave's judgment just then, but more likely it was getting tossed like a rag doll—twice—that did it.

He dived after the man, catching him behind the legs and bringing them both to the floor with a hard thump. The man groaned and put a hand to his forehead. He was hurt, but not badly, and would now be furious. Meaning

Dave had better hit him, probably many times, to keep him on the floor. He crawled up the man's back and punched him hard between the shoulder blades, twice, preparing to strike again at the back of the head. But a leather-clad elbow shot up and hit Dave square in the face. Cracking his nose and sending him reeling onto his left side. The big man was on his feet much too quickly. This was not going as planned. Oh, right, there had been no plan.

Face or gut, face or gut? Trying to cover both, Dave put his arm over his face and rolled his knees up. So when the boot struck it hit only ribs. Possibly cracking a few, but he did not puke up his bagel and that had to count for something. The man cocked his foot back again as a figure appeared in the doorway.

"What the fuck?" said Audrey. Dave could not help but notice she sounded more surprised than upset.

The big man hesitated, then kicked Dave anyway. Which, in fairness, was what Dave would have done in his shoes. Boots.

"Stop that," Audrey insisted. "What are you doing?"

"Where did you find this clown?"

"He's a friend. Why are you kicking him?"

"A friend you were meeting at a motel."

"What's that to you?"

"Nothing," the man said, feeling around his forehead. "Am I bleeding, can you see?"

"You're not bleeding, dipshit. He is."

Dave levered himself into a sitting position and leaned gently back against the bed. The ribs would trouble him for days, but at the moment the nose hurt more. He tasted blood in his mouth. Audrey crouched beside him, examining his face with a certain degree of fascination.

"That could be broken."

"Unph," Dave agreed.

"Why are we here?" the big man asked. "Does he have the money?"

"Shut up," said Audrey, peering more closely at the nose. "Do you have ice?"

"There's a machine," Dave wheezed. "By the manager's office."

She grabbed a handful of his hair and squeezed, in what he supposed was meant as a comforting gesture. Then she stood.

"Come on," Audrey said to the goon. "We can talk while—"

"I'm not going anywhere," he replied petulantly.

"He's got nothing to do with this," Audrey said sharply. "You want one more person involved?"

"Did you bring the cash?"

"What we said. Okay? So come on." She started out of the room without waiting for his answer. "Hang in there, Davie, I'll be back with ice."

The big man followed, not giving Dave another glance. In the minutes they were gone, Dave managed to pull himself onto the bed and retrieve his phone. Her message did refer to a meeting, and she had clearly expected to arrive first. Otherwise, it was not terribly illuminating. He tossed the phone aside and closed his eyes. Only to hear the pickup's engine roar to life. As it pulled away, Audrey strode into the room with a bag of ice.

"Now we need a couple of towels," she announced, heading for the bathroom.

"Audrey," he said, too quietly. Then louder, "Audrey."

She poked her head out of the bathroom door. Her face all innocent attention.

"Leave the ice in the sink and go," he said.

"This will just take a second, I have to—"

"I'm not asking you," he said harshly.

"I owe you an explanation."

"I don't want an explanation. I want you out of my room. Now."

"Look, I'm going to wet one towel with cold water, put ice in the other, and bring them to you. Then I'll leave, okay?"

As she slid off him for the second time, Dave had to concede the day was shot. He was not completely unhappy about it. The endorphins dulled the pain considerably, and his blues had faded. Temporary relief being the only kind available, he was grateful. Even if this was a terrible idea.

"I knew you had another one in you," said Audrey, her ample chest lifting and falling rapidly. She lay in a curvy heap, smiling at him through a curtain of hair.

"You kidding?" he replied, breathing even harder. "Give me a few minutes and I'll be ready for more."

"No *way*," she said, eyes getting big.

"That's right," Dave laughed. "No way. Unless you want to explain my corpse to the police."

"Screw that," she said. "I'd be long gone before they showed."

They both found this very funny. Endorphins were great.

She took his left hand loosely in her right. He thought she might kiss it, but she only held it and said, "Thanks."

For what? Not throwing her out? Rallying for a second round after the not-so-great first? She had waited until his head was numb from Advil and the ice pack on his nose. Then she'd unbuttoned his shirt and worked gently on the sore ribs. At some point the towel was replaced by her lips and tongue, and one thing had led to another. She was cautious at first, not what he expected, but she warmed to the task. Her urgency became infectious, and he was far too ready when she climbed on top. The second time was better. It was wonderful, actually, for both of them. Assuming she had not been manufacturing those moans and spasms. There you go again, Dave, poisoning the fun.

"You did all the work," was all he said.

"The least I could do," she said, crawling back to him. Damp and spicy, with a trace of vodka. Like she was sweating it. "Given your delicate condition."

He groaned as she fell against his side.

"Yes, and who's responsible for my delicate condition?"

"Um, let me think," she murmured into his armpit. "You?"

"Did I summon that goon to my room?"

"No, but apparently you jumped him." She propped her head on her hand and stared at him in puzzlement. "Why the hell did you do that?"

"I don't know. He seemed scary, and the way he acted when he saw your car…"

Perplexity, suspicion, then delight, all within moments. Her face was a magic show, but you had to be looking closely.

"You were defending me," she laughed, slapping his stomach. "You idiot."

"Not so hard," he said, feeling a little bad. His motives were more mixed than he was letting her believe.

"You've got a flat belly for an old guy," Audrey observed, smoothing her hand over it. "How old are you, anyway?"

"Too old for you."

"Clearly not," she said gleefully. "My ex-husband is older, too. Almost seven years."

"I'm older than that," Dave replied. "So you owe this guy money?"

"Rick does. My ex. Gambling, mostly."

"And what does Rick do?"

"Oh, everything," she said sarcastically. "He's what you call an entrepreneur. In other words, I married my father."

"I see. So why is this guy…"

"Zeke," she supplied.

"Zeke. That's perfect. So why is Zeke after you for the debt?"

"Because Rick is on a kind of permanent vacation. Nobody knows where to find him."

"How does that make you responsible?"

"This is a lot of questions, Dave." She tried waiting him out, but he had nowhere to be. "Zeke looks at it as a shared debt," she said, breaking eye contact. Meaning she was not telling the whole story, but that was fine. "He knows I don't have much money, so he only asks for a grand here or there. Then he heard about my grandfather dying."

"Ah, of course. So he thinks his ship has come in."

"Right," she said, sitting up and flipping the hair from her face. "I tried telling him things don't happen that fast.

I don't even know what I'm getting, if I'm getting anything. He doesn't want to hear. He was going to show up
at the house, which would have been a frigging disaster."

"So you redirected him here."

"I didn't know he would get here so fast," she protested.

"Why involve me?"

"I had to meet him someplace. Private. But I didn't want
to be all alone with him, if you know what I mean."

It was plausible enough, if not completely convincing.
Dave ran a finger along her smooth thigh.

"How did you know where to find me?" he asked, which
is where he had meant to start.

Audrey shrugged.

"Once I knew where you weren't, there were only a
couple of logical places."

He replayed last night's talk, which seemed so casual
at the time. She had eliminated B and Bs, places in New
Haven, and she knew he was somewhere it was raining.
Christ, was she looking at the radar on her phone? He was
going to have to take her more seriously.

"Would have served you right if I wasn't here."

"I'd have dealt with Zeke on my own," she answered.
"That would have been better than you getting beat up."

"Hey, I got some punches in."

"Of course you did, tough guy."

"How much do you owe him, Audrey?"

She slid away. All the way out of the bed, and began to
retrieve her clothes.

"I should get back."

"Okay," he replied. "How are things at the house?"

"Under control. Everyone's a little on edge."

"About the cause of death, you mean?"

"Not that," she snorted, pulling on her jeans. "Actually, the autopsy results came back. Heart attack, plain and simple."

"As you predicted," he said. "Thanks for telling me."

"Philip would have anyway."

"So what are they on edge about?"

"The will," Audrey replied. "Who gets the house, the paintings. What nasty surprises the old man left for each of us."

"When do you find out?"

"Soon as Grandpa's lawyer decides. Maybe right after the funeral."

"Which is tomorrow?"

"Yes," she confirmed. "You coming?"

"I don't think I'm invited," Dave replied.

"I'm inviting you," she said as her head emerged from the turtleneck. She tugged it down over those stunning breasts and flipped back her hair. "So who is Luisa?"

"What?" He felt punched in the gut. "Why are you asking that?"

"You said her name. In your sleep."

"In my… I wasn't sleeping."

"You were," she laughed, slipping her feet into low black boots. "Just for a little while, you know, between. Not going to tell me, huh? That's all right, I can guess."

He fell asleep? How could he not remember? Dave fought not to let his gaze shift to the messy pile of research on the other bed. How long was he out? Had she read any of it? Fully dressed, Audrey marched over to the bed and kissed him hard, then more softly.

"God, you're a wreck," she said smiling. "Look, there's been someone prowling around the property. My brother saw him. I think my cousin did, too."

"Huh. Any idea who?"

"Ideas, yeah. But I don't want to bias your own conclusions. So come to the funeral, and keep your eyes open. Never know who you'll see."

10

The plot was on a hillside, between a cherry tree and a Japanese maple, and far from the larger monuments. A simple granite stone bore the word "Morse" in capital letters, with Dorothy's and Alfred's names below. Alfred's date of death had not yet been carved, which was common, but for some reason disturbed Teresa.

She gazed over the broad vista of lawn, her eye drawn to the orange flare of sugar maples, just turning. It was a beautiful place. Across the way was the stone chapel where the ceremony had been held. A very brief ceremony, with the casket closed. That was both a relief and a reminder. She had dared to hope they would find a way to restore his face, so she could remember him looking regal and placid. No such luck. That awful mask remained fixed in her mind. The blue sky dimmed suddenly. The hillside fell into shadow, and figures moved furtively behind the trees. *It is all a surface, my Teresita. All that you see. Like a painting.*

Some of us are able to look through, to see below that surface. It is a gift, but a strange and sometimes terrible one. The vision lasted only a moment, but Teresa was left breathless and weak. She did not lean left, upon her mother, but the other way. Upon James. Without a word, without turning, he caught her upper arm in his strong hand. She was buoyed, she would not fall. Teresa closed her eyes and listened to the priest's singsong muttering.

She'd spent the previous day in bed, assaulted by memories, real and false. Walking the streets of Madrid as a girl. Her father above, his large hand enclosing hers. They spoke Spanish, which she only ever spoke now in dreams. They were in the Prado Museum. He had taken her to see the Black Paintings. Miranda would give him hell for it—you let a child look at *those*? But Teresa had not been frightened. Or a little frightened, in a way that made the experience exciting. Serious. She would never forget those works, would know them instantly in the bad reproductions of college textbooks, or old postcards pinned to corkboards.

Other memories felt just as real. Wandering along a river until they reached a small house, overgrown with vines. Inside were the same works painted onto the walls. The black horns of Satan's goat. The mad and bulging faces. More damaged and faded, yet also more powerful. But how could they be both in the museum and here? *Always questions,* mi pequeña. *The skeptic sees only lies. The open heart sees the truth. Just look.* He gestured her through a doorway, but she knew what was there and hesitated in fear. He became angry, and she had to turn away from his face. That terrible face.

Teresa blinked back tears. The priest droned, and all

eyes were focused on the shiny casket suspended above the open earth. Such a fancy case for a used-up form. No one looked at her, which was the main thing. She wiped her eyes quickly. Tears were normal at a funeral, right? She need tell no one they were for her father. Ramón had never been angry at her that Teresa could remember. And Goya's house by the river was demolished a hundred years ago. Yet the memory was so real. She missed her father profoundly today. An oddly timed grief, but Grandpa would understand.

Turning her head to take in James' profile, Teresa caught sight of a figure beyond. Twenty yards down the slope, near the hearse. A dark blazer and jeans. Brown hair touched with gray, and even at this distance she could see something was wrong with his face. His nose was swollen and discolored; the aviator sunglasses sat uneasily upon it. It was ridiculous to think he was looking at her. She could not see his eyes. The family was gathered in a tight mass of mourning. He could have been looking at any of them, all of them. Yet she felt certain those hidden eyes were locked upon her own. She was wondering who he might be when a second man came into focus behind him. Another twenty yards back, on the far side of the lane and half-hidden by the tomb he leaned against. Faded green military jacket. Tangled blond hair and beard. It had been a long time, but Teresa knew he must be Jenny's brother, Pete. Part of her had been looking for him all morning.

Proving that he had, in fact, been watching Teresa, the first man followed her gaze to where Pete stood. The two men stared at one another awhile, until Pete slid backward out of view. Moments later, the first man turned and strolled after him, also disappearing. The priest had stopped talking.

When Teresa turned back, the coffin was being mechanically lowered into the hole. It took longer than expected, and they all shuffled in place awkwardly. Miranda dabbed her eyes. Her brothers were stony-faced. Kenny looked like an advertisement for the suit he wore, while Audrey tugged at her ill-fitting skirt. Across from her, Cynthia—back from Paris last night—wore the elegant dress and jacket Audrey otherwise would have nabbed. She would have looked better in them, too, but it was good to see Audrey lose a fight.

No roses, no last words from the family, except those said under the breath. Miranda threw a handful of dirt on the coffin and Philip and Fred each did the same. Ilsa, clutching her sister's arm, seemed unsure what to do. No one had seen her until this morning at the chapel. She had refused to come to the house, and would tell no one where she was staying. Teresa remembered her as a commanding presence. Gray-eyed, silver-haired, ramrod straight in her bearing, with a quiet voice you did not contradict. She looked old now. Older than her seventy years, and frightened. Freddie stepped forward and encouraged her to toss some dirt on the coffin of her deceased employer, friend and—if the whispers were true—lover of decades. Ilsa did so, staring a long time at the casket, then at the dirt on her hand. Until Fred and her sister led her away from the hole. Then they wandered back to their cars. The little slope nearly made Miranda tumble off her heels, and she grabbed Teresa's arm for balance.

"Thanks, hon. I shouldn't lean on you when you're not feeling well."

"I'm fine today," Teresa lied. Pointlessly.

"Good. That's good. You took your medication this morning?"

"Yes, Mother."

"No need for that tone. It was brave of you to come. It would have been fine for you to rest another day."

"No, it would not have been fine."

There had been no way in hell that Teresa was going to replay her part from fifteen years ago. To be immortalized in family myth as The Sick Girl. She would have crawled to this ceremony on her hands and knees, brain on fire and blood seeping from her eyes. In fact, she did not feel that bad today, between bouts of the heebie-jeebies. And yesterday's rest had given her time to think. Or not think, to let ideas drop fully formed into her unresisting brain.

Such as the cause of Audrey's disappearances the last two days. She went off cranky and keyed up and returned glowing and calm. Duh. She was seeing a guy. Whatever else she might be doing, she was getting some action off the premises. Also, Philip and Cynthia were not living together. No one had mentioned it, but it was clear from their body language. This was a formal appearance only, for the family. They were no longer a couple. How long had that been true? What other truths was she missing? The secrets eating at James and Kenny had not announced themselves, yet her certainty that such secrets existed was stronger than ever. James' involved the lost painting. His interest was not abstract but personal, and driven by fear. Kenny was still a complete puzzle.

Teresa helped her mother into the back seat of Philip's Mercedes, then went around to the other side, scanning the grounds. There was no sign of Pete, but she spotted broken-nose forty yards away. Talking to Audrey, of course. And there was Philip, striding rapidly toward the two of them. Just before her uncle arrived, Audrey brushed her hand lightly over the mystery man's cheek. Then sauntered away.

"Thank you for joining me," said the attorney, targeting each of them in turn with his rheumy-eyed gaze. "I know it's been a difficult day."

"Cut the formalities," said Audrey, "and let's get to it."

"Shut up, Audrey," said Kenny in his calmest lawyerly voice. For some reason, she did. James and Teresa said nothing.

It was just the four of them. The cousins, seated in a half circle around their grandfather's ancient attorney. Mitchell had wanted to use the study, but there were heated protests to that plan. The other rooms downstairs were too open, not sufficiently private, so they dragged extra chairs into Alfred's bedroom. An intern from Mitchell's firm was posted outside the door. Officially to see people in and out and call the next group, but quite obviously to prevent eavesdropping.

To everyone's surprise, Ilsa had been called first. It was only with great difficulty that she had been convinced to come to the house, and purely for the sake of these legal matters. She'd spent twenty minutes sequestered with the lawyer, then staggered down the stairs in tears and went straight out to her car. "Guess she didn't like the retirement package," Freddie had said, a very full glass of scotch in his hand. Her sister Frieda made apologies and said goodbyes to all, then drove Ilsa away. The grandchildren were called next. Kenny had bounded ahead of them while Audrey and Teresa practically dragged James up the stairs.

"It is customary in these modern times," the lawyer continued, in a voice as wet as his eyes, "to simply mail the will to all appropriate parties. But your grandfather wanted things done a certain way."

With trembling hands, he reached to the desk beside him for a slender pile of documents. Then handed one to each of them. Teresa could read Last Will and Testament at the top of the first page, but the paragraphs below were covered by an envelope paper-clipped to the front. A sealed, cream-colored envelope with her name written on it in a shaky but elegant hand. She glanced over to see that each of them had received a similar envelope. Kenny was speed-reading the will itself while Audrey turned pages at random. James stared out the window, ignoring the papers in his lap as he would an overfriendly cat.

"You will see on the first page that I am named executor," said Mitchell after a few moments. "You will also note that a separate party is named artistic executor, overseeing the disbursement of the art collection."

"Hah," said Kenny in amusement. "Makes sense."

"What?" said Teresa, curious for the first time. "Who?"

"You," said Audrey, squinting as she read. "You don't keep the money, though."

"There is a fee provided for the position," Mitchell clarified.

"Forty grand," said Audrey, jutting her lip out. "Not bad."

"That figure can be adjusted at my discretion," the lawyer added. "Depending upon the time and effort required."

"Stop," said Teresa, trying to take in this bizarre turn. "I'm still in school. I'm not qualified to oversee a collection like his."

"There are detailed instructions," Mitchell replied, shifting uncomfortably in the hard chair. "Which I will present to you upon the assumption of your duties. Little has been left to your discretion. I will, of course, assist with the legal ins and outs."

"I don't know about this."

"You're free to refuse. But I will say that your grandfather and I discussed your level of experience, and he was quite satisfied that you could execute the task."

"Suck it up, Tay," said Kenny. "It's a good job for you."

"I'll help if you want," Audrey offered.

"Sure you will," Kenny sneered. "For half the money."

"I'd settle for ten."

Teresa sat back and massaged her forehead. What a ridiculous development. Had her mother known? What would she think, what would the aunts and uncles think? Would they be as indulgent as her cousins?

"Why are you seeing us before our parents?" she asked Mitchell.

"The order is your grandfather's," Mitchell replied. Then, almost as an afterthought: "Starting with beneficiaries and moving outward to other concerned parties."

Audrey's head shot up from the paper.

"Wait. Are you saying that our parents aren't beneficiaries?"

"Look at the document," said Kenny. "Page four."

They all flipped to that page, including Teresa and James. Their four names were in a row at the bottom, each fol-

lowed by a string of legalese and a number. The same number in each case: $250,000

"The cheap bastard," Audrey said under her breath, yet
more than loud enough for all to hear.

"Maybe we don't deserve more," said James morosely.

"You'll be lucky to see this," Kenny informed them.
"Between taxes, liquidation costs, what happens in probate. And the conditions precedent."

"The conditions…" Audrey read the passage in question
with growing alarm. "To be satisfied before the disbursement of any funds. Detailed in the accompanying document, specific to each beneficiary."

Kenny waved his still-sealed envelope, a rueful smile on
his face. None of the envelopes had been opened yet, and
no one hurried to unseal his or hers. James had gone still,
but there was a look of such anguish about his eyes that
Teresa reached for his hand. To her surprise, he seized hers
with a fierce energy, squeezing his eyes shut.

"So we have to do whatever it says in here before we get
our money?" Audrey asked, her voice pitching up a notch.

"That's correct," Mitchell confirmed.

"And our parents get nothing?"

"The beneficiaries are all named in the document."

"You know my father will contest," Kenny said, matter-
of-factly.

Mitchell gave him a long look. Despite his hangdog expression, there was ice in those eyes.

"He will act in whatever manner seems right to him.
But he will find that the document has been very carefully prepared."

"Doesn't mean he can't hang the whole thing up for

months, or years. But I guess that's good for the lawyers, right, Mr. Mitchell?"

The old man shook his head.

"I'm not a litigator, son. I am not even in regular practice. Your grandfather was my last client. Nothing would please me more than to see these arrangements settled in my lifetime."

"Wait a minute," Audrey interjected. "Who gets the money? Who gets the house and, and everything? Is it going to charity?"

"That's not the last page," Kenny said. "Flip over."

James was still holding Teresa's right hand, and she fumbled the document hopelessly with her left. Not sure if she even wanted to see what was there. Audrey gasped, then growled out three words.

"No. Fucking. Way."

"What?" Teresa asked, barely above a whisper.

"I can't believe this. She gets it all? She gets everything?"

"Who?"

Audrey's murderous blue gaze swung upon her.

"That old witch. Ilsa."

11

The brick pillars marking Owl's Point appeared on the left, but Dave slowed only briefly. The wooded part of the property lay west of the house, and the road shaped it closely. Within a quarter mile he saw what he was expecting. A lime green Chevy parked on the grass, half-hidden by pine branches. Dave pulled in behind it and killed the motor. He moved carefully getting out, but still tweaked his ribs. Almost any motion hurt. Breathing deeply against the pain, he approached the empty-looking vehicle. There was rust on the quarter panels, and the windshield was dirty. Balled up fast-food bags sat on the passenger seat, and an Irish cross was glued to the dashboard. Shiny gold plastic. Nothing else of note. Dave turned from the car to the silent woods. Not silent, woods were never really silent. You had to listen closely, separate the sounds. The chatter of sparrows. The distant pock-pocking of a woodpecker. The weighty swish of wind through pine boughs.

And what might be feet shuffling in the underbrush. The direction was a guess, but Dave picked a spot and started into the trees.

It was funny how things went. He had not intended to go to the funeral. It was not his place to be there, and it might have annoyed Philip Morse. Yet morning found him throwing on the darkest clothes he had and seeking directions for Cedar Hill Cemetery. Philip only nodded when he spotted him, standing well back from the grave. Dave assumed his hardest task would be not staring lustfully at Audrey. It was not Audrey who caught his eye, though, but a petite, dark-haired young woman. Her resemblance to Luisa was unnerving. Even now the memory brought him to a halt, hand braced on a damp tree trunk. Teresa, the sickly cousin, Audrey told him afterward. Instantly suspicious of his interest. You could not keep things from women, or at least Dave couldn't.

He was certain that Teresa was staring back at him, but then followed her gaze over his shoulder to the lurking man. He had never met Peter Mulhane. The groundskeeper went into hiding after the theft, and was then arrested, but Dave saw him once in a courtroom. Prison had not been kind to Pete. He had the edginess and paranoia of many ex-cons, and he bolted the cemetery grounds before Dave could catch up. The last sign of him was a green car racing away. You might expect a man so unwilling to talk to keep his distance after that, but Dave bet otherwise, and the empty vehicle by the roadside looked like his payoff.

A hundred yards into the woods he came to a tumbled iron fence, surely the property line. He stopped to listen, but the footfalls—if they had ever been there—were no longer audible. Once again he chose a direction at random and continued into the trees, which were thickly clustered now. The occasional oak or maple opened up the view, but it was mostly pine, and for long stretches he could not see more than a few yards in any direction. He was not easily spooked, but this place was creepy. He would be glad to reach the other side.

His senses were alert before the stimulus registered. He had not seen or heard anything unusual, but even with his nose so swollen he smelled something. Cigarette smoke. Dave shouldered through branches as quietly as possible. He found a cigarette butt near the base of a big oak, where the scent was sharpest. After a few moments the smell dissipated. But not that eerie feeling which fretted him. Indeed, it seemed strongest right here, almost a malevolent presence. A sound reached him, not part of the natural repertoire. A soft laugh. He waited most of a minute, but it did not repeat. A swath of green was visible through the branches. The lawn of Owl's Point. He moved in that direction until he made out figures wandering about, members of the returned funeral party. One of them might be the smoker. Had Mulhane come to meet someone? Was the car even his, or was Dave on a wild-goose chase?

A heavy thud spun him around. He slapped branches aside and was quickly in front of the creepy oak again. The muddy ground was gashed, and a crumpled pack of Lucky Strikes lay there. Directly above were the remains of a tree house that he had missed before. It had been on the far side of the trunk, but still, all he needed to do was look up. Idiot. Someone had been standing ten feet above, laughing at him. Dave heard footfalls rushing away through the woods. He scooped up the cigarette pack and pursued.

In half a minute he caught sight of a figure scrabbling over the broken base of the fallen iron fence. Faded army jacket, wild blond hair. The man from the cemetery. There was a hitch in his step that Dave had not noticed before. Probably he bruised something falling out of the oak, so the laugh was on him. Even so, he would reach his car before Dave could catch him. Only to find himself blocked by the Taurus.

"Hey," Dave shouted, dodging small trees as the road appeared ahead. "Come on, I just want to talk."

The figure did not slow down.

"Peter Mulhane," Dave said clearly. "What are you running from?"

Fifty feet ahead and maybe thirty feet from his Chevy, the other man stopped and turned.

"What do you want?" Mulhane demanded, hands on his knees. Obviously winded. It was a long time since his Marine Corps days.

"Only trying to give you these," Dave said, waving the pack of Luckys while continuing forward. "But it looks like maybe you should quit."

"Stop there," Pete replied, straightening up. "I have a gun in my pants."

"In your pants? Well, heck, be careful."

"No joke, man. You stay right there."

Dave stopped and looked over the other man. Mud on his jeans, leaf debris in his beard.

"You hurt yourself falling out of that tree?"

"I didn't fall. Ladder gave way."

"Uh-huh," Dave replied, examining the cigarette pack. "That sounds like falling. Only three of these left."

"You keep 'em," Pete said, walking backward. Dave did not necessarily believe in the gun, but it wasn't worth finding out.

"Saw you at the funeral," he said, keeping pace with the retreating man.

"Just paying respects to the old man."

"After he let you do ten years for a crime you didn't commit?"

That stopped him, as Dave knew it would.

"How do you know I didn't do it?"

"I don't," Dave admitted. "But it seems to be the general consensus."

"General consensus," Pete spat. "Who are you, anyway? Her boyfriend?"

"Whose?"

"*Whose*, he says. That prick tease. Audrey."

Where did he get that? Maybe Audrey had a lot of boyfriends, so it was an obvious guess. And why had Dave been confused about the "her" in question?

"Did she tell you that?"

"Nah," Pete said, shaking his head. "I ain't talked to her in a while. But she was looking at you that whole time by the graveside."

Which meant Mulhane had been looking long and hard at her.

"I'm an investigator," said Dave. Figuring, what the hell. "Philip Morse hired me."

"To do what?" Pete asked, backing up again.

"Find out who really took that painting."

"Bullshit," Pete shot back. "Why would he have waited all this time?"

"Good question. Maybe you should ask him."

"He don't want to talk to me."

Pete came up against his car and halted. Dave did also, twenty feet away.

"So you tried to speak to him. About what?"

"Hell, man, if you work for the guy, shouldn't he tell you this stuff?" Pete cackled. It was a good point, certainly.

"Is that why you've been hanging around here? Looking for another chance to talk?"

"Why would I do that? I'd go to his house, like before. I just wanted to visit the old place. Wasn't here ten minutes when you showed up."

"I don't mean today. The last few days."

"I don't know what you're talking about," Mulhane said, narrowing his eyes.

"Come on, Pete. You were seen in these woods, a couple of times."

"Screw this," Pete said, yanking the driver's door open and sliding into the car.

"Wait." Dave rushed forward, only to see the other man tug something free from his waistband. Maybe the gun was real, after all. He stopped again. "Take these."

Dave tossed the cigarette pack through the open window. Pete shook it, sliding a cigarette into his mouth and tucking the pack in his jacket.

"Thanks," he said.

"Let's get a beer," Dave suggested. "I'm buying."

"Nah," Pete said, gunning the car to life as he lit up. "If Philip wants to talk, he knows how to reach me."

"Some message I can give him?"

Pete gazed at him several moments with those pale, nervous eyes.

"Did you know he testified for me?"

"Philip?" Dave replied. He had been to an early hearing, but off the case before the actual trial started. "No, I didn't."

"His idea, I didn't ask. Character witness. Kind of funny, since he barely spoke two words to me in my whole life before that."

"That is odd."

"Ain't it? And I'll tell you something else, mister. I haven't been in these woods for fifteen years until today. See you later."

"Hang on, I'll move my—"

But Mulhane was not waiting for anything. He reversed into the Taurus with a loud crunch, knocking it back a few feet. Then he cut the wheel hard to the right as he put the Chevy in Drive. Pine branches scraped against the hood and roof, but the car sprang free and zipped off down Long Hill Road.

12

She stared at her closed bedroom door, willing James to knock. Knowing he would not. Neither of them knew how to seek comfort, to ask for help. Teresa pictured him doing what she was now. Sitting on his bed with the letter beside him. Lost in dark thoughts, hounded beyond the wall of death by their bitter, controlling grandfather. Damn the man. Though that probably was unnecessary.

They had all gone their separate ways after meeting Mitchell, but curiosity or common cause would draw them together before long. What would she reveal? James and Kenny knew what they would find in their letters. It was Audrey and Teresa getting the nasty surprise, yet in the end was it surprising? *Go to the place that's most private to you. Most humiliating. That's right where he would have put his finger.* Kenny had warned her, and her unconscious had gnawed at his words ever since. She tore open the envelope believing its contents a mystery, yet as soon as she began reading Teresa grasped the old man's intent. She did not read closely, just scanned words and phrases. *Impaired functioning. Occipital lobe epilepsy.* The names of surgeons. The second paragraph dealt with her father, and with a young person's tendency to romanticize mental illness. Teresa tossed the letter aside then. At some point she would read it through, but the meaning was clear enough. She was a broken thing. She needed fixing.

Another part of her understood that this was a long-delayed reckoning. Not with her grandfather, but herself. She had suppressed certain questions for so long that they stopped being questions, just shut-up rooms in her brain. The shock of the sprawled body on the sofa blew open those doors. She had found the courage to enter that room of death, and she would need the same courage to explore her interior chambers. To wipe the dust off old uncertainties and seek answers. Who had her father really been, and what had he done that severed him from his family? What did her visions mean, or did they mean anything? Would she be the same person without them? Was she brave enough to find out?

Oh, and a late addition: What or who had killed her grandfather?

She stood and paced. Hard questions for someone un-skilled at extracting information. She needed more than courage; she needed an ally. Up to now she had assumed it was James. But he could not even speak of his own trouble, and he would make a terrible detective. Audrey was the obvious choice, but she could not be trusted. Kenny was too removed from everything. Philip was the only one seeking answers, but why would he share them with her? He wanted the estate, which meant a fight with Ilsa, of which Teresa wanted no part.

The front doorbell surprised her. Family and friends had been in and out all afternoon without observing niceties. Curiosity sent her down the hall to the top of the wide, carpeted stairs. Audrey was below, changed into jeans and a dark blouse. She had the door open two feet, her frame filling the space. Blocking the man standing outside, or requiring that he push through her to enter. The man stayed put, speaking in a low voice.

"Come in," Audrey said, stepping aside. "But good luck speaking to Philip."

He moved stealthily into the hall. Dark blazer, dark circles under his eyes. Swollen nose. The man from the cemetery.

"Where is our Phil?" he asked.

"Beats me. Probably upstairs strangling the lawyer. Have you eaten?"

"Uh, no."

"Figures," Audrey said, with affectionate disdain. Her speech was vaguely slurred, and there was a sway in her step. "Come back to the kitchen. There's a ton of food."

They set off down the hall, and Teresa retreated to her room. Philip's investigator, he had to be. What was he doing here? What had he learned, and why did he make Teresa so uneasy? She slipped off her boots and went carefully down the back stairs. From the lower flight she could see the closed door of the study and the open kitchen entry. She sat on the second to bottom step. She could not see into the kitchen from here, but could easily hear anyone inside. Especially anyone as loud as Audrey.

"These are tasty. Not sure what's in them."

"Something indigestible," he replied with his mouth full. "I'll stick with the fruit."

"That's how you keep that flat belly."

"It was only flat because I was on my back."

"Yeah." She giggled. "Mine ain't flat in any position, as you know."

That answered one question, Teresa thought, shaking her head in wonder. Quick work even for Audrey.

"Are you okay?" he asked.

"You mean am I drunk," Audrey declared, exaggerating the slur. "Yes, sir, I am."

"Well, funerals…"

"If you must know, I've had a financial setback."

"Ah. Zeke won't be happy."

"Fuck Zeke," she said viciously. Who the heck was Zeke?

"I leave that to you."

"You think I'm doing him? You think I sleep with every guy I meet?"

"Only the hopeless cases."

"Did you catch up with Pete?" she asked, her tone more casual.

"I did, yeah."

"You going to tell me?"

"You going to split my fee with Philip?"

"Philip," Audrey said acidly, "owes me more than he can ever repay. What's he giving you, anyway?"

"I got the impression you and Pete have been in contact. I mean, since he's been out of prison."

"You did, huh?" She was quiet for a bit. Ice shifted in a glass. "He came to see me. Year or two ago."

"To catch up? Were you two pals before the theft?"

"I was fifteen, dickhead. But yeah, I was friendly with him, maybe he remembered that. I wasn't the only one he visited either."

"Who else?"

"Philip. Ilsa, I think. Maybe others."

"What did he want?"

"You are getting seriously boring with these questions, Davie."

There was no reply, just more ice slushing against glass. Audrey tossing back another vodka, no doubt.

"He asked about the family," she finally said. "How everybody was doing. Mostly he wanted money."

"Did you give him any?"

"Few bucks, out of pity. What did he tell you?"

"That Philip was a character witness at his trial."

"Oh yeah," said Audrey in a flat voice. "That was kind of weird."

"You know why he did it?"

"Philip? Why would I know that?"

"Because you know things. You keep your ears open."

"I have to watch what I say to you."

"He also claimed not to have been in those woods for fifteen years."

"Huh," she mumbled. "You believe him?"

"He was convincing. I haven't been around him long enough to know when he's lying."

"That a skill of yours? Lie detection?"

"Yes," he said.

One of their phones buzzed. The first bars of a pop song, so Audrey's.

"I've got to take this," she said. Teresa stood, preparing to flee, but Audrey's voice went the other way, toward the dining room. Teresa sat again. This was her moment to confront him, while Audrey was out of the room. What would she ask? She was sitting there puzzling it out when he magically appeared. Standing in the doorway, profile to her. A glass of something clear in his hand and an anxious look around his eyes. His eyes, which were dark and round and hypnotic. She did not move. His head went left to right, from the basement door to the hallway, the study, the stairs. The merest shock registered in those eyes, a quick flare around the irises, at finding her so close. Then he simply stared. Teresa should have felt unease, but there was something so tender in his face, and so forlorn, that she was disarmed. She could not look away. He blinked and stepped back, breaking the spell.

"I'm Teresa," she said, standing and extending her hand. With the stair giving her a boost, she looked him straight in the face. "Marías. I guess you know that."

He took her hand carefully, as if she were an animal that might startle.

"Nice to meet you, Teresa. Dave Webster. I work for your uncle."

"I know."

"Yes. No secrets in this family."

"There's nothing but secrets," she countered. "That's just not one of them."

His smile transformed his face nicely, but lasted only a moment. The face looked less swollen up close, but more colorful.

"What happened to your nose?" she asked.

"That, yeah."

"You don't have to tell me."

"It ran into an unfriendly boot."

"Ouch." She had an urge to touch it. "No one I know, hopefully."

"I wouldn't presume to know your pals, but I doubt it."

"Vodka?" she asked, looking at his glass.

"Gin," he answered, taking a large swig.

"I don't think there's any gin in the house."

"That explains the lack of kick," he replied. "Just water, then. So you were, uh, having a quiet moment back here?"

"No, I was eavesdropping on you and Audrey."

Dave nodded agreeably. He knew exactly what she was doing, of course. He had the manner of someone who was never surprised, but his casualness felt forced. Teresa would swear that she made him nervous. Strangely, she was no longer nervous at all.

"Sorry we weren't more entertaining," he said.

"Actually, I was riveted. Does Philip know you're sleeping with her?"

"He's probably figuring it out." He gazed at the floor sheepishly. "It was only one time."

"Won't happen again, officer."

"I'd like to promise that, but…"

"She's a force of nature," Teresa commiserated. He smiled again.

"She is," he agreed. "Anyway, it wasn't very professional of me."

"You must be good at what you do if Philip hired you."

"No," he said. "I mean my abilities have nothing to do with it. I have prior history with the case."

"I don't understand," Teresa said, her mind chasing possibilities. "My grandfather only died a few days ago."

He looked blankly at her until comprehension came.

"I'm not investigating your grandfather's death. I understand an autopsy was performed and nothing suspicious turned up."

"Maybe not in the autopsy. So what are you investigating?"

"Wait," he said, stepping forward. "Do you have a reason to think there was something odd about his death?"

"Did Audrey tell you?" she asked, trying to keep the quaver from her voice. "About the, um, about his body? The condition of the body?"

"She said something," Dave replied, weighing words carefully. "Did you see him, or did she tell you about it?"

"I found him."

"You did?" He seemed perplexed, then nodded slowly. "She said that she had."

"Of course she did," Teresa snapped. "She always has to be the center of attention."

"Or," he proposed reasonably, "she was trying to protect you from intrusive questions. Like these."

"Yeah," she conceded, exasperated with herself again. "That could be it. She's been watching out for me. I don't know why I'm being bitchy."

"There you are," a none-too-friendly voice said from the hall. Philip strode toward them in an obviously foul mood, the source of which was no mystery. "If you can take a short break from seducing my nieces, I need you to meet with my brother and sister."

Instead of jumping at Philip's command, Dave looked

to Teresa. As if awaiting her leave to go. His gaze touched her. However unwise it was to assume, she felt they had made a connection.

"Nice to meet you, Dave," she said, ignoring Philip's stare. "I'm sure we'll talk again."

13

Night was falling, the last they would all spend together under this roof. There was no formal dinner. People took what they wanted from the kitchen. Laurena and Cynthia sat at the table and gossiped. Miranda and her brothers stayed holed up in the old man's room, long after Dave left. Kenny and Audrey shot pool. Teresa worked feverishly in her room. From memory, not her preferred method, but she wanted no witnesses in case she needed to destroy the result. Her marks were quick and sure for someone so out of practice. Her fingers cramped around the pencil, but it felt good to be working. She stared at the sketch awhile, then went to look for James. He was not in his room, or on the lawn, or in the wine cellar. If he had gone into the pines, Teresa was not following him there in darkness. Then she thought of the attic.

The stairs were at the back of the house. She had not been up in years and could not remember where the switch

was, but there was just enough light to see. Modest bedrooms lined one side of a narrow passage. Servants' quarters.
There was a storage area and at the far end an unfinished
room that had been intended as a studio. From the stairs,
Teresa could see a light within. She did not call out, but
went quietly to the door. James sat on the floor, or what
there was of one. Some spots were just exposed insulation.
His back was against a wooden beam, and his face averted.
Beside him was a candlestick from the dining room with
a lit taper.

"Mind if I join you?" she asked.

"No," he replied without enthusiasm. "Careful of the
floor."

She made her cautious way to him and sat down.

"This is where you've been hiding out, huh?"

"Sometimes." He rubbed his palm over his knee. "They
sealed up that place in the cellar."

"I know. Audrey was outraged."

"Audrey?" He looked at her in surprise. "What's it got
to do with her?"

"You showed it to her once, I guess."

"I did?" He went away in thought. "I didn't remember."

"I made this for you," she said, handing him the small
sketch. He stared a long time at the loose, impressionistic
version of his face. The swiftness of her lines made him
look slightly unhinged, Teresa noticed, and nearly stole
the page back.

"It's not very good," she said anxiously. "I haven't worked
in months. I don't know why. I just haven't felt the urge."

"No," he murmured. "No, it's wonderful. It's the grown-
up me."

"I guess it is."

"I almost didn't recognize myself. This is great. Thank you, Tay."

"Don't thank me. I should thank you, I get very few requests for my services. I'll do better next time."

"Maybe a real portrait?" he said, smiling hopefully at her. "With paints and everything? This can be the preliminary sketch."

"Only if you wear a lab coat and stethoscope," she said, trying to laugh off the idea. "Are you happy to be leaving? To get back to school?"

"I don't know. Are you?"

"I'm not escaping so easily. I'll need a leave of absence to deal with the collection."

"Shall I stay and help?" he asked, taking her hand. Sounding neither eager nor hesitant. Just serious. Always so serious. His hand was large and a little clammy. It made her think of Dave Webster's warm, steady grasp. She leaned her head on James' shoulder.

"That's a sweet offer, but I'm not sure what you could do. I'm not even sure what I'm supposed to do."

"I could keep you company. We could talk about things."

"Family stuff?"

"No," James said. "Paintings. Old paintings."

"What about them?"

"How they were made, and preserved. Or restored. How they're understood."

How demons get into them, Teresa thought, but she refused to tease him.

"I know you know those things," he pressed, squeezing her hand. "And in your spare time you can work on my portrait."

"You have to get back to school. Medicine is serious, you can't miss classes."

"Do you ever wonder?" James said in a different tone. Sadder. "Do you wonder what our lives would be like if Grandpa never bought the Goya?"

"Well," she said, searching for an honest reply, "I don't know if I've thought of it like that. I wonder about the theft. How things might have gone differently that day if I didn't get sick. I wonder about my dad. Why he left, what we could have done to make him stay."

"None of it is your fault," James said urgently. "You mustn't think that. You couldn't help getting sick, and your father... It wasn't his fault either. He had a high resistance to the painting, but that only got him into more trouble. He was always in there looking at it. Both of them. In that room conspiring, remember?"

Remember what? she almost said. She only knew of Ramón's obsession secondhand, but then a vision pushed in upon her. The two of them, James and Teresa, standing outside the study. Sweaty hands clasped, like now. Very close to the door, listening to the men talk inside. It was not a unique memory. They had stood there several times. They had heard many scary and fascinating things. It was almost certainly the source of what she knew of the painting and its history. The source of James' strange—and strangely familiar—tale the other night. How the hell could she have forgotten? Yet she had, completely, until now.

"Anyway, it started before," James continued. "From the time Grandpa got ahold of the work. It warped our parents. Made them greedy and frightened people. It killed that man, that art historian. It made my mother not want to live, and it made Grandma say cruel things. Things she never would have said before. It changed us all."

His hand was gripping hers painfully now, but she would not pull free. Would not abandon him. Nor would she accept his words blindly.

"The painting changed our lives, but it didn't change us," Teresa said. "It only brought out the worst. It made us more what we already were."

"No," he seethed, shaking his hand loose as if hers was on fire. "That's not right. That's not right at all."

"James." There was nothing to say. She could listen, she could try to draw him out, but she could not indulge dangerous fantasies. "I'm sorry."

The stairs at the end of the hall creaked. Loudly, then again more softly. Someone was coming up. They froze. Like two terrified children in a horror movie. Not snuffing the candle, not hiding, just sitting there, numbly awaiting the monster. A dark form with spectral white hair slipped in the doorway and stopped.

"We're crashing your party," slurred Audrey. She held a glass of blood-dark wine, and the guttering candle made her face jump. Kenny stood behind her, sipping a beer and gazing about the room.

"I don't remember this place."

"You've never been up here," James said bitterly. Implying that they should not be here now.

Audrey took a careless step onto the spongy insulation, and would have fallen on her face if Kenny had not grabbed her. She shook off his hand with a shiver of anger.

"You're welcome," Kenny said.

They stepped carefully to where the other two sat, forming an awkward ring about the low flame. Audrey passed the wineglass, and Teresa took a deep drink. The taste was earthy and potent. James had a slug of Kenny's beer. He did not want it, but that didn't matter. There was a ritual quality to it. As if they were swearing an oath, without words.

"You two figuring things out?" Audrey asked, tugging a pack of cigarettes from Kenny's shirt pocket.

"You can't smoke in the house," said James automatically.

"Why not?" Audrey scoffed, lighting up. "You think Grandma's ghost is going to come scold me?"

"Serve you right if she did," Kenny said. But he took the cigarette when she passed it.

"What are we supposed to be figuring out?" Teresa asked.

"So many things," Audrey said breathily. "Did you like Dave?"

"Who's Dave?" asked James.

"The guy my dad hired," Kenny answered gloomily. "With the broken nose."

"He seemed nice," Teresa said.

"Nice," Audrey spat. "He's not nice. You better watch out for him, little girl."

"You think?" Teresa took the cigarette from Kenny and had a pull. Then blew the smoke in a narrow jet at Audrey. "That's funny, because we made a date."

Audrey's face went rigid. Then relaxed slowly into a smile.

"Lying bitch," she said proudly. "I'm just saying, he's dangerous."

"What was he doing here?" James asked.

"Supposedly investigating the theft of the painting," Audrey informed them. "He's the same guy Grandpa hired."

"No," Teresa said in disbelief. "He's not old enough."

"Pushing forty," Audrey replied, stealing back the cigarette. "He was working for his father-in-law back then. That's how he got the case. Truth is, Philip's just paying him to say stuff to my dad and your mother."

"What stuff?" Kenny asked sharply.

"Do we want to talk about this?"

"Talk about what?" Teresa asked.

"He knows," said Audrey.

There was silence while the elder cousins stared each other down.

"Say whatever you want," Kenny replied.

"Grandpa thought that Philip stole the painting," Audrey said, softly enough that Teresa had to lean in to catch the words. "That's why he was left out of the will. Philip is paying Dave to say he didn't do it. Or something like that."

"Why?"

"So they'll agree to join him in a suit. For the property. The three of them have to act together to have a chance."

Kenny had no reaction, which could only mean...

"You *did* know," Teresa said.

"Know what?" he snapped. "That the old man thought it? Yeah, he told me. In our little chat on Saturday. But it's bullshit. My father never would have done that to him."

"Of course," Teresa agreed. Not knowing what to believe. It certainly did not sound like Philip, but their grandfather must have had reason to think so.

"And *my* dad is obvious," Audrey continued. "He's

blown all his money so many times that Grandpa just figured, you know, why give him more? Which leaves your mother," she added, pointing the cigarette at Teresa.

Who said nothing at first. It was odd to know something Audrey did not, and Teresa had only heard it an hour earlier. Her mother claimed not to know the reasons, but she had somehow learned that her brothers were cut off. Maybe her father told her, maybe Ilsa had. Miranda informed the old man that if Philip and Freddie got nothing, she would prefer to get nothing, as well. Clearly, he had honored her request. Just as clearly, no one but Teresa would believe it. They would call it a self-serving fairy tale by Miranda.

"She was pretty wild when she was young," Teresa said. "So maybe it's the same as your dad. Grandpa thought she would waste it. Or maybe it just seemed more fair to make it a clean sweep."

Audrey nodded, satisfied with the lie.

"So much for them. What about us?"

"I'm not playing," said Kenny, finishing his beer with a long swallow.

James got up and went to the window, forcing it open with a loud squeak. He crouched before it, breathing the night air. Audrey shook her head at both of them, mashing the cigarette out on a floorboard. Then she looked at Teresa.

"How about it, *Teresita*? Some kind of brain surgery? A mental health screening to prove you're not nuts?"

"Jesus, Audie," said Kenny in disgust.

"Yes," Teresa said, staring back at her witchy cousin. Unblinking, voice steady. "That's about right. You?"

"I was guessing. You can do the same, can't you?"

"A dry-out clinic in the desert, maybe?"

"That's about right," Audrey replied, then emptied the wine in one gulp.

"Drugs?" Kenny asked. "Booze? Bestiality?"

"It's a three-in-one deal," Audrey shot back. "You still not playing?"

"Nope."

"Fine," Audrey said, leaning toward him aggressively. "But answer me this, you big pussy. Whatever it is you won't tell us, are you going to do it to get your money?"

There was that adolescent rage again, twisting Kenny's pretty face. Another vision intruded on Teresa's mind. The four of them swimming by the bridge. Audrey teasing Kenny. Yelling, slapping, then Kenny twisting Audrey's hair in his fist and holding her head underwater for too long. Teresa and James had to scream at him to let go, and Audrey emerged pale and choking. Had there been other incidents over the years? Could that hidden temper be connected to Grandpa's instructions? The condition too shameful for Kenny to name?

Instead of striking his cousin, Kenny slapped the empty beer bottle, which flew to the center of the room and spun. They all watched until it came to a stop, pointing at Audrey.

"So?" she asked coyly. "You going to kiss me?"

"Pass," he grumbled, the anger dissipating.

"Wouldn't be the first time. I won't stick my tongue down your throat."

"Please," groaned Teresa, "do I have to know this?"

"Come on," Audrey laughed. "We were, like, thirteen. You have to learn somehow."

"No," Kenny said with a hard finality. "To answer your

question, I'm not doing what he asked. I tore up the letter. Unlike others in this room, I don't need the money that badly."

Though she knew he meant Audrey, Teresa felt her cheeks burn. Student loans, sketchy employment. Graduate school was on scholarship, but there was no stipend. She could really use the money. But it was impossible.

Audrey bit her thumbnail, as Teresa had seen her do when the wheels of calculation were turning.

"You made it sound like we would never see that money," Audrey noted. "Won't it get tied up in probate or something?"

"I'm guessing neither side will contest the grants to the grandchildren," Kenny explained. "Yeah, it could take a while, but you'll need that money just as much in six months or a year. Maybe more."

Audrey rolled onto her hip and pulled the folded envelope out of her back pocket. Teresa nearly laughed, as her letter was in exactly the same place. None of them were going to leave the incriminating words lying around.

"I need it, sure." Audrey unfolded the envelope and slid the letter out. "But I'll be damned if I'm going to be blackmailed by a dead man." She glanced at the note once more, then extended her arm until the corner of the paper met the candle flame. It took a moment to catch, but soon the creamy sheet flared to life, illuminating the dim corners of the room. The letter curled and blackened, vanishing inch by inch. Audrey let go and the final unburnt shred drifted slowly to the floor, as the room grew dark again.

"Fuck the money," she said.

Teresa let out the breath she had held for half a minute.

Mesmerized by her cousin's performance, and inspired. Audrey had nailed it. It was not tough love Alfred offered, but blackmail. Which is why she must refuse. She tugged her own letter out of her back pocket. She had meant to read it properly, but that would not happen now, and maybe it was for the best. Before she could reconsider, Teresa touched the letter to the flame and stared in fascination as it ignited. Feeling heat on her face and her fingers. Releasing the corner at the last moment.

"Fuck the money," Teresa said.

Audrey hooted and clapped her hands. Kenny stood and marched out of the room.

"Screw him," said Audrey, with a dismissive wave. She was very drunk. Was it wise, Teresa wondered too late, to emulate a drunken person?

"Turn around," James said to them, having moved away from the window.

"Huh?"

"Turn around," he repeated. Then more insistently, "Turn your backs to me."

Teresa and Audrey exchanged a look, but complied. There was the sound of scraping wood. A floorboard or panel being shifted. Teresa tried to remember a hidden compartment in this room, but nothing came to her. He never told them to stop averting their gaze, but they both turned back when the room brightened a third time. James wore a deeply solemn expression as he gave his own letter to the greedy candle. Determined to get the job right. Yet Teresa saw something unusual in his face. A restrained joy, perhaps, at doing something so reckless. Or maybe it was only the flames dancing in his dark eyes.

"Fuck the money," he said softly, just as Kenny strode back into the room. In his hand were the half dozen torn strips of his own letter. He knelt down and fed them to the flame one by one, until they were gone.

"Fuck the money," said Kenny, arms dropping to his side.

And they were done. Ashes skittered along the floor, and the room smelled of smoke and beer and rebellion. Teresa felt a tingling throughout her body and took deep breaths to stay calm.

"So that's that," said Audrey. "And may the demon take any of us who goes back on his word. Now, Kenny, honey. How would you feel about making your favorite cousin a loan?"

14

"Mr. Webster?"

Dave looked up from the glossy magazine to the woman behind the desk. A long article on Matthew Barney had stupefied him into near speechlessness.

"Sorry, yes?"

"Mr. DeGross is off the phone." She had been stealing glances at his bruised face for the last ten minutes, and now took the opportunity to stare openly. "If you would like to go in."

Dave tossed the magazine aside and went through the door to her left. Where the outer office was full of the sounds of Madison Avenue two stories below, the inner sanctum was quiet. A swaying locust tree filled most of the back window, and the furnishings were spare. An old sofa, a few chairs, a bookcase and some second-rate landscapes. Either Charles DeGross had no taste or was anxious that you should not know what his tastes were. The man himself was short with curly gray hair and lively eyes behind thick lenses. His suit was expensive, but hung awkwardly on his squat frame. He did not hide behind his desk as Alfred Morse had, but came straight to Dave with a smile and a firm handshake.

"Mr. Webster, welcome. Very good to meet you."

"Thanks for making the time."

"Nonsense, thank you for breaking up the dull routine of my day. Please, sit."

Dave did so, laboring to order his thoughts. He had come to expect anything from civility to open hostility from his interview subjects, and was comfortable with that. He grew calm in direct proportion to their agitation. The collector's warmth threw him. He had hoped to leave DeGross for later, collecting clues from others first. But Philip's siblings were no help, Fred drunk and hostile, Miranda cagey and silent. Ilsa Graff would not talk at all, and no one knew where to find Jenny Mulhane. DeGross, whom Dave expected to be elusive, agreed to an appointment at once. And here he was.

"Tell me, how is the Morse family?" DeGross asked, with a convincing tone of concern, as he settled behind the desk.

"Bit of a mixed bag. There's a lot for them to sort out."

"They are not a close family, I think."

"I think that's fair." Get off this subject, Dave. "I was hoping we could discuss your relationship with them."

"So you said on the phone. This is on behalf of Philip?"

"He's the one who hired me, yes."

"This time," DeGross said. He did not actually wink, but it was in his voice. Dave had wondered if the man would remember him from those years before, when DeGross had adamantly refused to speak. Had threatened legal action against Dave if he so much as telephoned him a second time. "Hired you to...?"

"Review past events which might have a bearing on the estate," Dave said, being as vague as possible. "I can't say more than that."

"Of course. In truth, Philip is the only member of the family I can claim to know. I am somewhat surprised not to have heard from him regarding this visit."

"He's allowed me a degree of latitude," said Dave, improvising. It had become clear to him that Philip was focused on the will. Reopening the investigation into the theft had dropped from his mind. He had written Dave another check—barely enough to cover the damage to the Taurus—but had not directed him what to do next. So Dave was winging it.

"You mean that he does not know you are here," De-Gross concluded.

"He wouldn't be surprised," Dave lied. "We talked about your association. If you want to call him, I'll wait. Or we can reschedule."

"Not necessary," the collector replied with a wave of his hand. "Our association was brief, and I don't know what I can tell you that Philip has not already. You are welcome to ask whatever you want."

Like, did you steal the painting? Maybe better not to start there.

"You say Philip is the only Morse you know. Did you not know his father?"

"A little. We met once or twice, I think. At auctions. Exchanged a few words."

"Did you use intermediaries when you offered for the Goya?"

"At first," DeGross said. "But we were both dealers, in addition to being collectors. Both forthright by nature, I would say, so we ended up speaking."

"Not in person?"

"By telephone. I made the first offer to his assistant, the second directly to him."

"I wasn't aware of an assistant," said Dave. Though it made sense for a man like Morse to have one.

"A German woman," DeGross specified. "Or Swiss, maybe. Formidable."

"Ilsa Graff?"

"That's the name."

"She was his housekeeper," said Dave. And heir, as it turned out.

"More than that, surely. I understood her to be involved in all of his important decisions."

"Philip told you this?"

"He might have," DeGross allowed. "Anyway, that was the impression I received."

"It may be true," said Dave. There was so much he did not know. "Seven million and then ten million dollars."

"Correct," the man replied, not feigning a cloudy memory.

"That's a lot of money, Mr. DeGross."

"Not enough for Morse. Though he did consider the second offer for a few days."

That was interesting. A man who would not sell at any price would not need to consider. Alfred Morse never told

Dave his reasons for refusing the offers, or whether there was a magic number that would have changed his mind.

"I remember a figure of twenty million dollars bandied about," DeGross added, before Dave could ask. "Which was absurd, of course. Yet there was no promise he would sell even for that."

"Some would say ten million was absurd."

"Many would, yes."

"What compelled you to go that high?"

"An excellent question," the collector said. Yet no answer followed.

Then another question, the most obvious question in the world—though it had struck him only now—occurred to Dave.

"Wait, when did you see the work?"

The man smiled thinly. As you might at a slow student who finally solved a difficult problem.

"Do you think me so brave, Mr. Webster?"

"Meaning?"

"I never saw the work."

Though it was the answer Dave expected, his reason rebelled.

"You offered ten million dollars for a painting you had never seen?"

DeGross smiled wider and nodded. Like they were laughing together at the foolish doings of a mutual friend.

"That's…" Dave struggled to say what it was.

"Madness? It's a hard thing to explain, but I had no doubt of the painting's existence. Nor any doubt that I should know it for authentic when it was in my possession."

"Why wouldn't you demand a viewing?"

"There was no need to demand," DeGross answered. "Morse invited me to come see it."

"You didn't want to," Dave said, nearly in a whisper. "Did you *ever* intend to look at it? You know, after you bought it maybe?"

"I had not really made up my mind about that."

"Why did you want it at all?"

"My apologies for not offering before—would you like a drink, Mr. Webster?"

"No," Dave said, though he must have looked like he needed it. And the thought was suddenly tempting, despite the earliness of the hour.

"Did you know that Philip Morse wanted to be an artist?" DeGross asked.

"I didn't."

"No reason you would. His father, who revered artists above all men, mocked him. Humiliated poor Philip for such an indulgent and grandiose idea. The boy considered art history, then settled for history, then finally went to law school."

"As his father intended."

"Yes," the collector sighed. "Mustn't disappoint Daddy. But I'll tell you this, he was a pretty fair artist at one time. He had the makings."

He let the words sit, and Dave's mind circled them hungrily. DeGross was not the sort of man to tell pointless anecdotes.

"My God," Dave breathed. "He saw it. He was the only child to see the Goya."

"Yes," DeGross purred.

"So, what, he painted it?"

"You're quick, David. Not a painting, a sketch. From memory. But, oh, what a sketch. What an awful and beautiful thing. It was enough for me. Both the image itself and what it cost him to make it, to show it to me. It convinced me that all I had heard and read was true."

Dave felt unmoored. Sick. As he had those years before. A sickness that sent him hunting a cure more poisonous, a cure he never found. Though he lost plenty.

"You know what I mean," said DeGross.

"Pretend I don't."

"That first expert. The one sent to examine the paintings while they were still on the walls of the quinta, one hundred and fifty years ago. Illness, insanity, suicide. Then the marvelous Marquis de Salamanca, the first owner."

"Alleged," Dave managed to say.

"Of course. It's all alleged, David, don't be a pedant. He saw what use could be made of the thing. Creating an aura, frightening enemies, not to mention the inexplicable luck in business which attaches itself to the owner. At first. Fortunes made and lost. Yes, José Salamanca had a great time of it, until he was ruined and had to sell. Alfred Morse had less flair, but he used the painting the same way. Don't believe he was upset by that art historian expiring in front of it. Perfect for burnishing the legend. It wouldn't surprise me...ah, but I risk saying too much."

"You believed all that, and you still *wanted* the thing?"

"Who would not want that?" DeGross demanded to know.

"Most people."

The collector resettled himself in his chair and gazed at Dave with something like disappointment in his eyes.

"Thank you. I accept the compliment. Not everyone would have the courage to take possession of such a painting, that's true."

"You weren't buying a painting. You were buying an idea, a ghost."

"A demon, you mean."

Here it was, out in the open. There was no smile on the man's face. He was deadly serious, and Dave now understood Philip Morse's frustration with his father. How many men like this were there in the world? Wise enough to know the risk, mad enough to want to take it. Rich enough to pay for it.

"Would you have gone higher than ten million? If he pushed you?"

"Probably," DeGross said after a pause. "I wish now that I had."

"Do you know what happened to the work?"

"What do you think?"

He was not faking his passion, Dave would bet anything on that. It was equally clear that it had gone unrequited. Still troubling him like a great love that should have been.

"Did you ever try to find out?"

"I made inquiries," DeGross admitted. "Not among the family. Morse and the police would not have tolerated that. I put out feelers to the sort of people to whom such a work might eventually come. Really, even that should not have been necessary."

"Because anyone who knew what he was doing would come to you. Who else would possibly offer more?"

DeGross let his silence be his assent. They sat in that unhurried silence for a little while, until the collector spoke again. In a hushed voice.

"Do you have a guess? Any guess at all where it might be, Mr. Webster? I know you made inquiries, too, after you were removed from the case."

Dave clenched his left hand into a fist to avoid any other outward sign of distress. It was a pointless exercise. Everyone involved knew his story, and someone like DeGross would not even find it odd.

"It was hard for me to let go," he said. "I knew the artist so well, knew the other works. I had been longing for a job like that. To have to leave it unfinished…"

"And go back to insurance cases. Which was your father-in-law's primary business."

"Yes. But all I did was waste my time. Researching. Seeking out people who wouldn't speak to me. I had too little experience, no useful contacts. I learned nothing."

"I suppose we would not be sitting here if either of us knew the work's whereabouts," DeGross said sadly. "Still, if any small clue were to come your way."

"I would be obliged to share it with Philip."

"Philip," DeGross snorted, as if the name were a joke. Though he had been speaking compassionately about him just minutes before. "I can recompense your time and trouble far beyond the limited imagination of Philip Morse, I promise you. Don't say anything now, just keep that in mind."

"I have to ask," said Dave, "do you still have the sketch?"

"No. I never had it, he only showed it to me."

"So it's in his possession?"

"I should have said…" DeGross hesitated, with a little shake of the head, but then continued. "He burned it. Right there in front of me."

"Burned it," said Dave numbly. Tasting the dry ash on his tongue.

"It wasn't the first time, nor probably the last. He drew it over and over again, you see. Never the same way twice, or so he said. And he burned them all. It was a sort of expiation, I suppose."

"Or exorcism."

"A better word," DeGross agreed.

"And if he did it again and again…"

The collector nodded slowly, watching Dave's troubled eyes.

"Yes. Then it clearly did not work."

15

Fred met her at the train. She was spooked to see him driving his father's Jaguar, but more alarmed to smell whisky on his breath. Yet they made it to the house without incident. Teresa looked out the windshield at the brick mansion and sighed. Forty hours away, now back to this haunted place. She could have remained longer in the city. Could have gone downtown to inventory the works in storage, which were the more valuable ones. Could have seen Marc, or caught up with her pal Julian, or spent more than two blessed nights in her own bed. But Teresa knew that if she stayed away from Owl's Point for too long she would not be able to return. Especially with everyone gone.

Not everyone, of course. Not with all that art on the walls. Teresa being there alone was acceptable to no one. Ilsa had communicated her intentions. She would not support Philip in contesting the will; indeed she would fight for ownership. Not from any strong desire, but because it was Alfred's long deliberated wish. She had no interest in taking up residence, however. Philip wanted to hire a security firm, but Fred insisted he had nothing to do for a while, and there were guns in the house. Guns, booze and jangled nerves, thought Teresa. Great.

"Well," Freddie muttered. "Let's go inside."

"Yeah," she agreed, popping her door and stepping into the autumn chill.

The season had advanced dramatically in a few days. October was here, and leaves were yellowing. Her eyes strayed to the pines across the lawn, and she halted. Had a figure stepped back into the trees? Not a branch swayed; nothing was visible. Don't do this, she told herself. Do not give in to this, you don't have time. And you don't want poor Freddie to have to lock you in the cellar.

"What is it?" Fred asked. Teresa noted that his suspicious gaze was aimed not at her but the tree line.

"Nothing," she said. "Those pines always creep me out."

"Christ, you spent enough time in them," Fred grumbled, continuing toward the house. "I guess kids like to be scared."

"Am I still a kid?"

"You are to me."

The job would take days. She started in the attic and worked her way down. Match the painting with the inventory list. Make sure it was the correct work—subject, style, dimensions. Check the condition. Warping, holes, nicks in the frame, those were easy. Harder was determining residue buildup on the surface, discoloration, the degree of craquelure. Especially with her lack of training and the poor light. Some pieces had been photographed at the time of purchase, some had not. Several were by major artists, but none were famous, so the records were spotty. Teresa knew she should not overworry it. Institutions to which works were promised would soon send their own appraisers. Her focus should be on the lesser pieces whose fate had not been decided. But the bigger works interested her more, and overworrying is what she did.

On a wall of the second-floor corridor, the face of Anton Raphael Mengs gazed out from a dark and unfinished background. Teresa leaned in with her flashlight and magnifying glass. There were wide, curved cracks in the "French" pattern, but no obvious paint loss. It was in good shape. If it was a real Mengs, not a student or copy, it might fetch forty or fifty thousand. She straightened up and looked again at the broad forehead and black eyes. She remembered a self-portrait of Mengs she had seen in Europe. Open gold jacket and brown hair to his shoulders, haughty and beautiful. Not here. The flesh had begun to loosen, troubled eyes were sunken in shadow. It was a more handsome face to Teresa, weary and revealing. He would die at fifty, impoverished and with too many children.

Something in the expression made her think of Dave Webster. Not a comparison he would welcome, perhaps, but her mind needed little excuse to fix on him. What was he doing now? Had Philip dismissed him or was he still on the case? If so, why had he not contacted Teresa? She had been at the house during the theft; she had found the body. She knew more about the artist than any of them, and her father had been a suspect. She could help him. They could help each other. Had he been told to stay away? By Philip, or Audrey? The idea made her angry. Then the anger made her smile. Which was good. This was not about her. He did not owe her an audience. She did not even know what he was investigating, but if it was for Philip it was surely about money and property. Not a missing Goya.

Teresa looked to the window and saw the light fading. Enough for today, she would check on her uncle and dinner. The kitchen was empty, but a pot simmered on the stove, and she heard noises. She went to the door of the mudroom and there was Fred. In stained jeans and a denim shirt, cleaning the shotgun. A glass of scotch sat on the windowsill beside him.

"Isn't this a picture."

"If you say so," he replied, laying down a long brush and wiping his hands on a rag.

"Whisky and weapons, so American. Anything you need? Crackers? Cocaine? A hand grenade?"

"You could check on that stew," he said.

Teresa stirred the pot and turned down the heat. A shadow passed the window, but she did not look. She had been seeing movement at the edge of her vision all day, and ignoring it. She could not take the pills and be sharp enough to work. So she must be calm and disciplined. But she was not working now, and there was the Balvenie on the counter. Teresa poured a generous glass and returned to the mudroom. Fred occupied one bench, and she shoved coats aside to sit on the other. The room smelled of oil, metal and earth. She liked it.

"Didn't figure you for a scotch drinker," Freddie said.

"Just being sociable."

"As long as you appreciate it. How goes the work?"

"Well. To the extent I have any idea what I'm doing," she qualified. "I'm suited to it."

"Then I guess you made the right choice. About school."

"Only took me three years to figure it out."

"Three years is no big deal," he said dismissively. Staring down the steel barrel for any recalcitrant bits of grime. "Not at your age. With both your dad and grandfather pushing you that way, it's no wonder you'd resist."

This thoughtful Fred was new to Teresa. She remembered the fun-loving goof who made her laugh. Not as tall or handsome as the other Morse men, but more charismatic. And she had seen flashes of the tyrant who beat his daughter and terrorized his son. Audrey forgave the beatings, which she claimed to have earned, but hated him for the endless business trips and slow emotional withdrawal. James feared him, though Teresa was sure there was love mixed up in it. Fred had been kind to Ilsa during the funeral, the only one of the children to show any warmth. People were never as simple as you wanted them to be.

"Where's Laurena?"

"In the city. We're thinking of selling the apartment. She likes California, and I'm in Asia most of the time now, so it makes sense."

"How's your own work going?" Teresa asked.

"My work," Freddie echoed disdainfully. He put the gun down with care and picked up his scotch. "What I do can't exactly be called work. Closer to gambling."

"Isn't that why you like it?"

"Hah," he said, then took a big swallow. "Oh, that's smooth."

"Grandpa had good taste."

"Too smooth for me, I prefer a little edge. I like it when it's going well. I like winning. Nobody likes losing millions of dollars, least of all my investors."

"You were counting on money from the estate," she said, the whisky loosening her tongue. Fred did not look offended.

"I haven't counted on anything from the old man in years," he said, running a hand through his thinning hair. "And there isn't enough money to really change things. But it would have helped. Kept the wolves at bay."

"Couldn't you say that to Ilsa?"

"Say what? I'm not going to beg that battle-axe for a handout."

"Not beg," Teresa said. "Appeal to her on a human level. You've been kind to her, she likes you."

"She doesn't like any of us," Freddie said sourly. "She might hold me in the least contempt, but she totally absorbed Dad's disgust. More than absorbed it, she…well, no use talking about that."

She what? Teresa wondered. Abetted it? Caused it?

"Why is everyone so hostile in this family?" she asked. Not expecting an answer.

"It always comes from the top, right?" Fred replied. "I don't know why Dad had children. It's what you do, I guess. Carry on the line. But he had absolutely no use for us, and he wouldn't pretend. The art was all he cared about, if he even cared about that. Big hole in the center of that man. Sometimes I pity him."

"What about Grandma?"

"She tried to be good to us, but she wasn't equipped.

She liked nice clothes and parties and that stuff. Like her daughter, and granddaughter. Sorry, I shouldn't—"

"It's all right," Teresa said.

"She cared about making Dad happy. She did try there, but it was hopeless. We were raised by nannies and house-keepers. Ilsa was the last, and the toughest. She had to be. We were teenagers. Heck, Phil was in college. Mean, calculating, self-centered monsters. She wouldn't have survived a month if she didn't find a way to control us, or at least protect herself."

"And how did she do that?"

Freddie looked mournfully at his empty scotch glass.

"By learning our secrets."

"Yeah? What secrets?"

"Kid stuff, at first. Then worse stuff. I can't speak for Phil or your mother. That was the thing. She knew us better than we knew each other."

"And she told your father?"

"When it served her purposes. Or just threatened, to make us behave."

Could Ilsa be behind it? Not the shocked recipient of unexpected wealth she portrayed, but a skilled manipulator who poisoned Alfred's mind against his children. Teresa found it hard to accept, but then why? She knew Ilsa even less well than she knew the others.

"She was good to me," Teresa said, stupidly. She put the glass down and stumbled on. "Not warm, that's not her nature. But kind, attentive. Fair."

"I think she does like you," Fred said, without rancor. "You don't make trouble. Then there was your dad."

"What about him?"

He looked at her closely. As if trying to see if she were pulling his leg, and Teresa felt suddenly nervous.

"I guess you were pretty young," he said, breaking eye contact.

"Come on, Fred, don't mess with me. Why would Ilsa like my dad?"

"Well, my father loved him," he replied reasonably, "so she may have responded to that."

"That isn't what you meant."

"Talk to your mother about it."

"I'm talking to you," Teresa said.

"Don't take that tone with me," he growled. A momentary wave of unease passed over her. She was alone in the house with this guy. Who was known to be a mean drunk.

"I'm sorry," she said. Because it was just good old Fred, after all, and her tone *had* been too sharp. He sighed and toyed with his empty glass. Teresa handed hers over, and he quickly downed what was left.

"Ilsa had a thing for your father. I thought everyone knew that."

"What? No, she was, she was older." Which meant what? Teresa asked herself. And it was not even true. Her father was forty-two when he married Miranda, forty-three when Teresa was born, only two or three years younger than Ilsa.

"I didn't say he had a thing for her. Or that anything happened, I don't know about that."

"She was in love with Grandpa, I thought."

"Hard to picture her in love with anyone," Fred replied with distaste. "But yeah, that was understood. He'd stopped paying her attention by then. I mean that kind of attention. She had his ear until the end. Look, all women had a crush on your dad. My wife certainly did."

Teresa was stroking the sleeve of an old coat hard enough to burn her hand. You asked for it, honey. Would her mother confirm this? Could she bring herself to ask?

"Anyway, it's not a case of her liking kids," Fred went on. "She hates mine."

"Audrey made her life difficult," Teresa said numbly.

"Christ, she made all our lives difficult. Drove her mother around the bend." He quickly realized what he had said. "I don't mean it like that."

"I didn't take it—"

"It was an aneurysm. Anything else you've heard is bullshit."

"Okay," Teresa agreed, watching him wrestle with himself. That same fury that was in Kenny and Audrey. Was it in Philip and Miranda, as well? And if so, how had she and James avoided it?

"It's not just Audrey," he finally said. "And it's less that she hates them than, well, she's afraid of them."

"Afraid? Why?"

"I don't know, because they're nuts?"

"I was recently informed that we're all nuts."

"What, the whole family?"

"Yup."

That got a small smile from him.

"I won't deny it. They aren't terrible kids," he said sadly. "Just a bit off. I wasn't a very good father. Too rough on them, or not around enough. Ah, you don't need to hear this."

Teresa was trying to think of something comforting to

say, or if she wanted to be comforting at all, when two things happened. First, she noticed that the sleeve she was mauling belonged to an old coat that had lived in this room forever. Everyone used it. Audrey had it on one morning last week. Worn canvas, faded green. The same exact shade as Pete Mulhane's army jacket, or the coat that the man in the woods had worn.

Next, a shadow fell across the floor. A figure stood in the window right behind Fred. Inches away through the glass. Don't look, Teresa. You've been doing so well today. It will vanish if you ignore it. Do not look. But she couldn't help herself.

Freddie was up and facing the window before Teresa even realized she had screamed.

"What?" he demanded. "What is it?"

"Someone," she gasped. No face. But an unmistakably human form beneath a speckled gray shroud. There for a moment and then gone. "Someone was right behind you."

"Who?"

"I couldn't tell."

He grabbed at the shotgun, dropped it, then picked it up and went to the outside door.

"Don't take that," Teresa said, not knowing why.

"It's not even loaded," Fred replied in exasperation. He turned back to point a stained finger at her. "Stay here. You stay right here."

Then he went out, closing the door behind him. Teresa could do nothing at first, only take deep breaths and try to blink away the afterimage of that figure. So still and so sinister. Well, of course it was sinister, she berated herself. What kind of creep peers in windows with a cloth over

his head? That did not make it something, something...
unnatural.

Freddie passed by the window, looking left and right.
Clearly he had not spotted anyone. As he turned toward
the trees she saw him halt abruptly, squinting at something
outside Teresa's line of sight. Then he broke into a run.
She took one more deep breath to steady herself, jumped
up and rushed out onto the lawn.

Her uncle was halfway down the slope, looping around
the angel statue. Teresa followed as fast as she could, losing ground. He had vanished into the pines well before
she reached them. She pulled up before the wall of green,
the adrenaline rush abandoning her. Don't be a girl, go in
there, she commanded herself. Go. But where? What direction? She listened closely, waiting for the shotgun blast,
despite knowing it was not loaded. For no good reason she
drifted to the nearly invisible entry point that led to the
tree house, pulled a branch aside and went in.

She could not see beyond the next pine, and with every
step she imagined a shrouded figure suddenly appearing.
Now, or now. Panic rose up, but she controlled it. In under
a minute she caught sight of the old oak, and Fred standing
beneath it. The shotgun pointed at the ground. He glanced
at her quickly as she approached, but did not turn.

"I told you to stay put."

"Where is he?" Teresa asked, trying to follow where his
eyes looked. But he was not looking at anything. Instead
he seemed lost in thought. "What did you see?"

"Not sure," he murmured, shaking his head.

"But you saw something," she said desperately. Her tone
brought him out of his reverie, and he looked at her.

"Yeah. Didn't get a clear look. I lost him right about here."

"So you didn't notice anything, like, strange?"

"Such as?" he asked. She had heard that tone before. The sane and reasonable speaking to the mad. After a few moments Freddie continued, "Let's go. You were right about this place being creepy."

"I couldn't see him because he had something over his face," Teresa made herself say. "Like a cloth, draped over his head."

She had Fred's full attention now.

"That's what you saw?" His tone did not sound patronizing, but uneasy.

"Did you see it, too?" she asked. Hoping. Needing someone else to be with her in this.

"Not me," he answered. "But that's exactly what Ilsa reported to the police. A figure with something draped over his head, wandering through the house on the night your grandfather died."

16

He was tired and annoyed, and the F train took its usual eternity to deliver him to this borderland of Carroll Gardens and Red Hook, where he had lived the last six years. On top of which he was being followed.

Dave had been stood up for a coffee date in Manhattan. There was relief mixed with his irritation, but it had wasted two hours and allowed him too much time to meditate on frustrations. Ilsa Graff was still not talking. He had identified sixteen Jenny Mulhanes in the Tri-State region, and ruled out nine based on age or circumstance. He would need to contact the others, assuming they would speak and assuming that was all the Jenny Mulhanes there were from New Jersey to Connecticut, which he doubted. An old friend in Corrections had passed along some info on Pete Mulhane's prison time, but Pete himself was not to be found. The meeting with DeGross had been intriguing, but added no new avenues for inquiry. Except pointing him straight back at Philip Morse. Just as talking to Pete had done. Philip, who had paid Dave enough to repair his car and cover a month's rent, and would not return calls now. It was possible that Dave worked for no one at the moment. Which would hardly be a new experience.

He hit the liquor store on the corner of Third Place to buy a bottle of vodka, though he had not drunk the stuff in years. Then he crossed Court and went into Caputo's, picking up a few things he did not need while keeping an eye on the street. There. Lingering by the grocer's across the way, back turned to him. By the time he emerged from the narrow shop of fine Italian foods, his stalker was no longer in sight. It did not matter. Dave had gotten a good look, and he relaxed a bit.

Past Saint Mary Star of the Sea, under the rumbling shadow of the Brooklyn-Queens Expressway, he turned right and went halfway down the block to a brick town house. Then he sat on the concrete steps and waited. In less than a minute his stalker sauntered down the street and stopped in front of him. Black today. Black boots, jeans, jacket, sunglasses. Dark red lipstick. Right hip shot out like a Greek statue. She looked good. Good enough to push up against that car behind her and—

"Hey, Davie," said Audrey.

"No one has ever called me that."

"I have," she corrected. "So this is where you live?"

"Basement apartment. There's a garden in back."

"That's cute. You out there like the old Italian guys, planting your tomatoes?"

"I wish," Dave said truthfully. "Why this game? If you

wanted to know where I lived you could have asked. At our coffee date you missed."

"I didn't miss it. You just didn't see me."

"Clearly," he conceded. Wondering where she had been hiding. Watching him. Then following him all the way out here. It was weird.

"Would you have told me?"

"No."

"See, I knew that," she said, stepping forward and butting her knee against his. Her eyes were unreadable behind the shades. "We'd make a good team, but you don't trust me."

"That's true."

"So I can't trust you either, even though I want to. Anyway, thought I'd see what you were up to. Who you were meeting, how the investigation was going."

"There is no investigation," Dave said, sounding more sullen than he liked.

"What, Philip pulled the plug?"

"Not that he's told me. Everything is just a little hazy right now."

"Not me," said Audrey. "I'm not hazy."

"No, you're not."

"I have a plan, and I want you in it. But we've got to figure out this trust thing. Are you going to invite me in, or did you buy that wine for yourself?"

Not wine, but vodka. Her drink. He had known exactly who was following him and what he was doing, even as he pretended otherwise. The idea disturbed him. Dave stood abruptly, expecting her to step back. She did not, of course, and he had to push past her to reach the basement steps. It was not until he got to the bottom and unlocked the door that he saw she had not moved. She just stood there, hands jammed in her jacket pockets, looking down at him. Like a vampire awaiting an invitation.

"Come on," Dave said. "Come in."

She wanted to try it a different way.

"Ow."

"Sorry, how should—"

"No, I like it."

"*Ow* you like it?"

"Yeah. Hold my knee higher," she instructed. "And move this leg a little. Yes."

"Yes?"

"Yes. Now harder. Oh. Good, that's... Yes."

"My feet are going to cramp."

"Shut up. Shut up and just...just..."

She descended into a stream of banal but effective obscenities. Only to scale the heights of eloquent inarticulacy, hips jerking wildly. Moments later and without warning, he climaxed so intensely that his soul was ejected from his body. Floating briefly in a bright ether of pure sensation. Returning cleansed, and most reluctantly, to his tainted and collapsed form.

"You don't make any noise," Audrey complained.

Because my pleasure is none of your business, he thought. Recognizing how contrary to the spirit of the thing that was. And hypocritical. His pleasure was predicated almost completely upon his partner's, always. Luisa had been the same, which made them a poor match in that regard. Some-one needed to be greedy.

"I was kind of focused on the mechanics."

"Did you not enjoy it?" she asked, rolling toward him. She looked so happy after sex. Her round face lit up. Her eyes seemed a brighter shade of blue.

"No, it was great," he insisted, or tried to. There was no energy in him; he felt loose and limp. It was a good feeling. "A real toe curler."

"Did your feet cramp?"

"Yeah, but I didn't care."

"Good," she said, slapping him on the ass. "Show a little enthusiasm next time."

Then she jumped off the bed and went to the kitchen. The moment she was out of view his paranoia struck. It was all he could do not to follow her, but he only sat up and made himself wait. In half a minute she returned with the vodka she had left in the freezer. She did not go long between drinks.

"Here," Audrey said, handing him the cold glass. He meant to refuse but took a drink. Then another. He did not like vodka, but it was good this way. Biting.

"You don't drink," she said.

"Not much. A beer now and then. I abused the privilege."

"Me, too," she sighed. "But I can't go more than a couple days before everything gets me down. I've got to have either the booze or the cancer sticks. Right now it's both."

He had tasted smoke on her, but had not seen fit to mention it.

"You going to tell me why you came here?"

"I don't know yet," she replied, taking the glass back and downing most of it. "Are you ready to ditch Philip?"

"Pretty close. He may have ditched me already."

"Pretty close isn't good enough. You want to know what's going on? Like, solve the case or whatever? For yourself, I mean. For your own satisfaction."

"I can't live on satisfaction," Dave said.

"There would be money," said Audrey.

"Whose? You don't have any money."

"That could change."

"So your scheme is about solving the theft?"

"My scheme is about paying back Zeke and getting out of this frigging hole I'm in."

"And how certain is it?"

"Not certain at all," she said defiantly. "You'd be taking a flier."

"I'd have to trust you."

"That's right." She looked away from him and finished the vodka. "This isn't going like I hoped."

"You need to tell me more, Audrey. I can't commit to something this vague."

"And I can't tell you unless you commit," she said. "So I guess we're done."

They sat in silence. Dave very much wanted to know her scheme, but was not willing to say whatever she needed just to learn it. And she would know if he was lying. Probably it was something ridiculous, yet there could be a clue in it.

"How is your brother?" he asked.

"Fine. Back at school. What you want to ask is how is my cousin, right?"

He had thought about her, on and off. Mysterious Teresa. The mother and both uncles had warned Dave off of talking to her. She had a condition. Fainting spells or something. There were hints of a more serious disorder. Philip alluded to mental instability in the father, Ramón, who had jumped off a bridge in Argentina a dozen years back. Dave had only met her the one time, and briefly. She was small and quiet, but she did not seem fragile. He would have said that she seemed strong.

"All right, how is she?"

"Don't know," said Audrey. "I haven't seen her since the day of the funeral."

"She also back at school?"

"No," Audrey replied, leaning off the bed to dig through her jacket. She came up with a pack of cigarettes and a lighter.

"Don't do it," Dave said.

"Seriously?"

"Not in here. You can go out in the garden if you want."

"Well, shit, Dave." She seemed more perplexed than angry, and threw the instruments of death back on the floor. "She's in the worst possible place for her."

"Which is where?"

"Back in that house. They've got her overseeing the paintings. Donations to museums and all that."

"Sounds like a good thing," Dave said. "Hands-on training, making useful contacts."

"It's a good job," Audrey agreed stiffly. "I guess. But it's a bad place for her. She had, like, five attacks when we were there those few days. And now she has no one watching over her but my alcoholic dad."

"You're saying she's more at risk for these attacks at Owl's Point?"

"Haunted houses tend to bring out the worst in people, don't you think?"

That fear again. Dave had not seen it in her since their breakfast date, over a week ago. She had it under better control now. She had her big plan to steady her.

"It's just a house, Audrey. Maybe the painting was haunted, but it's long gone."

"Go spend a couple of nights there and then talk to me. I mean it, Dave. Somebody needs to get her out of that place."

"Have you said this to anyone?"

"They won't hear it from me. They'll think I'm jealous that she has this important job. Hey, what time is it?"

She sat up, breasts flattened on her knees, regarding her scattered clothing. Dave could see from her distracted look that she had grown bored of the conversation. Bored of him. In a moment she would make one of her quick exits. Which was for the best, but he might not have this chance again. He needed to get whatever he could, right now.

"Charles DeGross," he said. She gazed at him blankly. "The collector who offered ten million for the Goya," he elaborated. "You asked me his name a few times. Pretending you didn't care."

She narrowed her eyes.

"Why are you telling me?"

"Trust isn't a leap. It's a process. Like this, for instance. I tell you something you want to know, you reciprocate. Who knows where we might end up?"

"You always surprise me," she said, shaking her head.

"Thing is, I already found out his name, so you'll have to come up with something else."

"You found it," he answered, taking a calculated risk, "by reading my notes while I was sleeping in that motel room." Her eyes widened, but she did not object swiftly enough, and she understood immediately that he saw it.

"What if I did?"

"Then, in a manner of speaking, it is something I told you. Along with who knows what else. So not only do you owe me, you're late."

"You don't feel like I've given you anything?" she said, smirking suggestively.

"We both had our fun. One thing is not another thing."

"I'm not saying I agree with any of this, but what do you want to know?"

"Lots of things," Dave replied. "Right now I'd settle for Jenny Mulhane's whereabouts."

"And why would I know that?"

"Couldn't say. Pete might have mentioned it when you spoke to him."

She bit her thumbnail, thinking it over. Looking for the trap. But in the end the game was too much her style to refuse.

"Okay," Audrey said, sliding toward him. Dave made himself focus on her face and voice. "I don't have an address or anything, but Pete did say she was working at a restaurant on the Jersey Shore. In the kitchen."

"You remember the name?"

"Something lame. The River Café, maybe? In Toms River. And she's cleaning people's houses on the side. Kind of sad."

"A steep fall from Owl's Point," Dave agreed. "Thanks for that."

"It isn't a favor, right? It's a trade. Now it's your turn again."

His phone was buzzing on the night table. It had rung earlier, but Dave had been in no position to answer. Audrey looked at the screen.

"It's Philip."

"I'll call him back." He did not want to speak in front of her, but he also did not feel like jumping just because the lawyer had finally gotten around to calling.

"You should take it," she said, holding the phone out to him.

Dave grabbed the device and accepted the call.

"Hello."

"There you are," Philip boomed, loud enough for Dave's neighbors to hear. "I've tried you three times. Where the hell have you been?"

Fucking your niece, Audrey mouthed at him. *Say it*. But Dave said nothing.

"Are you there, Webster?"

Dave nearly hung up, but he had heard something in Philip's tone. A shakiness. A sharp worry underlying the bluster. The attorney had experienced a recent scare.

"We should meet, Philip."

"No doubt, but something pressing has come up. I need you to do a job that's outside of your usual line."

This had better be good, thought Dave. Strangely enough, it was.

17

She should not be here.

"This is James. You can leave a message."

Teresa ended the call and put the phone back in her pocket. That was so him. Not "please leave a message" and certainly not "I'll get back to you." More like "speak if you must, maybe I'll play it next week." She pictured him in the overlit basement of some grim medical facility. Carving up cadavers with intense concentration. Preparing himself to save the world. It was a ghoulish vision, but it amused her.

Uncle Fred snored through whisky dreams, and Teresa wandered the dark and empty house. At least she prayed it was empty. All the doors and windows were locked—the alarm would not engage otherwise. No one could get in. But who or what might already be inside? Unseen, yet always here. Someday you will stop being such a scared child, she scolded herself. Not tonight.

No one on the back stairs. No one in the billiard room. No one in the study.

They had not called the police about the hooded figure. Fred said he would, then called Philip instead. He told Teresa "reinforcements" were coming, whatever that meant. On her own, she had begun to dial Detective Waldron, then stopped. Why? Because she and Fred could not agree on what they had seen? Because she could not stand being looked at like she was crazy by one more person? Some other reason that she was not yet willing to confess to herself?

No one in the kitchen, pantry or mudroom.

Her days were busy. She had met two museum curators in the last two days, and spoken to a famous gallerist on the phone. She had filled out all her checklists, and most of the paintings were crated. Half had already been taken away to the storage facility. It was the nights that were hard. Sleep did not come easily, and Fred was poor company. He was no threat, but she was not sure how much good he would be in a real crisis. And though the phantom had not reappeared, she kept seeing things from the corners of her eyes. She needed to leave this house.

Dining room and sitting room both empty, so up the wide and silent stairs she went.

Teresa wished that James was here. She would tolerate his obsession with demons in exchange for his peculiar company. Yet she wondered how much relief his presence would bring if he suddenly appeared. What she truly yearned for was childhood, when the two of them understood each other in a few words, or none. When they could jam their small bodies into some hidey-hole and feel safe. There were no safe places now.

Ilsa's room was next to her grandfather's, and bare as a monk's cell. The narrow bed looked as if no one had ever slept in it. Housekeeping ledgers, bound in green leather, lined one shelf. All in German. There was a print by Dürer on the wall, probably valuable. A cloaked figure lost in a gloomy wood. It was a gift from Alfred, the sort of cheerful thing they both liked. If there were any clues in this chamber, Teresa could not find them. All the bedrooms were empty but the one in which Fred grunted and thrashed. She wondered how Laurena got any sleep. On this night the noise was comforting, but Teresa moved away. Down the hall to the narrow stairs at the back. She had been to the attic several times in daylight, when it seemed another place. A low-ceilinged, dusty storage dump without much character. It would be different now. Sinister. Yet up she must go.

Her eyes had grown used to the dark, and she made her way without stumbling. At the top she found the big square flashlight she had left behind yesterday, the rooms up here being dim even at noon. The powerful beam lacked a candle's warmth, but it illuminated her path far better. She went straight to the unfinished room, running the light across the broken floor and stepping carefully. Here. Somewhere right around here was James' hidden compartment. This would be easier in daylight, but she kept not getting to it, and anyway Fred might be hovering. Now was the time. The wall panels were solid; she could find no give in any of them. Several floorboards shifted under her weight, but none would come loose. She worked from the center of the room toward the interior wall. She had not been at it ten minutes when her head snapped up suddenly.

What was it? A creak? Teresa forced herself to pick up the flashlight and go to the door. Nothing was visible down the long corridor. Two minutes passed and the sound did not repeat. Back to work.

She was about ready to quit when she found it. A shortened floorboard right against the wall. So obvious, she should have checked it first. The nails only lightly gripped the beam below, and by pushing them one way she could release the board. It was tricky. James must have practiced often to do it so swiftly. She grabbed the bulky flashlight and shone it into the compartment. A child's treasure chest. Three marbles, two creamy with swirls and one clear with a green cat's eye. She recalled flicking them with her thumb across a rutted wooden floor. Perhaps in this very room. James had tried to teach her the rules, but she ignored them. Next to the marbles was a cheap brass medal with a faded ribbon. A piece of pink quartz. A 1943 zinc penny. A scallop shell. A crow feather. All sitting upon a folded sheet of artist's paper. Something touched her thigh.

She yelped and sat up. Her phone. It was the phone vibrating in her pocket. Teresa tried to laugh but shivered instead. She pulled the device out and checked the screen.

"James. What are you doing awake?"

"Why did you call if you thought I was sleeping?"

"Sorry, I lost track of time. What time is it, anyway?"

"I don't know," he said. "Late. Or early. Maybe two o'clock."

"So I guess you weren't sleeping. You sound odd. Are you in your room?"

"No, out walking. Where are you?"

"Still at the house," she replied.

"I know, but where in the house?"

Why the hell was he asking her that?

"The attic." They might withhold information, but they did not lie to each other.

"Did you find my place?" His voice stayed neutral. He did not sound suspicious or wonder aloud why she was in the attic at 2:00 a.m.

"Yes."

"It's okay. I don't mind you finding it. But tell me if you take something."

"Why would I do that?" she asked, gently sliding the paper out from under the other objects and unfolding it.

"For reassurance, maybe? Like a good luck charm."

"A talisman," she said. It was the sketch he'd mentioned last week, the one she did when they were young. Not terrible work. The details were nice, his lips and nose especially, but the features were not in proportion to each other. The expression was lifeless, even before it was changed. "I thought there were more marbles."

"There were dozens," James said. "I'm not sure where the others went. Those three were my favorites. Take the cat's eye. As a…talisman, you said?"

"That's all right." Someone, likely Audrey, had taken a black marker to the sketch. The eyes were made pointed and evil-looking. Two horns stuck out of the wavy hair. Someone else, likely James, had tried hard to erase them, but the stubborn ghost of the marker remained. "I don't need to take anything."

"Are you looking at the sketch? I'm sorry about what happened to it. I'm happy to have the new one you made."

"I'm honored you took it with you."

"Of course I did. Are you working on my portrait?"

"It's been busy." She could not tell if it was his attempt at a joke, but he kept mentioning the imaginary portrait. As if talking himself into its existence. At the bottom of the hole was scattered debris that must have predated James' use. Small rusted nails and chips of wood or paint. She slid the refolded sketch back into its place.

"I hope my father has been treating you well."

"Yeah, he's been great," Teresa replied. A heavy sleepiness was coming over her. Caused by his gentle monotone, perhaps. "He's a good cook."

"He's been on his own a lot. When he was young. Between wives, or even while he's been married. Living overseas so often. He believes in self-sufficiency."

It was not much, but more than she was used to hearing James say about his father.

"I shouldn't tell tales," she said. "But he and I have talked a lot this week. He feels bad about the way he treated you and Audrey. I don't know if he's told you that."

James was quiet for a time, and Teresa felt herself nodding off.

"He said something like it once. When he was drunk. Truthfully, I don't care. He's never been much of a father to me. It's Audrey he should apologize to."

She did not believe him, and knew that even to the extent it was true, it was just emotional self-defense. Yet the coldness of his tone chilled her.

"Does Audrey care?" she asked.

"She says she doesn't, but it's a lie. She always wanted his attention, even if she had to make him angry to get it."

"All of that stuff she did as a teenager. You know, drinking and drugs and breaking into houses. You think that was about getting a reaction from your dad?"

"I'm not her psychiatrist. I guess it started there, then it just became who she was."

How sad, Teresa thought. And how thoughtless of her not to have understood. On some level she must have, but she was too busy resenting Audrey to really grasp it.

"That had to be rough for you," she said. "Watching that happen."

"It was unpleasant."

"Did he beat her badly?"

"It got worse over time. The more she resisted, or fought back. He broke her nose once. We had to take her to the hospital, and my mother almost had him arrested."

"You're kidding! Jesus, I had no idea."

"Later, Audrey broke his hand with a hammer. She threatened to kill him. They were going to send her to one of those camps for troubled teens. Dad and my stepmother, Joyce."

"When was this?"

"The same year Grandma died. Just a few months before. She was on her best behavior after that. She was terrified of being locked up."

Wow, Teresa thought. Imagine Audrey afraid of something.

"Did he ever beat you?"

"He hit me sometimes. Not hard. Whenever I was in

line for a real beating Audrey made sure to do something worse, so she got it instead."

"She really did protect you."

"I suppose," he allowed. "Honestly, I think she was just jealous."

"Jealous of…of him hurting you instead of her?"

"Yes," he said simply. Not seeming to find the idea odd in the least. "Also, I was her creature. If anyone got to torture me, it was going to be her."

Teresa felt called upon to express horror, or grief, or anything at all. To say aloud how wrong it was, but she had no words. She should not have called him so late, she was exhausted in body and spirit. She wanted to roll back time to earlier this evening. To earlier this lifetime. She wanted to protect them, James and Audrey both. She wanted to go downstairs right now and cave in Freddie's head with a lamp. The idea exhilarated her, then a moment later made her sick with fear. What was wrong with her? What was wrong with all of them? What was this demon in the blood of the entire family?

"I've upset you," said James. "I'm sorry."

"You have to stop apologizing. I wanted to know."

"Do you think all families are like ours?"

"They all have issues," Teresa said. "Some worse than us. But I don't think this is normal either. Nobody should have to endure a childhood like you just described."

"There were good parts," he said dutifully. "Trips to see my father. In London once, and Hawaii. There was you. All of us together for the summers. There were never any beatings at Owl's Point."

No, just a cruel old man and his death-dealing painting.

"James, I have to go to sleep. I'm about to pass out on the floor."

"I should be with you. We should be together. Don't you feel that way?"

She had been feeling nothing but that for days and days. Years, maybe. Now she was not so sure. It seemed possible that they were not good for each other. That each brought out the other's fears and weaknesses, instead of their strengths.

"You can't leave school," she said gently. "I'll come to you when I'm done with my work here."

"What if that's too late?"

"What do you mean? Too late for what?"

"I don't know," he mumbled.

"Tell me," she insisted. "What are you afraid of?"

"I said I don't know." A rare annoyance in his voice. "I have this feeling that more bad things are going to happen. Don't you feel it, too?"

"Nothing is simply going to happen. But somebody might do something. Whom do you fear?"

"All of us."

"Me, too?"

"Yes. And me. I don't trust myself, Tay."

Join the club, she thought. Her feelings were vaguely hurt that he did not trust her, but why should he? Did she completely trust herself? Was she aware of everything she said or did when her episodes occurred? What were those shreds of memory that kept surfacing? Conversations that seemed so real, yet must be dreams.

"You're a good soul, James. You have to believe that."

"I should let you sleep. Please, don't worry about me.

Just look out for yourself. And don't trust anyone, Teresa. Good night."

"James, wait."

He had disconnected. She was wide-awake now, and considered calling him back. To what end? It was a small miracle he had said so much. He was unlikely to say more, or to even answer. Her work here would be done in another day or two, then there would be a break before taking it up again in the city. She must use that break to pursue the questions she had posed herself last week, and come no closer to answering. First she must sleep. And she would, after one more perambulation around the lonely house.

The lonely house by the river. The Quinta del Sordo, empty but for Teresa and Ramón. Again he gestures her through a door to the room beyond. A room she has never seen, and must never enter. The room of terror. He is not angry this time, but gentle and encouraging. The father she knows. Entering the chamber first, he kneels and gestures to her. *There is nothing to fear, my child. Not for you. You have seen the others, now look upon this last, their master. Together we will make sense of it.* Slowly, so slowly she goes forward. One step, then another. Into the room of dark wood and books. She turns her head and...

Sat up. Half her face was hot and there was drool on her cheek. Drool on the rock-hard settee, upon which she had somehow fallen asleep. She was in the sitting room. It was morning, and a noise had startled her. The doorbell. Which rang again, too loudly. Freddie would come stumbling downstairs with a hangover and the shotgun in a moment. Teresa stood too fast and nearly fell, gray spots darting about her muzzy head. Then she righted herself and went into the hall. First disarming the alarm, she fumbled with the front door locks. At last she pulled it open, squinting against the harsh sun.

"Dave?"

"Hello, Teresa."

His eyes were less brooding and more alert. Maybe he was a morning person.

"Your nose looks better."

"Thanks, it feels better."

"What are you doing here?"

"Philip sent me. Can I come in?"

"Oh." She realized she was blocking him. "Sorry, I'm not awake." She shuffled out of the way slowly. Uncertain. *Don't trust anyone, Teresa.* He stayed on the steps, eyeing her. The guy missed nothing. "Please come in," she said. "But be careful of my uncle. He might shoot first and ask questions later."

"Philip spoke to him," said Dave, stepping inside. "I'm told Fred has to get back to Los Angeles in a hurry."

"He didn't mention it. You mean you're the reinforcements?"

"I guess. Phil wants me to play security guard for a day or two."

"So it would be just you and me?"

"If you're uncomfortable with that we can—"

"No," Teresa said, too eagerly. "This is good. This is perfect, in fact. I've been waiting for you to show. We have a lot to talk about."

18

Fred had no intention of leaving. Dave had sensed the man's contempt during their meeting the day of the funeral. Who knew what Philip had said about him? Maybe it was enough that he had worked for their hated father, and was now employed by the overbearing Philip himself. Dave would feel the same way in Alfred Junior's shoes, so he did not take it personally. But he was not going to stick around and swallow abuse, especially since Fred's presence made Dave's unnecessary. Teresa thought otherwise.

"You're not going anywhere," she said, whisking eggs expertly. "Philip gave you a job and you accepted. Sit down."

Dave sat while Uncle Fred made coffee.

"Fred," Teresa continued, pouring the eggs into a hot pan. "You should help Laurena with the apartment. You've been in this house too long."

"So have you," he grumbled, putting a mug of coffee in

front of Dave. "I'm not leaving you with a stranger. Your mother would skin me."

"He's not a stranger. Philip hired him to help us."

"I don't know why Philip hired him," Fred said, staring hard at Dave. "How about this? You come with me and we leave Magnum PI here to watch things."

"I have a truck and four specialists arriving in one hour to load paintings."

"Fine. Then we all stay."

Knowing his silence bothered the other man, Dave kept it up. Though he did compliment Teresa on her eggs, which beat the heck out of that diner. He was pleasantly surprised to see her wolf down the food. No anorexic nibbling. Fred ground his teeth and ate little. When his phone buzzed, he jumped up and left the room to answer.

"Do you have to?" Teresa asked, corralling eggs with a heel of toast.

"What?" said Dave.

"Get him worked up. Not that it takes much."

"I didn't say a thing."

"I know. It's the smug way you sit there quietly that does it." Then she sighed and waved a hand. "Sorry, I've been around him too long."

"Well," said Dave. Shamed, and annoyed about feeling that way. "You're not wrong. I don't like your uncles much."

"You're working for one of them."

"It's not unusual to work for people you dislike. Anyway, I'm with Fred, I don't know what Philip wants out of me anymore."

"What do you want?" she asked, locking him in place

with her black eyes. The similarity to Luisa seemed super-
ficial now. A little in the face and build, nothing at all in
the voice and manner. He preferred seeing her like this.
Her own person.

"What do you imagine I want?"

"Save the mystery-man bullshit for Audrey," she said
bluntly. Dave felt slapped. Had he read her wrong?

"All right. I want to get paid so I can get away from your
disturbed family."

"No, you don't," she said, not offended or put off. "You
knew how disturbed we were before. You came back for
some reason."

"Masochism."

"Maybe," she allowed. "What else?"

"Leave it alone," Dave said, menace creeping into his
words. She did not flinch.

"No."

He pushed his plate away and rubbed a hand over his
face.

"What business is it of yours? Maybe I want to get some
closure for an old wound." Now why the hell did he say
that? If she pressed him one inch farther he would go. Just
get up and walk away, however much it might embarrass
him later.

"Yeah," Teresa said softly. "Me, too."

Dave's hands shook, so he put them in his lap. She had
gotten under his skin too easily. Probably because the attack was unexpected. Yet he saw no meanness or manipu-
lation in her. She needed a friend. Perhaps she had already
made him one in her mind, and finding the real him stubbornly reticent had set her off. He would not easily excuse

such behavior in someone else, and wondered why he was doing it for her.

"I'm happy to listen," he said. "I'm curious. But don't expect reciprocation. I don't find that sharing pain helps anything."

"Never mind. Something is going on, Dave. Not fifteen years ago, right now."

"And you say that because..."

"I don't believe my grandfather died a natural death. And I've seen someone creeping around this property at least twice. Probably more than twice."

"Okay," he said, grabbing the coffee mug to keep his hands busy. Here was something solid to wrestle with. "You saw him and I didn't. But dead people often have ugly expressions, especially if they die in pain." She did not speak, only waited for him to continue. "The prowler is a different story. It's hard to guess what his presence means without knowing who he is. I gather it's you and James who saw him?"

"Right, the crazy ones."

"Come on, I didn't say that."

"Audrey said it to you," Teresa maintained. "Some version, I'd bet any money."

"It's cute how you all talk about money when none of you seems to have any. Is that some affectation of the formerly rich?"

"I was never rich. Fred saw the prowler, too. You can ask him."

"I'll take your word for it," Dave replied. Swirling the coffee as if a vision might appear there in the tiny vortex. "What did he look like?"

"The first time he wore dark pants and a green jacket. I couldn't see his face. He started toward me and I ran. The second time…" She looked away.

"Tell me," he urged.

"The second time I couldn't see anything. Because he had a cloth draped over him."

"Over his head?"

"Yeah." Her voice had become small and tight. "Head and shoulders. But I think he could see through it, because he was looking in the window."

"And Fred saw this, too?"

"I don't know what he saw exactly, but he chased some-one into the woods. There's an oak tree just a little way in, with a crumbling fort."

"I've seen it."

"He lost him right around there."

"That's where I ran into Pete Mulhane," Dave told her. "Up in that fort, laughing at me. He swore it was the first time he'd been in those woods since prison."

"I heard you tell Audrey." She rubbed her nose. "It might be true. There's this jacket the same color in the mudroom. Everyone uses it."

"So you're thinking not a prowler? Someone in the fam-ily?"

"It's only me and Fred staying here."

"Who has keys?"

"Good question," she said, forehead creasing in thought. Or irritation that she had not considered this before. "The lawyer gave me Grandpa's to use this week. Philip has a set that he gave to Fred. I don't know who else. Ilsa, for sure."

"Your mother?"

"No. But maybe... When we were kids, Audrey was always stealing keys. She could get into any part of the house."

"Imagine that," said Dave. "This person would also have to know the house alarm code."

"Right. Which Fred changes every few days. But there's only a couple of words he uses, and I think he got them from Philip."

"Megaphone mouth," Dave said, making her smile for the first time. "So we can safely assume any number of people might know."

"Who do you think is out there?" she asked earnestly.

"I don't know, Teresa."

"Who do you think stole the painting?"

"I don't know that either. There was someone I suspected for years, but now..."

"Look sharp," said Fred, striding back into the room. Squeezing his phone as if he would like to shatter it. "Your moving guys are coming up the drive."

Dave headed for the woods. Both to get out of the way, and because patrolling the grounds seemed like part of the job. The morning mist had burned away, but a smoky residue clung to the pines. And the temperature seemed to drop steeply as soon as he got under the trees. Generally speaking, he enjoyed woods, but this claustrophobic patch was hard to love. He found the old oak without much trouble and circled it. Definitely no one in the fort this time, but that malignant aura remained. Like it was in the tree itself, or the soil. This was an unhappy place. Dave knew he could not cure that, no matter what he uncovered, but nor could he run. Not while Teresa remained. There was no reason he should feel responsible for her, yet he did. Audrey had hectored him about the girl's vulnerability, then Philip had stuck him here. Almost as if they had conspired to trap him. He should take Audrey's advice and get Teresa out, but he knew she would not leave until her work was done. He circled the dense wood once, feeling invisible eyes upon him the whole way. Then he walked the seaward edge of the lawn to the circular drive. And finally to the marshy inlet near Long Hill Road. Nothing visible to the eye, yet a dozen places where someone who knew the ground better might hide.

Heading back to the house, he ran into Fred walking rapidly toward his car.

"Leaving us, after all?"

"Something came up that I have to deal with," Fred replied, looking agitated. "Be back as soon as I can."

"We'll take good care of the house."

"Screw the house. It's going to end up with that pinched old Austrian bitch anyway. You take care of my niece. Be careful with her, you hear me?"

Dave only nodded. Fred swept back his thinning hair and jumped into the forest green Jaguar. Then he tore around the gravel circle and out through the rhododendrons. Clearly he had been Audrey's driving teacher. Dave took a last look around, then walked into the swirl of high-end professional packing.

"I wouldn't have picked you for a whisky drinker."

"Why does everyone say that?" Teresa replied in exasperation. She had encouraged him to sit facing the Sound, but Dave chose the opposite side of the moldering gazebo. Where he could keep an eye on the house. It was the sort of unconscious decision that defined his life. Though in this case it carried the bonus of watching the sun's last rays catch her lovely face. "What would you have picked?" she asked. "White wine?"

"Nah," he said. "I'll give you a real drink. Martini, maybe."

"Never had one. I'm sure it would knock me on my ass."

"You say that like it's a bad thing. Okay, a dark gamey red. Spanish, of course."

"Of course," she agreed. "I used to know a little about Spanish wine."

"From your father?" he guessed.

"Yes." She tossed back the last of her scotch. Dave nursed his. It was friendly support against the cool, damp evening, but he had to be careful. "He did favor things from the Iberian Peninsula," Teresa said, refilling her glass. Either she or Fred had been hitting the bottle hard; there was not much left. "Which you might call cultural chauvinism, but he could defend his choices. He knew his stuff. Art, music, religion. Wine."

"You remember him well."

"I was fourteen when he died. Not a child."

Fourteen will seem like a child when you're forty, Dave thought.

"That must have been really hard. I mean, at that age. Then he's in a different country, and there isn't even…"

"A body," she supplied, staring down at the warped floorboards. "Yeah, it was bad. We had to wait a year before the Argentine government declared him dead. Like he might be pulling a trick on them."

"Did he leave a note, or was there any indication... I'm sorry, ignore me if this—"

"There was no note, at least I never heard about one. He was there on a fellowship, but he may have gotten mixed up in some bad business." She gave him a long look from under her black hair. "You'll have to ask my mother for details. She wouldn't tell me anything else. She may not know. Apparently he sounded more and more erratic with each phone call. Like he was losing his grip. She begged him to come home."

"Had he acted that way before?" Dave asked. Unable to curb the investigative impulse, though she seemed willing enough to talk.

"Not that I saw. He was eccentric, maybe. Not crazy, whatever anybody thought."

"He didn't seem crazy to me," Dave offered. She looked momentarily stunned.

"I didn't know you met him."

"Only once, when I was interviewing the family after the theft." Dave remembered a handsome but defeated figure, slumped in a wing chair. Refusing eye contact and answering in monosyllables. Suffering like a martyr until the interview was over. "My overriding memory is that he seemed sad."

"I guess he was. He had serious depression. My grandmother's death hit him hard. They got along well. Then the theft. I don't know if it was the loss of friendship with my grandfather, or if he sensed that people suspected him."

"Why did they suspect him?" Dave pressed.

"Because he had a special relationship with that painting. He could look at it for hours. Everyone else was frightened and wanted it gone." Her glass was empty again, which surprised them both. She picked up the bottle, contemplating whether or not to pour. "Hey, Dave, I'm doing all the talking."

"That's okay with me."

"Well, not with me. If you think you can get me drunk so I'll spill my—"

"*I'm* getting you drunk?"

"Okay, it's a team effort. But you have to pick up the pace."

"I can't, Teresa."

"Oh," she said, understanding. "How stupid of me. Don't drink that."

"I'm enjoying it, but one is enough. What do you want to know?"

"Everything." She gazed at him with a sincerity only possible with intoxication. "I want to know everything, Dave."

He finished his scotch, thought it over for a moment, then started talking. About Charles DeGross, and Philip's relationship with him. About Philip's haunted sketches. The details of his run-in with Pete, and trying to locate sister Jenny. Audrey's face would have told him which parts she already knew and what was a surprise, but Teresa's face told him nothing.

"Huh," she said at last. "That's heavy stuff. I'm not sure what it all means."

"Me, neither. Tell me what I'm missing."

She recalled her uncles' moods and behaviors. Which

revealed little, except that they were both more financially strained than Dave had realized. That could push people to do drastic things. She talked of the four cousins burning their letters, which made him smile. Did such an act rule out money as a motivating factor? Surely not, Audrey needed money badly. So her hatred of whatever was in the old man's note trumped that need. Curious.

"Tell me about James," Dave asked. "I haven't been able to get near him."

"He's very private," she said, pausing a long time. "Very gentle. And very dear to me. We tell each other things we wouldn't tell other people."

"Including me. Okay, what about Ken?"

"The straight arrow," she said. "Smart, charming, high achiever."

"Sounds unbearable. And suspicious."

"Well, he has a bad temper. And he is hiding something, darned if I know what. Do you do this with Audrey?" she asked suddenly. "Trade information?"

"We have done something like this, yes."

"Are you naked when you do it?"

The tone was so neutral he could not tell whether she was teasing, accusing, or what.

"Um, we were, yeah," Dave replied. "That was incidental. I think. I've said more to you tonight than I ever said to her."

"Do you know what she's up to?"

His impulse was to toss the question back, but that had not gone well so far, and he did not feel like being coldly professional with her.

"No, I don't. I had a chance to find out, but it meant throwing in with her completely."

"Which you weren't willing to do?" she asked. "Too committed to your buddy Philip?"

"Are those my only choices?"

"Couldn't you have pretended to throw in with her?"

"In theory," he said glumly. "But no, I couldn't. I owed her that much honesty."

"Wow, an honest man." She sniggered. "You think she gives a shit about your honesty?"

"You know," he said, standing up and walking a few steps onto the lawn. "If whisky makes you this nasty, I'm not sure you should drink it."

"Sorry," she said, hiding her face from him, though it was now too dark to see. "I don't know why I'm doing that."

"You're angry at somebody," he said. "Just make sure it's me."

"Please, come back and sit down."

He did, feeling childish for having gotten up in the first place. He knew she was drunk, worn-out and blunt by nature. Why did her words bother him? They sat quietly for a while, letting evening settle in around them.

"What's the next step?" Teresa asked. "What would you be doing now if they didn't have you playing nursemaid for me?"

"Audrey gave me a lead on Jenny Mulhane. I'd be in Toms River trying to find her."

"Why?"

"I never interviewed Jenny. She and Pete were stealing from your grandparents. Maybe not the painting, but other stuff, and I would bet your squandered Morse riches that they never told everything they know. There's no good reason anybody in the family should give Pete the time of day, yet several of them have."

"What, blackmail?"

"Maybe," he replied. "Anyway, it's the only lead I have right now. It's getting cold. We should go inside."

Before they could move, his phone rang. Philip. Again he thought about not answering, and again he relented.

"You're there, thank God."

"Philip?" The voice was so hoarse with panic that Dave was unsure for a moment.

"Don't talk, just listen to me. All right? In fact, write this down."

"Say it, I'll remember."

"It's important, Dave. Jesus, I really need your help here."

"Philip, calm down and tell me what's up."

"There's a park. A large, public park, about twenty minutes north of you. I'll give you directions."

"Now?" Dave said. Teresa was staring at him in rising apprehension.

"It's Pete. Peter Mulhane. He's there, or he may be there. I need you to find out."

"So I'm meeting Pete in this park." Was he drunk, having a breakdown? "Why? And why tonight? I'd rather meet a guy like that in daylight."

"He's not going to… Christ." Philip took a ragged breath. "He'll be in the wooded part in back. If he's there."

"Why don't you give me his number and I'll—"

"You're not understanding me. I need you to find his body."

19

"Turn right."

"That's not what he said."

"Turn," she insisted. So Dave turned.

It had proven impossible to leave Teresa behind. Beyond her fierce determination to come was the fact that both Fred and Miranda were far more concerned about her than the house or its contents. Dave was not to abandon her for anything. Which meant staying at Owl's Point and ignoring Philip, or bringing her along. Given the task Philip had laid out, ignoring him did not seem an option.

"I told you, I know this park," Teresa said, leaning against the seat belt's restraint like a dog on a short leash. She had sobered up swiftly. "Philip's directions are crap. You would be lost out here."

There was a GPS in the glove compartment, but Dave did not argue. They had passed the bright lights of a shopping center and always-busy Route 95, but otherwise it was back roads.

"How do you know this place, anyway?"

"My grandmother took us when I was little. Then I found it again while I was at school. Like a nostalgia thing, I guess. I still don't understand why we haven't called the cops."

"Philip told me not to."

"But someone could be dead."

"In which case he'll still be dead when we get there, and then we'll call the police. On the other hand, if Philip has made a big drama out of nothing, it's better we leave the authorities out of it." He did not add that his history made calling police an absolute last resort. All they had to do was punch his name into a database, and he was facing days of hassle, minimum. Worse if there was a body involved.

"Do you have a gun?" she asked.

"There won't be need for that."

"You don't know."

"Guns escalate things," Dave said. "Come on, I'm an art investigator."

"Audrey said you were dangerous."

"She did, huh? Well, she wants to believe that. Or she wants to scare you."

"So it's not true?"

"A few years back," Dave said reluctantly. "After my life took a nosedive, I worked for some unsavory types. Down in Florida, finding art that one thief stole from another."

"Sounds exciting."

"It was. The first client was a white-collar type. Lawyer, collector, entrepreneur. Charming guy and upstanding citizen, except for being a thief. The longer I stayed at it, the farther down the food chain I fell, until one of my clients was murdered an hour before our meeting. I found him. That's when I got out, moved back here. Doing research, surveillance, security, whatever I could find. Philip did a pretty complete background check on me, and he must have told Audrey some things."

"Wow," Teresa said after a few moments.

"You sure you still want to be in this car with me?"

"Keep straight here," she instructed. "It will be coming up on the right."

They were in a sleepy neighborhood of middle-income houses built close to the road. Then the houses fell away on one side and there were stately trees and paths of cracked asphalt. Half of the old-fashioned lamps were dark. Connecticut needed to invest in infrastructure. Dave pulled over slowly.

"Teresa, listen to me."

"I should not even think about getting out of the car, right?"

"Thank you."

"Do you watch any slasher movies? Do you know what happens to the girl who stays in the car?"

"Here." He handed her the keys. "Drive around if you want, but swing by every five or ten minutes, okay?"

She took the keys silently and handed him the flashlight. He could see that she was both energized and frightened, and he squeezed her shoulder.

"Thanks for getting us here. Hang tight now. This is probably nothing."

"Be careful."

"Always."

The park was still and empty. There was a dog walker

across the street who might be coming this way, or possibly just leaving. Not another soul. The trees were mostly oaks, their broad branches forming a pale and susurrating ceiling. His breath misted, and he jammed his hands into his jacket pockets so they would not get stiff with cold. To his right was a large band shell. To the left a pond, with a monument on the far side. Bronze soldiers frozen in action, he could not tell which war. Dead ahead was a copse of tightly packed trees. He could see nothing within, but anyone there would see him approaching. Damn it. Why did he have to do this at night? Why couldn't he say no to people?

On the swath of grass between the path and trees, an object caught Dave's eye. A crushed cigarette box. Lucky Strikes, Pete's brand. Him and a million others. Not far away was a plastic lighter, and the grass was disturbed and even gouged in places. Two men had struggled here. A few yards on, at the edge of the trees, some saplings were bent. Dave crept over, trying not to step on anything. Trying to separate sounds within the night woods. Peering in, all he could tell was that the copse was larger than he had guessed, and ran downhill into a little gulley. Without a light source, he would find a prone body in there only by tripping on it. No choice. He reached the flashlight out of his jacket and flicked it on.

If the light was not sufficient giveaway, an army of twigs and weeds exploded under his shoes with every step. It would have taken considerable imagination to engineer a way that he might have made *more* noise. The trees were mostly birch, with oak and maple mixed in. Dave lost the path of broken twigs, or any path at all. He might have stumbled around a long time if the flashlight beam did not catch a pale object. Stepping over fallen branches, he arrived at a spot where the weeds had been flattened. A blood-stained rag was bunched there, and more drops of blood were scattered about the leaves and brambles. Someone had lain here, hurt.

A moment later it was Dave facedown on the weeds. The flashlight beam was in his face and the air had been punched out of his lungs. After a stunned delay, pain erupted across his just-healed ribs, not sparing his spine. He pulled for breath, but it would not come.

"You saw my flag," said a voice so slack it was almost indecipherable. A branch hit the ground near Dave's head—the club that had struck him. A man bent to retrieve the bloody rag. His shaggy hair made a blond halo in the light beam. Bending and straightening took some time. "Must have thought it was a surrender flag." Pete cackled, but the sound was horrible through his ruined face.

Dave tried again and was able to breathe, but the pain in his ribs doubled. Small breaths, he told himself. Gentle, gentle. Pete squatted beside him. One eye was swollen shut, he had the bloated lips of a corpse, and there was blood all over his face and shirt.

"You," Pete said. "They send you to do the dirty work, huh? That used to be my job. You poor, stupid dick."

Dave rolled onto his side and tried to speak, but what emerged was the noise a child might make imitating a dinosaur.

"Whoa there," said Pete. "Don't make me hit you again."

"Who did that to you?" Dave whispered.

"Hell," Pete laughed. "Don't they tell you anything?

You need to reconsider your line of work, friend. Where's my pistol?"

"Don't know."

"I saw you picking up stuff out there."

"Cigarettes," Dave wheezed. "No pistol."

"Damn," Pete growled, but the tone shifted quickly to whining. "That's my only gun, man. I need it."

"What for?"

"Business, you know?"

"Blackmail business?"

"Shut up. You shut up or I'll kick you where it hurts."

"That should be easy." The pain was backing off somewhat, and Dave thought he might not be too badly hurt. "What happened, Pete?"

"Man don't like hearing the truth, that's all." He stood and reeled a few steps. "I thought you were one of them. That's why I hit you so hard."

"You should go to the hospital. We both should."

"Nah, I got to get out of here. They might have called the cops. Make it all my fault, you wait and see. I didn't break your back or nothing, did I?"

Dave sat up very slowly, though not slowly enough. He tipped his head, thinking he would vomit, but nothing came. Mulhane was already moving away, disappearing noisily into the surrounding darkness.

"Pete," Dave called after him. The heavy steps stalled, but Dave was not sure what he wanted to say. "What happened to the painting?"

"He didn't really hire you to find it, did he?"

"No," Dave admitted, both to the other man and to himself. "That was a lie to pull me in. I just want to know."

"I didn't take it."

"But you know who did."

"What did she tell you?"

"Who?" But that was wrong, Dave knew. He should have guessed, or kept quiet. The footfalls started again. "Stay away from them, Pete. You hear?"

"Why should I?" the disembodied voice asked.

"Because those types always come out on top."

"That's what they think, but I *know* things."

"What do you know?" Nothing. "Well, it doesn't matter," Dave said in a tired voice. "They're poison. They poison anyone who comes near them. You stay away."

"Yeah," the other man said after a few moments. "Maybe. You do the same."

Dave retrieved the flashlight and made a pathetic attempt at pursuit. Even in his battered condition, Mulhane managed to disappear completely before Dave freed himself from the trees. No more woods, he thought as he staggered over the damp grass toward the street. Go back to the city and stay there.

The street was empty. Where was the damn car? Had Teresa driven off? Had Mulhane taken her hostage? But, no, there it was fifty yards away. It was Dave who had come out in the wrong spot. Teresa sprang out of the passenger seat as soon as she saw him, eyes wide with worry and phone plastered to her ear.

"Are you all right?" she asked, looking him up and down.

"More or less."

"It's Philip," she said, holding the phone out to him. Dave grabbed it too roughly.

"What is she doing with you?" the lawyer demanded.

His voice sounded stronger but also thicker. Dave suspected whisky courage.

"I'd still be driving in circles if she wasn't here."

"I didn't tell you to—"

"Pete's alive."

"He is? Thank God. What shape is he in?"

"Good enough to club me with a tree branch. But you worked him over pretty good, or someone did."

"Is he there, do you have him?"

"No, he got away from me."

"Damn it, Webster. The man's dangerous, he could say anything."

"He's badly banged up, he's lost his gun, and I think I convinced him to keep his distance from you. Philip, what is going on?"

"Okay, okay, we'll just have to… Go back to the house, and I'll call you tomorrow."

"Philip," he said savagely, then held the phone against his chest while he breathed deeply and painfully. Why the ribs again? He brought the device back to his ear and spoke calmly. "If you do not tell me what the hell is going on right now, I am going to drive to your house and beat it out of you."

"I have to think this through," the lawyer insisted. "Be patient. I'll call in the morning."

"Philip, no. Philip?"

The connection was cut. That high-handed little dick, Dave would bounce his head off the walls of his pretty white kitchen. He would grind his… Teresa was watching him.

"What?" he said furiously.

"Are you sure you're okay?"

"Yes," Dave said more gently. He was not angry with her, and anyway she was utterly unimpressed with his rage. "I'm good. Probably cracked ribs."

"Should we get you to a doctor?"

"There's nothing to do for ribs. They don't even bind them anymore, just give you painkillers."

"Pete's all right, too?" she asked cautiously.

"I wouldn't say that. He was all right enough to give me the slip a second time."

"What do we do now?"

Right. Get with the program, Dave. He levered himself very slowly into the passenger seat as Teresa scampered around to the driver's side and swung in.

"Now," Dave breathed, when the pain had subsided enough to speak. "We go show your uncle that I do not make idle threats."

The house was dark, except for a light in the kitchen. No sign of the Mercedes in the driveway or the garage. No way to know if someone lurked in the bushes. Dave had felt eyes upon him since walking the Owl's Point woods, and all nature was suspect now. They went to the kitchen window and peered in. Chairs were knocked over, and there was broken glass on the table and floor. He could just glimpse a painting askew in the hall.

"Quite a brawl."

"Do you think Pete came here after we talked to Philip?" Teresa asked.

"Doubt it. He was in no shape to do this kind of damage. Let's take a closer look."

He used a potted geranium to shatter one pane of the window and unlock it. No alarm sounded. He began to pull himself up, but Teresa grabbed his forearm.

"You aren't in any condition for that."

"I can't ask you to break into your uncle's house," Dave said, pleased at recovering so quickly. The pressure of her hand had shut his brain down briefly.

"I'm guilty by association just standing here. I'm also lighter and smaller, but you have to give me a boost. I'm not exactly athletic."

"Okay. Be very careful of the glass. And don't touch anything you don't have to."

"You want me to levitate?"

"That would be best."

She may not have been an athlete, but her legs were strong, and she was a good climber. He held her a little too long, which was better than letting go too soon. Half a minute later she let him in the door.

The worst damage was in the kitchen, and it was not too bad. Overturned chairs and a few broken glasses. From the impact marks on the wall, Dave guessed they had been thrown at someone. The coffee table in the living room was tipped over and the sofa knocked back a foot. In the cramped study in back, a cut crystal glass with a faint scotch residue sat on the desk. Beneath it was a check and a note. The check was made out to David Webster for $10,000. The note said: *We'll talk soon. Keep your mouth shut.*

"He knew you would break in," Teresa said, amazed.

"Yes," Dave agreed.

"And what? He ran off so he wouldn't have to face you?"

"Possibly. Possibly he was running from someone else."

"Like Pete," she said.

"Maybe. He may also have been chasing someone."

"You know, don't you?"

"No," Dave said. Which was true, strictly speaking. Though he had a theory or two.

"This is hush money," Teresa said, flicking the check with her finger. Her moral vehemence amused him.

"It's just money."

"We need to call the police now. Let them figure this out."

"Teresa." How should he say it? "Some men have beaten one another for reasons they understand and we don't. I would be very surprised if any of them pressed charges, and no one involved wants the police called."

"Then what do we do next?"

"The wise thing would be to go back to the house and finish your work."

"Do you usually do the wise thing?"

That made him laugh, though it hurt. "Almost never."

"My work is essentially done," Teresa said. "I want to understand what's happening to my family, Dave. It's important to me. So I'm asking you again, what do we do next?"

20

When she woke, they were on the Garden State Parkway.

"What time is it?" Teresa asked, stretching. She had been dreaming again. Something upsetting involving her father. In fact, she felt on the verge of a seizure, there inside the dream. Awake now, the threat had passed. "Did I snore?"

"Not that I noticed," Dave replied. His eyes were fixed on the sun-bleached highway. The urban sprawl of northern New Jersey had given way to parched grass, wildflowers and stunted pine. "Do you normally?"

"I didn't think so, but my last boyfriend complained."

"And that was the end of him."

"I have a one-strike rule about insulting my womanly perfection," she quipped. "Come on, you could at least smile."

"I'm smiling on the inside," he said, a sliver of amusement reaching his lips. She knew he was in pain. He had refused her spare Vicodin in favor of Advil—apparently alcohol was not his only demon. Contrary to the latest medical wisdom, they wrapped his ribs in cloth bandages this morning, before setting out from Owl's Point. Any awkwardness she felt handling his bare torso was dispelled by his acute discomfort, and the ugly bruising.

"Look at this traffic," Teresa said.

"This is nothing. I should have come down in October all those years."

"You a Jersey Shore guy?" she asked, surprised.

"Used to be, before I got married. July and August this road is a parking lot."

"Your wife didn't like it?"

"It never occurred to me to bring Luisa to Surf City or Barnegat Light. She's more a Greek islands or Costa del Sol kind of girl."

"I've never been there," Teresa said. Without envy, but with some wonder at why she had been so few places in her life. "Must be beautiful."

"Some of it. They wrecked the Spanish coast with over-building. I prefer Madrid."

"I love Madrid," she gushed. "I mean I used to. I haven't been in a long time."

"Dad's hometown."

"Yes." Of course he would know that. "What happened with your wife? If I can ask."

"I made the mistake of working for her father."

"Before or after you got married?"

"It all happened together," he said in a weary voice. She left it to him to continue or not, and after a while he did. "We met in graduate school. Your field, art history."

"No kidding? I guess that makes sense, given your work."

"We were terrible students." He shook his head and grinned, so Teresa did also. He had an oddly contagious smile. "Luisa wasn't really that interested. But her dad investigated stolen fine art and she worshipped her dad, so she tried. I was more into it, especially the Spanish stuff. Your field again. But I was also lazy and undisciplined. I only cared about what I cared about. The oddballs and mysteries. Like, whatever happened to *Storm on the Sea of Galilee*? From the Gardner heist, you know? What was in the lost top half of El Greco's *Vision of Saint John*? Where was Goya's demonic self-portrait?"

"You knew about that in school? Before you took the case?"

"Yes," he said fervently. "It was one of those rumors that got passed down through the generations of art wackos. The people I gravitate toward. I was obsessed with it."

"So you got your degree and what?"

"Never got the degree," Dave said. "I dropped out and went to work for Luisa's father. The great Ricardo Reál, also known as Richard Real. She and I had gotten serious. More serious than I was about my studies. Luisa had worked through that youthful creative impulse and switched to law school. She was used to living a certain way. I needed to make money. And the work interested me, at first. Then less and less, until your grandfather called. Eighty-one, this is us."

They followed the long curve of the exit ramp and headed east on Lakehurst Road.

"It was one case," Teresa said.

"No," Dave answered. "It was *the* case."

"It's not your fault that it wasn't solved."

"Ricardo thought I mishandled it. That I told your grandfather too much, too soon. I came to agree with him, but either way I couldn't let go. I kept investigating in my free time. Then on work time, then all the time. Ricardo warned that I was slipping, but I wouldn't stop. He had to fire me. I starting drinking too much. Luisa and I had terrible fights. You find out some things about people too late. She preferred winners, like her dad. She had no stomach for adversity. Anyway, it's a sad story, and a common one."

And too simple, Teresa thought. At least in that version, but it was not her business.

"You reminded me of her," he said. "Luisa. When I first met you."

"Gee, Dave, I don't know what to say to that."

"Nothing. It was momentary. You are fully your own person now."

"Yeah? Which way did you like me better?" Teresa asked. Feeling her face redden and wondering who she had left in charge of her mouth. Dave only smiled, which was just as well.

They parked in a lot on Water Street, near the river from which the town took its name. Then they walked east toward The Riverside Grill, one of several businesses in a row of two-story brick-fronts, with a marina in back.

"You know her by sight," Dave said, "so go in and ask for her."

"What will you do?"

"There's a good chance she won't want to talk. There must be a kitchen entrance on the water side. If she's scared, that's the way she'll run."

"And you'll do what? Tackle her?"

"Make her see reason," he said impatiently. "I'm count-ing on her being worried about her brother. If she doesn't care, we've got no leverage."

Teresa tarried on the sidewalk, thinking. "Other way around," she said, before self-doubt could trip her. "You go in the front and I'll go around back."

She could see his skepticism, and waited for him to ex-plain why it was a stupid idea. Which for all she knew it was.

"Okay," Dave said instead. "I'll give you five minutes to get there. But look, if she shows one ounce of hostility, you get out of her way."

"Jenny isn't going to hurt me. What she might do to you, I can't say."

Teresa let him ponder that while she sought the nearest route to the water. There was an alley between a liquor store and a boat repair shop, but it ended at a fence. No gate was visible. Backtracking to find another way would take more than five minutes, or however long she had now. Flexing her fingers a few times, she took hold of the shaky wooden fence and climbed up, peering over the top. The drop did not look bad, so she swung herself over and let go. The concrete walkway she landed on connected to the boat piers and ran parallel to the back of The Riverside Grill. Teresa moved in that direction, waiting for some-one to challenge her presence. Her senses were sharp. Too sharp, yet she felt in control. Late-morning sun was bright on the water. A group of middle-aged men and women on a gleaming white yacht were laughing and listening to '80s rock. A young kitchen worker from the restaurant hosed out large plastic tubs.

When Teresa was within twenty yards, the door behind the kid opened fast, and a woman stepped out. She was in jeans, a T-shirt and windbreaker, and those clogs that chefs wore—good for arch support and keeping above a hot grease spill. Not so good for quick getaways. The woman tossed a soiled apron back through the door before closing it, then shuffled toward Teresa as quickly as she could move. Looking over her shoulder so often that she took no notice of the younger woman until they were face-to-face.

"Jenny," Teresa said, bringing the cook up short. She was heavier, and her strawberry hair had gone gray, but the lively green eyes were the same. Just now they were confused, bordering on hostile. "It's Teresa. Teresa Marías."

"Oh my goodness," the woman nearly shrieked. The smile was forced, but there was genuine warmth in her voice. "Little Tay. You're a grown woman."

"So they tell me."

"What are you doing here?" Then the penny dropped, and Jenny nodded slowly. She waved an arm back toward the restaurant. "That's your man inside?"

"My, um, yes," Teresa fumbled. Her man.

"It's lovely to see you, child, but this is a terrible time. I have to be getting—"

"Jenny, when did you last talk to Pete?"

"Pete." The word seemed foreign to her for a moment. "A few days ago. Why?"

"He's in trouble."

The woman deflated, shoulders falling as the breath went out of her. She swayed a moment, then pulled in a fresh lungful of river air, straightening up. Resilient. Or anyway, unsurprised.

"Of course he is. How bad?"

21

The tavern was small and dark, and far enough from The Riverside that Jenny did not fear meeting coworkers. She waited until noon on the dot to down her first Jameson, then nursed the second. Dave ordered a beer, to make her more comfortable. Teresa, still feeling last night's whisky and adrenaline, drank water.

"I was sorry to hear about Mr. Morse," said Jenny. "Your grandfather, I mean."

"That's generous of you," Teresa replied.

"Well, he treated me right for the most part. I suppose there was nothing he could do after all that fuss but let me go."

"Would you have wanted to stay?" Dave asked.

"Not really. But I'd been there a long time, and it was hard getting work with that blot on my record. And there's Pete going to jail for something he didn't even do."

"You mean steal the painting."

"What else would I mean?"

"But he did steal other things," Dave said casually.

"Small things that no one missed. And the old man knew he was doing it."

"He stole something large that day. A flat object that filled up a sack."

"It was a platter," Jenny insisted. "A silver serving platter that gathered dust in the pantry for years. No one used it. He stuck it in that hole in the big tree, to come back for later."

"The oak tree? Where we built the fort?"

"The same. He used to hide things there during the day, then return at night to pick them up. He'd park out on Long Hill Road and come in through trees so no one would see."

"He must have fenced it pretty quickly," Dave said.

"No, no." Jenny shook her head in frustration. "I thought everyone knew this. I wasn't using my head. I wasn't thinking about it being his *alibi* for a bigger crime. All I thought is they suspected him, and I had to do something. He knew enough to stay away, but I went out that night and got the damn thing. I brought it in and washed it up and put it back in the pantry, pretty as you please."

Destroying your brother's defense, Teresa understood, but managed not to blurt out.

"No witnesses," the woman said. Disconsolate. "No way to prove it happened. The lawyers laughed at me. It never even got entered into evidence."

"That's a heavy load," Dave said sympathetically. "But somebody did take the painting. And club poor Ilsa."

"He *never*—" Jenny jabbed a finger at him, pale fire in

her eyes "—he never would have done such a thing. He's not a violent man."

Dave laughed out loud, surprising both women.

"Your brother nearly broke my back last night. And I learned a few days ago that he would have been out of prison in five years, but he beat another inmate nearly to death."

"He was attacked, that's why he beat that man. Maybe you attacked him, too."

"Haven't laid a glove on him. He crushed my bumper and cracked my ribs, and all I've done so far is collect his cigarettes."

Dave's tone was so dismayed that in a moment Jenny's rage crystalized into laughter. Dave laughed, too, and then Jenny laughed harder. Teresa thought she must have blacked out and missed something.

"Lucky Strikes," Jenny guffawed.

"Lucky Strikes," Dave affirmed, and they tapped glasses. I'm not drinking, Teresa thought. That's the problem.

"Three people testified as character witnesses for your brother," Dave said after a swig of pale ale. "Audrey Morse. Philip Morse. And Ilsa Graff."

"If you say so, I don't remember that well."

"Take my word, then. Why those three? Were they all close to Pete?"

"None of them were. Audrey flirted, but there was nothing between them. Maybe she wanted to embarrass her father."

"Did Fred have it in for Pete?"

"Nah, hardly noticed him. He had it in for his own

daughter, though. My God, that man. Teresa knows what I'm talking about. They were terrible, those Morse boys."

"Philip and Fred?" Dave asked, and Jenny nodded behind her empty glass. "So why did Philip speak up for your brother?"

"Who knows?" she murmured, arching an eyebrow. "Maybe Audrey asked him to."

"What?" Teresa said. "Why would he listen to her?" A look from Dave told her not to pursue it. He knew things, she realized. He was holding out on her.

"And what about Ilsa?" Dave asked.

"Ilsa has been a good friend to me," Jenny replied, eyes shifting nervously. "And that's really all I can say. I have to get back to work."

"Actually, you're off this afternoon," Dave said, waving at the waitress. "That's why we got down here so early. Look, when I saw Pete last night he had been kicked to hell by someone. I mean it was bad. His face was swollen like a melon, and there was blood everywhere."

Jenny scrunched her own face in displeasure, but without the shock Teresa expected.

"It's not the first time," the older woman said.

"Jenny." Dave leaned across the table toward her. "Your brother is in an ugly dispute with those Morse boys. You know how they are. He is not going to get the best of this. He has no allies. He is in very deep trouble if you don't help us."

The besieged woman rocked back and forth on her chair as the waitress put a fresh drink in front of her. Jenny picked it up quickly and downed half.

"What do you want know?"

"How has Ilsa been good to you?" Teresa asked before Dave could speak. He let the question stand.

"She's called me, come to visit. She testified for Pete, like you said. She even, while I was looking for work, you know. She took care of me a little."

"Financially," Dave said. Jenny nodded.

"Why would she do that?"

"Kindness of her heart."

"Come on," Teresa said. "That's not Ilsa. Loyalty, maybe. Duty. But not kindness. Tell us the truth, Jenny."

"Damn you," the woman sighed. "Promise you won't tell her I said anything."

Teresa looked at Dave, who shrugged. He might not care about making such a promise, but Teresa did. She grabbed his glass of ale and took a long swig.

"We promise," she said.

"There was something Ilsa said to Pete. When they were alone, going over yard work." Jenny finished the third Jameson and leaned forward. "This was before the theft, mind you. She asked him… Now all I have is his word, but it was so strange that I didn't see him making it up. She asked him how he would go about stealing that hideous painting."

"You're joking," said Teresa.

"Swear to God. She didn't actually ask him to do it. More like she was curious how he might, you know…"

"Hypothetically."

"Exactly. Hypothetically, how he might take it. Later she said it was about checking if their security was up to snuff. But Pete didn't believe that for a minute."

"What did he say to her?" asked Dave.

"He thought it was some sort of test, so he just laughed it off."

"But after the theft," said Teresa, breathless. "Why wouldn't he have mentioned it?"

"There we are," said Jenny heavily. "His word against hers. Plus, she got bashed in the head. Concussion, in the hospital. A little hard to convince anyone she was the thief."

"He had nothing to lose," Dave pressed.

"That was the first time she came to me. We weren't friendly before, when I worked for her. But since then we've become sort of friends. I know you don't believe it, Tay, but I think she's sincere. Anyway, that first time she works her way around to saying that if Pete will forget a certain conversation, she'll help me out while he's in prison. You have to know Ilsa, Mr. Webster. She can say something like that and make it seem like she's doing you a favor. That there's nothing at stake for her. And honestly, Pete couldn't prove a thing."

"Well," said Dave, sitting back. He glanced at Teresa, who nodded in agreement. Then quickly scanned the room. There were only four other patrons. Older men drinking quietly, none of them looking her way. Yet she had felt eyes upon them. Dave had mentioned a similar feeling last night.

"How much did she give you?" Dave asked.

"Not a lot," Jenny replied. "I mean not at once. It was a little here and there."

"Thousands? Tens of thousands?"

"Sure, but that's over years. The old man was paying her good."

"Is this still going on?" Teresa asked.

"She stopped after I got full-time work. But Pete let her know he didn't like that, so she started up again."

"Pete went to see her when he got out."

"Yeah," Jenny agreed. "Felt he was owed. But he pushed too hard, wanted the old man himself to pay him! Ilsa told him where to get off. Said he had to be patient."

"Until…" Teresa said, the rest quickly falling into place. "Until Alfred died and she inherited it all? Is that it?" Her voice had grown harsh, and Jenny did not reply. But the way she hung her head was answer enough. "For God's sake."

"It's easy to judge," Jenny snapped. "You haven't had to work like a mule your whole life. No one helping you. Watching out for a brother bent on mischief."

"When did you last see Ilsa?" Dave asked, refocusing her.

"A few days ago."

"You must have discussed her new status."

"Of course. And the Morse children wanting their share. It was too much for the poor woman. She said she wanted to make things right with Pete once and for all, and now who knew when that would happen."

"And what else?"

"Things about the boys. Not nice things. Not things to repeat."

"But you did repeat them," Dave said, his tone sharpening. "Didn't you?"

Jenny turned her face away as tears began rolling down her rough and swollen cheeks.

"Yes," she gasped. "God help me."

"What things?" Teresa asked, leaning close enough to smell the woman's distress.

"It came up because of me wondering why everything went to her. Turned out the old man had consulted Ilsa. Not about what *she* got, but the children. He meant to cut them off, and wanted to see if she agreed. Freddie was obvious. He hadn't only bankrupted himself. He nearly bankrupted Philip and Alfred, too, with those crazy Asian investments."

"Right," said Teresa. "And Philip because Grandpa thought he stole the painting."

"See, I didn't know that," Jenny gurgled, fresh gossip temporarily soothing her grief. "But that's not the reason Ilsa said."

"No?"

"Philip," Jenny stage-whispered. Then looked around for added effect. "You may already know this, but Philip has a thing for girls. I don't mean twenty-five, I mean teenagers. We all knew that in the house. What only Ilsa knew was that he and Audrey had a…well, you understand what I'm saying."

"No," Teresa breathed. More in sorrow than disbelief. It was ugly, yes, but it also had a déjà vu quality about it. Once learned, it was as if she had always known. "How did Ilsa find out?"

Jenny tried to look properly appalled, but there was a mad glee in her eyes.

"She *saw* them doing it."

"When?"

"That summer before the theft. Everyone else was off doing something."

"She was fifteen years old," Teresa said.

"Yes," Jenny replied. "And we can't assume that was the only time. Who knows how old she was when it started?"

"That's prison for him," Dave noted, "if it's proven."

"No one's talking about prison," Jenny said in a panic. "The girl went along with it, obviously. She probably started it."

"That doesn't matter," said Teresa. "And how do you know she went along?"

"She told Ilsa."

"Ilsa confronted her?"

"No. Audrey knew they'd been seen, she cornered Ilsa. Told her to keep her mouth shut or she would kill her. *Kill* her, mind you. A fifteen-year-old girl! Well, Ilsa wasn't afraid of Audrey, but she kept quiet just the same. Then the old man heard somehow. I think maybe Cynthia found out. He asked Ilsa to confirm it, and she had no choice."

"Of course she didn't," Teresa said acidly. "Why did she tell you?"

"We'd had a few drinks. She was agonizing over using it to make Philip back off the estate fight. But she's too honorable a woman, wouldn't do it. Swore me to silence."

With that, the tears started once more.

"Which you violated," Dave said again. "By telling Pete."

"I didn't mean to," Jenny wailed. That turned a couple of heads in their direction, and she lowered her voice. "We only have each other in the world, me and Pete. It's natural for us to tell each other things. He hates those boys. I knew it would make him happy to hear Ilsa had it over them. I told him not to do anything with it. I begged him. But that way he smiled, I should have known."

"So you don't know his actual plans?"

"You showing up is the first I've heard of anything. You couldn't be wrong, could you? Maybe it's something else. Nothing to do with Philip."

Dave stared at the weeping woman with an odd expression. A kind of tempered pity. Teresa admired it in him, but felt none herself. Violent acts had been triggered because of gossip. Because of spite.

"Maybe," Dave allowed. "Anything is possible."

But no one at the table believed it.

22

They drove north again. Into the lowering gloom of evening. Teresa had been leaving it to Dave to speak first, her ire and anxiety growing with every silent mile. Until she realized that he was giving her room. It was her family, not his, and he was letting her sit with these new and wicked truths for as long as she needed.

"How much of that did you already know?" she finally asked.

"First," he said, "don't assume it's all true. We had her cornered, and thieves are liars."

"People are liars."

"Well. Yes."

"Do you believe her?"

"For the most part," Dave replied. "There's something between Audrey and Philip. Something unhealthy. And we already knew that Philip and Pete had tangled. What I couldn't make sense of was Pete's condition. You never know about people, but I just couldn't see Phil putting that beating on him."

"Freddie," she said. "That's where he was going in such a hurry yesterday."

"That's what I'm thinking also."

"So put this together for me."

"Not to lay any 'mystery man' bullshit on you," Dave replied, "but I'm more interested in your take."

"Starting where?"

"Good question. The more you peel it back, the more there is."

"Back to my grandfather buying that painting. And what it did to my father, and Philip, and James. And then what Freddie and Phil did to Audrey."

"Let's not…" Dave sighed. "I realize it takes a lot of pressure off to blame everything on the painting, but families have been screwed up for—"

"Fine," she said. "Take Jenny at her word. She blabs to Pete about Philip and Audrey, and now he has something. He doesn't have to wait for the will to get settled and Ilsa to pay him. So he calls Philip and says what's it worth to you for me to keep quiet?"

"Good. And Philip says?"

"Fuck off," Teresa replied. "If I know Philip. Or anyway, whatever he said wasn't good enough for Pete, because…"

"Because it doesn't end there," Dave supplied. "Next thing, Philip tells Fred to go back to California. And tells me to go to the house so that Fred will leave."

"Right," she said, slapping the seat. "He's trying to keep Pete and Fred apart. Knowing Pete will go to him next."

"But Fred won't leave. Pete calls him. Says meet me

somewhere private and I'll tell you a thing you need to hear."

"Jesus," Teresa breathed. "He must have lost his mind, or forgotten what kind of guy Fred is. Pete wouldn't be able to get to the blackmail part. As soon as he made the accusation, Freddie would go crazy. Beat the living crap out of him."

"Exactly," Dave said. "So badly that he might think later he killed him."

"But it's Philip who called us."

"Because where does Freddie go next?"

"God. To Philip's house, to see if it's true. And before Philip can deny it, Fred knocks him around, too. And somewhere in there he tells him about leaving Pete for dead. So Philip calls you, and… Okay, but where are they both now?"

"Another good question," Dave replied. "Philip was okay by the second time we spoke, so I assume he talked Fred down. Otherwise we would have found him beaten to death."

"But Fred never came back to the house. Where did he go?"

"My guess would be on a major bender."

"And Philip went looking for him?"

"Maybe."

Teresa felt herself getting too agitated and took a deep breath, letting it out slow. A deer stood on the grassy margin by the road, watching them drive by.

"What do we do? Do we call Laurena, or Cynthia?"

"Is anyone going to thank you for those calls?"

"So we do nothing?"

"I don't know, Teresa. I'm thinking it through."

"And what about Ilsa?" she demanded. "She connects everything. Don't tell me you believe she got tipsy and blurted out that secret. You don't know the woman, but Jenny Mulhane is the last person she would pick as a friend."

"I think we have to consider it a strategic leak," Dave agreed. "She knew Jenny would tell her brother, and Pete would try to use it."

"But how does Pete putting the screws to Philip help her?"

Dave nodded and tapped the steering wheel.

"Do you believe Ilsa was surprised at inheriting the estate?"

"I did at first," Teresa answered. "I don't see how I can anymore. Okay, he left most of the paintings to institutions, so she might have figured the other money went to charity. But he must have told her she would be taken care of. Maybe she intuited that the less the children got, the more she did."

"So she encouraged Alfred in cutting them off."

"Why stop there?" Teresa twisted sideways to face him. "Maybe it was her idea. She came up with the reasons, and reinforced them in his mind, day after day. They were alone together for years. He trusted her more than anyone, wife and children included. Maybe she's behind everything. Including bumping off Alfred when she got tired of waiting."

"Slow down," Dave said. "You're doing well, but don't get carried away. If that's true, Ilsa has two problems. Pete knowing her secret. Which we know bothered her enough to pay off his sister for more than a decade. And the Morse children banding together to contest the will. She needs to deal with both."

"On the will, she knows Philip is the key. Fred and Mom wouldn't have challenged on their own. Why doesn't she threaten Phil directly?"

"Maybe it's not her style," Dave tried. "Or maybe she knows that Philip will call her bluff."

"Then she knows he'll call Pete's bluff, as well." She waited for a response, but Dave only looked at her. Waiting for her to see the rest. "So Pete will move on to Fred. Who Ilsa knows is violent, especially regarding his daughter."

"You're right that Philip is the bandleader," Dave jumped in, "but he needs your mother and Fred on board to prevail. At the very least, Ilsa blows up that alliance."

"Without getting her hands dirty. And just possibly she gets Pete killed, which eliminates the other problem, as well." It was only after she spoke it that a shiver went through Teresa. Could people be that calculating? Could Ilsa be? "Are we reaching here, Dave?"

"Yes," he laughed. "We're totally reaching. And it's true that I don't know Ilsa well, though I've met her a few times. Pretty tough customer."

"It feels right to you."

"I don't know." He shrugged, working a crick out of his neck. "What do you think?"

That I would rather not know any of this, Teresa mused. Why was I so determined to dig into the diseased heart of things? I could be in Butler Library now, reading about the lives of dead artists.

"That I would like to say it to her face and see how she reacts."

"There's an idea," Dave said, uneasily. "She won't return my calls. Maybe you would have better luck. But it's a hell of thing to say to someone, Teresa."

"We're not going back far enough," she replied. Facing down the one revelation she had been avoiding, without even knowing it. "Why does Ilsa have a secret at all? Why did she ask Pete about stealing the painting?"

"Yeah, I've been chewing on that, too. It was years ago. Maybe she was impatient for a payoff. Maybe she thought it was an evil influence."

"Maybe she was asking for someone else."

"Huh," Dave said quietly. They stayed quiet for a while, the hum of the car on the road lulling them. Dave turned the headlights on. "Any idea who that would be?"

"You said there was someone you suspected for years. I assume that was the collector you met, DeGross?"

"Yes. Using Pete or one of the caterers. But after talking to the guy, I don't know. He's either the best actor I've ever met, or he's still mourning his failure."

"Idiot," Teresa said wearily. "He has no idea how lucky he is."

"You would have a hard time convincing him of that."

"I've been dreaming of my dad a lot lately."

"Yeah? Happy dreams, I hope."

"I don't do happy dreams. They're pretty intense, though I would probably be upset if they stopped. They're all I have of him."

"What happens in these dreams?" Dave asked.

"There are different ones. But I keep coming back to a dream where we talk about the painting. Where he tries to make me look at it."

"Did you two ever talk about it? Outside of dreams?"

"We talked about Goya." She closed her eyes and reached back for those exchanges. Memory was such a liar. "I know he said that I shouldn't be afraid of the portrait. I don't remember anything more specific. Nothing I trust."

"What does that mean?"

"I have conversations with my father. In my head. Sometimes sleeping and sometimes when I'm awake. Do you think that's strange?"

"Not at all," he replied.

"Well, I do. Later, I don't know what's memory, what's dream, what I made up. I've seen him, too. In museums, in train stations, on crowded streets."

"I'm sure that's also completely normal."

"For a couple of years I convinced myself he was still alive. That he faked his death to escape his enemies, and now he was following me around New York. My guardian angel. But I couldn't maintain the illusion."

"Not that I have a problem with it," Dave said cautiously, "but is there a reason we're talking about your father?"

"Fred said something to me. I didn't mention it in our information swap. It was too close to home. He said Ilsa was in love with my dad."

"Uh-huh. I see why that would be weird for you."

"And you see why I'm mentioning it now."

"He's obsessed with the painting. She's obsessed with him. It works. Asking Pete about stealing it was totally out of character for Ilsa. Love makes us do strange things."

"You probably know this already, since you see right through me."

"On the contrary, you are one of the hardest people to read that I've met."

"Really?" That perked her up. Why? Why should it please her to be opaque? And could she back out of this confession now? No, she could not. "I've given you these bullshit reasons why I want to know the truth. I'm worried about my family and blah-blah. The fact is I've been estranged from them for fifteen years. Not completely, but a bond was broken after the theft. Before last week, my mother had not been to one Morse family event in all that time. It has to do with most of them suspecting my father. All I've ever really wanted to do was prove he was innocent."

"Okay," Dave admitted. "I actually did know that."

"Instead, we seem to be closing in on the opposite. That he did it."

"My problem with your father as thief is the same as my problem with DeGross," Dave said. "The man I interviewed did not seem like a man hiding something. He seemed like a man whose best friend had died."

Sad as the words were, they lifted Teresa's mood more than anything had in weeks. So much so that she wanted to lean over and kiss him. On the cheek.

"Maybe he was upset about Pete taking the rap."

"Please, don't take offense," Dave said. "But was your father the type to get upset about the Pete Mulhanes of the world?"

"He wasn't a bad guy," Teresa protested. "He wasn't like Philip. But when he really wanted something, not much stood in his way. So you're probably right."

They drove in silence for a while as dusk turned into dark.

"Do you know where in Pennsylvania Ilsa's sister lives?" Teresa asked.

"Yes, more or less. Thought of dropping in on them myself, but we don't know if she's still there."

"From here, we can't be that far away, right?"

"A lot closer than we were in Owl's Point."

Teresa slid the phone from her jacket pocket and began to dial.

"You have her number?" Dave asked.

"Mitchell does."

"He's going to give it to you?"

"Yes," Teresa said, without a hint of doubt. "He is."

23

Sleep is for the dead.

Audrey sleeps in the window seat as rain pelts the glass. James' face is close, love and anger in his eyes. Then he is gone, and Audrey, too. Both vanish and then comes the scream. Demon hands hold her fevered body to the mattress. She cannot rise. A figure darts in and out of the room. *See it, my girl. See everything, do not look away.* Her father's hands. The demon is beside him. The demon is inside him. The demon is inside her.

Tay-ray, *qué pasa?*

Dónde está James? Qué has hecho con él?

An explosion of laughter. English, honey. My Spanish ain't that good.

Audrey?

Don't tell me you were sleeping.

It's the middle of the night. Why shouldn't I sleep?

Sleep is for the dead.

Who said that? Who just said that?

Where are you?

Here.

Another burst of laughter. Teresa, wake *up*. Where is here?

Pennsylvania, a motel. Too late that day for Ilsa. Tomorrow. She says none of this.

Are you at Owl's Point?

No. The Jersey Shore.

No way, really? Is Dave with you?

He drove me down. I had to get out.

That's what I said! I said that to Dave, she has to get out of that house. I can't believe he did it. And I can't believe he didn't tell me, the douche.

Are you high, Audrey?

As a motherfucking kite, my beach bunny. Is it cold there? I bet it's cold. You keeping each other warm? Hey, put him on, will you?

He's in the room next door.

What? What fun is that, go jump him. He's not bad for an old dude. Slow starter, but once he gets going—

Why did you call?

To see how my favorite cousin was doing, why else?

Have you heard from your father?

Did you think he was going to warn me before he showed up? Thank God Philip called, I'd be in frigging intensive care. Or he would. Then wouldn't you feel bad.

We didn't... I didn't realize that's where he'd go. I'm sorry.

This ain't your kind of game, Tay. But your new beau

should have known. In fact, I'm pretty pissed off at our Davie. You tell him that.

Where are you?

I'm on the run, sweets. Hey, can I use your place in the city? Is there a key under the doormat or something?

I'll call my super and tell him to let you in. You don't think Fred might look there?

You're right, better stay anonymous. Or I could try Kenny.

You mean go to San Fran?

You don't know? Kenny never left New York. Shacked up with his old flame for more than a week. Who knows what else he might be up to, right?

What's going on, Audrey?

Oh, it's all just a mess, isn't it? Just a shameful mess. Every girl for herself, know what I mean? You talk to my brother?

Not for a few days. Is he all right?

No, Teresa, he's not all right, and he's never going to be all right. And it's our fault, okay? Yours and mine. So if you see him, you take good care of him, understand?

I don't need you to tell me—

Shut up, you self-righteous bitch. Just stay where you are. Keep away until the smoke clears. Peace out.

Audrey. Audrey?

She punches keys, wrongly, again and again until: *This is James. You can leave a message.* Not good enough. She needs to speak to him, now. She must. And so she does. James, where are you? What's going on with Kenny?

I know his secret, and he knows mine. It's not safe.

Are you afraid of Kenny? Is he going to hurt you?

I don't know.

Don't wait to find out. Get out of Boston.

I'm not in Boston, I'm looking for you.

Are you at Owl's Point?

Nobody's there. I didn't go in the house. It scares me.

Go to New York. Go to my mother's apartment, do you know where that is?

I have to find you, Tay. We have to finish the portrait.

I have one more thing to do. I'll be back as soon as I can.

We should be together.

We will be.

Rest now, hon. You're getting overexcited.

Mom? Mom, can you take care of James? Please?

Sleep, my girl, the angels will watch over you both.

But sleep is for the dead.

No, my child. Our life is the sleep from which we all must awaken.

Dad? Dad? Come back.

24

"I'm confused," Dave said, turning onto a narrow road of broken tarmac. It ran straight as a ruler, with fields of cornstalks on either side. "These were real conversations or dreams?"

"I thought they were dreams," Teresa replied, slumped in the passenger seat and fighting sleep. "But the calls are on my phone. Very short. I'm almost positive that I spoke to Audrey. James could have been in my head. At one point he became my parents."

"For a hundred and seventy-five dollars I'll tell you what that means."

"Where is this place?"

"Should be coming right up."

Sure enough, over the next rise a red barn appeared. Behind it an orchard marched into the distance. In front was a gravel lot so full of pickups and SUVs that they spilled onto the muddy grass. Families with children shuffled to and from the huge, beckoning barn. Dave had to park a hundred yards away, and the walk in the cold morning air revived Teresa. Pumpkins were spread in stacks near the open barn door, and a white cat danced across the top of them. Around the side were pens with sheep, goats and chickens. Teresa had never gone to places like this as a child, and would have said she had no interest. Yet she had a sudden yearning to be a girl here. To grab the scampering barn cat and rub her face in its thick fur, despite her allergies. To buy a paper bag of pellets and feed the pushy goats. For one fleeting moment she was able to imagine an entirely different childhood, a different life. She felt her eyes misting and drove her ragged fingernails into her palms. Pull yourself together.

Dave went into the barn, but Teresa continued down the muddy lane toward the orchard. Beyond the duck pond, beneath the first apple tree, was a picnic table, and sitting there was a lone and austere figure. Black cashmere sweater and rain coat. Iron gray hair and eyes. No hint of either warmth or hostility. Teresa sat down across from her.

"Hello, Ilsa."

"Good morning."

"Thank you for meeting. Is your sister here?"

"No. Mr. Webster is with you?"

"Yes. I imagine he'll find us before long."

"He is a persistent man. What did you need to ask me so urgently?"

Straight to business. So be it.

"Did Jenny call you yesterday?"

"Hmm." Ilsa ran a hand over the rough plank of the table. "Jenny calls often."

"I'll take that as a yes. So you know that people have been hurt. Badly hurt, because of events you set in motion."

"Me? No. Events have been in motion for years, with predictable consequences. My part has been small."

"These are desperate, unstable men. To set them on each other just because you can—"

"I thought you brighter than this," Ilsa said. "I am sorry to spoil your illusions, but your uncles are vile men and have always been so. They wish to ruin me. To take what is mine."

"I would think there's enough for everyone."

"We have no idea what will be left when the accountants are done. Maybe nothing. But your grandfather was clear in his wishes."

"I don't believe he hated his own sons."

"No," Ilsa said, with a quick turn of the head that Teresa remembered. "He believed in responsibility for actions. He would have told you himself, had he lived."

"Was it him who believed that, or you?"

"Is that what you think?" Ilsa nodded slowly. "Your grandfather was his own man. He made the rules, always."

Dave sat down beside Teresa and placed a box with donuts and cups of hot cider on the table. Neither woman glanced at him.

"Even if you despise my uncles," Teresa pressed, "why involve Pete? You could have dealt with Philip directly."

"You think Peter is innocent? A thief, liar and extortionist?"

"All the more reason for you to steer clear of him."

Ilsa placed her palms flat on the table, and Teresa wondered if their talk was over. Just that fast.

"You know about Philip," Ilsa said. *"Ja?"*

"I know what you told my grandfather. I have no idea if it's true."

"Then ask Audrey," the older woman sighed. "In any case, my obstacle in talking to Philip about the matter is that Alfred forbade it. It was his absolute rule that it not be discussed within the family. Under any circumstances."

"But he's dead," Teresa said.

"Death does not remove my obligation. You may dismiss it, but throughout this difficult time I have tried to remain the custodian of your grandfather's wishes."

"More the letter than the spirit," Dave said, through a mouth full of donut. "Jenny's not family. That's why you used her. Makes sense now. And if Phil or Fred killed Pete to shut him up, that was just bonus points."

Ilsa looked at Dave as she might a goat that had bleated a credible counterfeit of speech. Teresa took a deep breath, thinking: now or never.

"Why did you ask Pete about stealing the painting?"

Ilsa took a tissue from her purse and blew her nose before speaking.

"I suspected that was your question. Are you prepared for the answer?"

I think I just got it, Teresa judged, her spirit sinking.

"As prepared as I'll ever be."

Ilsa swept the table again with her shaking hand, and Teresa realized it was a nervous gesture. That the older woman was as disturbed by this conversation as she was.

"I am not a religious person. Religious, spiritual, choose your own word. I have always been suspicious of those types. Your father was different. He was a true seeker.

By which I mean he was certain that he *did not* know the answers, but was open to what answers might come. He believed in good and evil, devils, angels. I think he understood them metaphorically, the soul at war with itself. But I am not certain."

"You talked about this stuff with him?" Teresa could not disguise her amazement.

"Later. At first I only overheard him with Alfred. They were both brought up to ignore servants. Especially women. I might have been offended, but I thought it a privilege to listen to them talk. Long and heated debates, Alfred on the side of the rational, your father the mystical. Alfred usually got the better of it. Yet I sensed that he wanted your father to win, ultimately. That he wanted to be convinced."

"Convinced of what?"

"The influence of the supernatural. The reality of the invisible world."

"So Grandpa didn't believe in the painting's power?"

Ilsa's gaze became sharp and anxious.

"It was layers beneath layers with your grandfather. His business dealings, his entire life was such a maze of deceit that he himself was lost in it. He certainly wanted others to believe. To fear the portrait, and him by extension. Also to desire it. In private, he would laugh at them, and declare the whole thing nonsense."

"But you didn't buy that," Teresa said.

"I asked him once," Ilsa replied, her mouth twisted oddly. Smiling at a memory, yet pained by it at the same time. "If you worship this *verdammte* painting so much, why is it on the wall *behind* you."

"He couldn't look at something like that all the time."

"Your father could."

"So he had...what? A higher tolerance for the work's influence? Higher than Grandpa, I mean?"

"Truthfully?" Ilsa eyed Dave with distrust. For a moment Teresa thought she would have to ask him to take a little walk, but the older woman overcame her hesitation. "I am not sure that comparison was ever tested."

"Holy shit," Dave whispered after a moment.

"Wait, what does that mean?"

"She means," said Dave, his voice hushed with wonder, "that Alfred Arthur Morse never looked at the portrait. My God, you have got to be kidding."

"No, that's, that can't..." Teresa felt stricken, and could discern a matching misery on Ilsa's face. Why? It was shocking, certainly, but why this pain? She sat with it for half a minute and then she knew. "He brought that thing into the house. Into all our lives. His own son never recovered from what he saw. That historian died. And he never even looked at it?"

"I do not know for certain. We didn't discuss it."

"You do. You know, or you never would have said such a thing."

"Perhaps now you understand your father's mind a little better, *ja*?" Ilsa pushed on. Reaching a hand across the table, but stopping short of Teresa's. "Why he might have found his own claim to the work superior to Alfred's."

"Did he know Grandpa never saw it?"

"If I am not sure, he could not have been. Yet he must have sensed the truth."

"And he asked you to arrange its theft?"

"His interest was not like other men's," Ilsa insisted. "He

did not want to sell it, or to inflate his stature. He did not care about ownership. As long as Alfred allowed him access, he was content. But Philip and the lawyers pushed Alfred to sell. Dorothy hated it and wanted it gone, and then she died so needlessly. Alfred felt terrible grief and guilt, and made up his mind to be rid of it. Ramón realized he would lose the work forever."

"But what did he want from it?" Teresa demanded.

"That he could not have said himself, I think. Except. He believed there was a demon in his blood. I use his own words. The thing that gave him strength and clarity also gave him those terrible depressions. And the mania, which was worse. He was institutionalized as a teenager."

"I didn't know that," Teresa said numbly. Bludgeoned by the knowledge.

"He saw in Goya a kindred spirit. Someone who had been through the fire, and found a way to defeat his demon. He thought that by looking closely enough, by meditating on the work, he might know the artist's mind. He might find his own way out. For himself, for your mother. For you. It was not greed or possessiveness, Teresa. It was love."

A green tractor rumbled by, towing a hay wagon full of squealing children. They made their slow way along the rutted lane, into the heart of the orchard. Teresa looked for the hidden lie, but could not discover it. She had always felt that her father loved her, however distantly. Love. How much harm had been perpetrated in its name? How much more was to come before they found the bottom of this?

"What then?" she asked, wiping the dampness from her face. "You asked Pete to steal it and he refused."

"He refused to even answer. He pretended not to take me

seriously. I put myself into his hands and achieved nothing. I told Ramón he must forget the whole matter."

"How did he take that?" Dave asked.

"Not well. He didn't argue, that was not his way."

"But he didn't give up the idea?"

"I believed that he had."

"Do you think he stole the painting?" Teresa asked. "Tell me honestly, Ilsa."

The woman bowed her head, and Teresa feared the worst. But a moment later Ilsa shook her gray crown vigorously.

"It was a long time before I could remember that day. I confess that in weaker moments I wondered. When I finally brought myself to ask him, Ramón swore he had not done it. He was offended. Offended and hurt. It was the last time we spoke." Teresa thought the woman would weep then, but her eyes remained dry. The tears were all in her voice. "He did not care for me as I did for him, but I do not believe he would have hurt me like that."

"Wait a minute," said Dave eagerly, leaning forward. "You're saying you *do* remember that day?"

"Much of it has come back. It took months, Mr. Webster. Years even. Much too late for the police, or your investigation."

"And no memory of who hit you?"

"It was from behind, I never saw. Just the boy there on the carpet."

"James," Teresa breathed.

"Yes," said Ilsa, her voice gone strange. She stared at a grassy patch near the table, but her mind was back in the study at Owl's Point. "Rolled into a ball. So still. As if there was no life in him. Then for just a moment before the room went dark, he looked up at me. And he smiled. An awful smile."

"What?" Teresa cried, standing and banging the table with her thigh. A cup of cider went over, and Dave stood also. "What the hell are you talking about? He was catatonic when they found him."

"Yes," Ilsa agreed. Her voice suddenly tired, as if the vision had emptied her. "It's true, yet the picture is in my mind. So clear. Probably something my bruised brain invented."

"Sit down," Dave said urgently. Why urgent? Because he sensed that her outburst had broken the mood. They might lose Ilsa any moment, and there was more he wanted to know. She didn't care. Not about Ilsa's secrets or Dave's needs or anything. It was all too much. The edges of her vision shimmered, and a sick feeling welled up in her. She sat.

"What else do you remember?" Dave asked.

"Bits and pieces," Ilsa mumbled. "Nothing useful. I went to Teresa's room to check on her. Ramón was worried. He was normally inattentive to children's illnesses, but he was very worried that day. I heard James scream, I ran down the back stairs to the study."

It started. A wash of bright light, and the world fractured. Don't close your eyes, Teresa commanded herself. That only makes it worse. *Yes, that's my girl. See it. See.*

"What's wrong?" Dave's hand grasped her upper arm. "Teresa?"

"She is having a seizure," Ilsa answered calmly.

"You were in the room," Teresa said between clenched teeth. Fighting to remain present.

"Yes," Ilsa replied. "Your room."

Not heading *to* her room, which Teresa had always believed, but actually in the room. She could see her there. Concerned gray eyes looking down, moments before James tore their world open. Teresa pulled breath downward from the base of her lungs, releasing it slowly. She stared at a single branch of the apple tree, willing it to stay solid.

"Where was Audrey?" she asked, her voice growing stronger.

"Sleeping by the window."

"Did you see her there?"

"No. You did."

"That's right," Teresa said. Herself again. The fractured world began to reassemble. Dave still held her arm, warm and close. Looking worried. Ilsa seemed shocked. She had not expected the young woman to shake off the fit. For the very good reason that Teresa had never done so before. "I saw her. No one else did. Dave, we have to go back. Now."

"Like, right now?"

"Yes, we have to go back to the house. Please, get the car, and I'll be right there."

"Right. All right." He looked at her with concern and suspicion both, but rose from the table and set off toward the barn. Ilsa had begun to rise.

"One more thing," Teresa said. "What did you see that night? The night Grandpa died."

"What do you mean?"

"You saw someone in the house."

"No, that was only shadows." Ilsa fell back onto the wooden bench and turned away. She looked as drained as

Teresa felt. "I found him in that, that state. I was frightened."

"A figure with something over its head. Ilsa, please."

"It was nothing. Nothing but my fear. Fear does the most terrible things to us, my child. It is the cause of all of this unhappiness."

I can't argue with that, Teresa thought. My child. Something her father said. Fred had been correct about the source of Ilsa's residual affection.

"You know," the older woman continued. "Later I decided it wasn't something covering its head. That it was hair. You see what I mean? Long thick hair to his shoulders."

"Like my dad's."

"Yes," Ilsa confirmed. With a smile so fragile that the faintest pressure would shatter it. "Like Ramón. But it was nothing, Teresa. There was no one there."

"Okay."

"Why did you ask me about it?"

"No reason. No reason at all."

25

They drove east, racing the waning light. Dave could not remember feeling so tired, which was saying something. Still, he guessed that he had slept more than Teresa. Her eyes were red and underlined in dark crescents, and her seizure had scared the wits out of him. She seemed on the verge of a severe physical or mental breakdown, for which he would feel responsible. Yet she was also locked in. Almost superhumanly focused on their mission of discovery. If she had been following his lead at first, they had switched roles. She was on a scent, and though he sat right beside her, Dave felt like he was running to keep up.

"What are you thinking?" Teresa asked.

"I thought you were asleep." The only sleep she seemed to get was in the car, so he had been staying quiet. She sat up and brushed the hair from her face.

"I was, but my dreams are freaky."

"Teresa, look. Is this safe?"

"Is what safe?"

"What we're doing. Is it safe for you? I mean, that attack you had."

"I'm okay. I was able to control it."

"Should you be trying to control it? Don't you have medication?"

"Did my mother tell you that?" she asked suspiciously.

"She says you don't take it."

"I do. Just not right now, I can't."

"What do you mean? Why can't you?"

"Dave, you have to trust me on this. Do you trust me?"

"Sure."

"The, um, what you call attacks. The episodes. They're messages."

"From who?"

"From…from me, from myself," she said, though Dave was sure she had been about to say something else.

"And what are they telling you?"

"You're going to feel like I'm doing tit for tat on the stuff you held back from me."

"I might very well feel that way," Dave acknowledged.

"There are things I can't say until I'm sure. Bad things that I won't be able to take back."

"Must be pretty bad. Why are we rushing back to the Owl's Point?"

"Because Audrey doesn't want us there. She wasn't worried about me. She was trying to get everyone out of the house."

Well, well. And why not? Dave felt sure that Audrey's concern had been real, but that did not mean it was the only thing on her mind.

"Why does she want the place to herself?"

"Yeah," said Teresa, running her pale hand across the dashboard. Like an echo of the devious and heartbroken Ilsa stroking the picnic table. "Dave, what if there was no theft? What if the painting never left the house?"

The car slowed until Dave realized his foot had gone slack. He picked up speed again, though it was all he could do not to pull onto the shoulder.

"Like misplaced or something? Come on, Teresa."

"No, deliberately moved. But still there."

"The house was searched."

"How soon, and how thoroughly?"

"I don't know. I only had the police report and your grandfather's word."

"They were looking to see what else was taken," Teresa said. "Not searching every cranny for something hidden. Right?"

"And after all this time nobody stumbled on it?"

"There are parts of that house where no one goes," Teresa replied. "Almost no one."

"So who hid it?"

"I don't know."

"You mean you won't say."

They hurtled down the steep ravine of 287 and shaped the long curve onto the Tappan Zee Bridge. Traffic was miraculously thin today. To the south, the towers of Manhattan sparkled distantly.

"Now you think Audrey is behind everything," he complained, not liking his own tone. "This morning it was Ilsa. Who will you accuse next?"

"Do you feel that protective of her?" Teresa asked, turning a sorrowful face on him.

"No." He fumbled with the E-ZPass scanner until Teresa took it from him, sticking it smoothly into the Velcro base on the windshield. "Yes," Dave admitted. "Obviously I do. She's a rude, crude, self-serving manipulator. But I like her."

"I like her, too," Teresa said sadly. "I suspect she likes us. But in a pinch she'll always put herself first."

"You could say that of most people."

"If you heard she had harmed someone to get a thing she wanted. Killed someone even. You might be a little shocked, but would you find it hard to believe?"

Dave did not answer right away. And kept not answering until it was apparent that he wasn't going to. He waited for the mechanical arm to rise, then shot out of the tollbooth like a jockey on a steel horse, racing eastward as fast as he dared to go.

On the far side of the little bridge, but still out of sight of the house, they pulled over. The lane was narrow. Rhododendrons blocked the passenger door, and Teresa had to climb out the driver's side. She took Dave's hand and squeezed it as they walked. He was startled, but did not pull away. Needing the comfort as much as she did. They cleared the last bushes, and there was the great pile of brick, awaiting them silently. The circular drive was empty of vehicles. There was no real way to hide, and Dave would have felt silly trying. Nevertheless, they walked on the grass margin, avoiding the gravel, and did not speak until they reached the front door. Teresa dug for her keys, and Dave touched her hand.

"Wait. I'm going to make a quick circuit of the house."

"I'll come with you."

"No, faster if it's just me. I'm used to doing this without being seen."

She did not like it, but said no more, and Dave set off. No one on the lawn or in the gazebo. No one visible in the woods. There was nothing of note until he reached the garage. Through the glass he could see that where the green Jaguar had been, Audrey's red Lexus was now parked. Carefully out of sight. Teresa's instincts were on target. Dave leaned his forehead on the little window and thought about Audrey as he had seen her last. Naked and grinning, panting obscenities. An ache passed through him that was equal parts desire and mourning. A dull thump seemed to happen inside his gut. Until it happened again.

He listened closely, but the thumps were more sensed than heard. Powerful but muffled. As if they came from underground. For the first time since a certain night in Miami, he got a bad attack of the heebie-jeebies. Audrey was right, this place was haunted. The fifth thump was the last. Then something caught his eye. A dozen yards into the trees, a figure moved. Tall and shuffling and making no attempt to hide. Dave lost sight of him and moved closer for a better look. This was a thinner part of the wood, less pine, more maple. He ought to be able to see. He thought about Teresa waiting at the door and knew he should go to her. But there was someone out there, and Dave had the jump on him. It was too good a chance to waste.

Within the trees, it was a different story. The lines of

sight were poorer than he had guessed, and he heard nothing but his own feet in the dead leaves. No more woods—you promised yourself two nights ago and here you are! After twenty yards, Dave began to turn back when he spotted something out of place. A loafer dangling off a foot. Then a leg, then a man in a beige raincoat, his back against a tree trunk. He blended into the surroundings so well that he was easy to miss. Dave did not think it was the same guy he saw a minute earlier, especially as this one was motionless, but he crept closer to investigate.

"Hey, Philip," he whispered as the face came into view. The hair was wildly messed, the glasses missing, the blue eyes at half-mast, not seeming to take much in. Yet Dave did not think he was dead. There was old bruising—two days old, Dave would bet—over the left side of the face, but a fresh and bleeding wound on the right temple. And another on the crown. "I see you've been having as much fun as me."

"Duff."

"Well said." Dave crouched and waved a hand in front of Philip's face. The eyes followed. That was a good sign. Which begged the question, why did Dave feel disappointed? Because some part of him had hoped to find Philip's head cracked open, his breath stopped. Even now, it would be so easy to place a firm hand over his mouth. To pinch his nostrils closed and watch the face turn red, feel the injured body tremble and jerk. Until it stopped. The man was in no condition to resist. And who could then say that the blows to the head were not the cause? Who could say you didn't have it coming? You sleazy, child-molesting piece of shit. "Who hit you?"

"Dave." Which was what he had tried to say before.

"I'm Dave, and it wasn't me. Why are you even here?"

"Peeth. Meeting Peeth."

"Pete, got it." So much for him staying away. The ex-Marine lived to dole out or receive punishment, it seemed. It was good to understand your purpose. "Why were you meeting Pete at all, let alone in these godforsaken woods?"

"His gun."

"What about it?" Dave asked. "He lost it in that park."

"Freddie took."

"Fred has Pete's gun?" That was a bad development, if true.

"No. I took it from Fred."

"So you have it now," Dave said, patting down the raincoat but finding nothing.

"Wanted it back."

"Pete did?"

"Yeah."

"So, what? You came here to give him his gun?"

It seemed unlikely, but a more credible conclusion occurred to Dave. Pete came to get his gun back, but Philip had a different use of the weapon in mind. Judging by his looks, things had not gone according to Phil's plan. Which meant that Pete had the gun again. Unless he was lying dead nearby.

"You five-star asshole. Why has no one killed you yet?"

Philip closed his eyes and said no more. Remaining crouched, Dave shifted around and looked out on the trees. Things had passed beyond an acceptable degree of risk. If not for him, then for Teresa. He slipped the phone out of his pocket and thumbed it on. Thirty yards away something swayed, as a thin trunk might do in the breeze. But there was no breeze. Dave looked once at the path he needed to follow back to the house, so he did not walk into a tree. Then he stood, fixed his eyes on the swaying form, and began to punch 911 into the phone as he shuffled sideways. Too many things at once, he told himself. You're dividing your attention. He had barely time to think it when something loomed to his immediate left and he turned.

"I guess both of us lied," Pete said, just before everything stopped.

26

Teresa held her breath, listening. The thuds were faint and evenly paced, and stopped after five repetitions. She could not pinpoint direction, but felt it in her knees more than she heard it. Dave was taking too long to circle the house. Maybe he had seen something. Maybe he had found the back door open and gone in. Wanting to protect her, that would be like him. Men were so annoying.

After five minutes, she started around the house in the opposite direction, to maximize their chance of intersecting. The sun was above the trees, but dropping fast. The light a low and melancholy yellow. Audrey's car was in the garage, which was no surprise, but sent Teresa's anxiety level up. The mudroom door was locked. No figures wandered the lawn or hid behind statues. She arrived at the front of the house again, and no Dave. Then she pulled her keys out and unlocked the door.

The house alarm did not chime its warning, and a quick

check of the control panel showed it unarmed. Someone was inside. Teresa took deep and slow breaths, trying to control her speeding heart. These were screwed-up people, but they were her family. She could deal with them. She made her way down the wide and shadowed hall toward the back of the house. The study door stood open, as it should—she had left it that way. Yet she could not help expecting to see her grandfather sitting at his desk. White hair swept back from his forehead and that superior expression he always wore. An expression, she now understood, serving mostly to hide the fear in his heart. And the portrait there behind his head, where he would not have to see it. But the room was empty. No painting or old man. Not even a shrouded ghoul.

She jumped before her mind registered the noise. The thump was not faint now, but a hammering bang. Followed by another, seconds later. Then a third. After each there was a brief clattering, as of crumbling masonry. The source was no longer a mystery. It came straight up through the floor. The wine cellar. The stairs to which were only steps away, and Teresa went to them in haste. The door was open a few inches, the light on above the stairs. The banging was unspeakably loud, as if someone was trying to take down the mansion's foundation. Hating the idea, Teresa forced herself down the creaking steps, the hammering masking her descent. At the bottom, a bizarre sight met her eyes.

The air was fogged with plaster dust. An empty wine rack had been dragged from its spot, and its former occupants were placed all about the chamber, frosted white. At least one had shattered, for the pungent scent of red wine filled the space. Along the near wall were a series of gouges

about three feet from the floor. Some were shallow but a
few were deep, no doubt requiring several blows. Deep
enough to expose different generations of plaster, concrete
and stone, piles of which lay smoking on the floor. Amid
this carnage stood a phantom. Dusted white from head to
foot, it lurked near one corner, a sledgehammer resting
on its right shoulder. The curvy thighs and heroic breasts
pushing the tank top's limits gave the game away before
she tugged the bandanna off her face.

"What's shaking, Tay-ray?" Audrey huffed into the
choked air.

"I didn't know you were so strong."

"Could have used you a few hours ago when I was moving this junk. Dave was supposed to do this part, but he
bailed on me."

"Men."

"What are you doing back here?"

"I knew that you would be," Teresa said, only then no-
ticing the shotgun leaning against the wall. Covered in dust
like everything else. Audrey followed her gaze.

"For intruders," she said, in a tone Teresa did not like.
"What do you think you know, little girl?"

"You going to patch up these walls and put everything
back when you're done?"

"Funny."

"Seriously, how are you going to explain this?"

"Easy," said Audrey. "Knock over a rack or two, spray-
paint some graffiti. Then go upstairs and do the same in a
bunch of other rooms."

"Hooligans? Who happen to know the alarm code?"

"I guess you and Davie forgot to set it when you left in

such a hurry." It was madness. Only Audrey would think it a viable plan. Or not even Audrey. She was working backward from desperation, not forward from reason. "Where is Dave, anyway?"

"Checking out the grounds. He'll be here in a minute."

"No, he won't," said Audrey, in that same threatening tone. "No way he would have let you come down here by yourself. Little Tay is all alone."

She could run. Audrey would be slowed by the heavy hammer, and would have to drop it to grab the shotgun. But Teresa knew she was not going to run.

"Nothing to say, *mi Teresita*?"

"You're in the wrong spot. I told you where it was."

"You did," Audrey agreed, catching a throat full of dust and coughing. "I didn't believe you," she croaked. "Wasn't where I remembered."

"Well, you must have been panicked," Teresa said reasonably. "Somebody might have shown up. You probably weren't sure how hard you hit Ilsa, how long she would be out."

"Think you're so smart," her cousin said, almost affectionately.

"Actually, I think I'm pretty stupid not to have figured it out years ago."

"Nobody wanted to figure it out. They had Pete, or Philip, or your father to choose from, if they needed a scapegoat. Everyone wanted to forget."

"I've never forgotten."

"Your dad was a mess his whole life. You can't lay that on me."

"James has never forgotten either, has he?"

Audrey took several quick steps toward her, squeezing the hammer shaft in both fists. Teresa had no doubt that if she turned to run she would get her head caved in. She shut her eyes and stood her ground. *Where are you, Dave? Where are you, Dad? Why are you making me face this alone?* When she opened her eyes Audrey was three feet away, breathing heavily.

"You're such a great victim, Teresa, but what's really happened to you? You have seizures, like millions of people. And what do you do? Not take your medication, so you can keep having them, so you can keep playing victim."

"I never asked for your sympathy."

"You lost your crazy dad, big deal. You can have mine. You have no idea what real suffering is. I live with what happened to James every day."

"How did it happen? Why was he in the study?"

Audrey took one more step forward, her breath and sweat filling Teresa's senses. Her smile was malicious, but there was pain her in eyes.

"He was trying to save you," she whispered harshly. Then she strode back to the corner of the chamber. "So, what, right about here?"

"How?" It was all she could say for a moment. "How was he trying…"

"You were both obsessed with that room. You would stand there with your ears to the door, listening to Ramón and Alfred discuss the fate of the universe, or whatever." She swung the hammer back, then struck the wall savagely. "I didn't really understand until last week. James decided the portrait was the reason for everything. Dad beating us and Mom getting wasted and Grandpa being cruel." She struck again. Plaster and concrete flew. "And you getting sick. Don't ask me where he got that, but he was convinced he had to do something or you would die."

I'm going to help you, Tay. The floor seemed to drop out from under Teresa.

"He wanted to destroy the portrait," she said. "To free the demon."

Audrey ceased hammering and looked thoughtful.

"I don't think he'd dreamed up that bullshit yet. But on some unconscious level, yeah, I guess. I didn't get it."

"Or you never would have let him into that room."

Audrey grimaced and looked at the floor.

"Why did you tell everyone I was still in your bedroom?"

"I thought you were," Teresa replied. "The last thing I remembered was you asleep in the window seat. I must have gone out for a while. James' scream woke me up, and I saw someone run out. It was Ilsa, but I thought it was you."

"Huh. And I thought you were covering for me. All these years I thought you knew."

"I should have known. You always had keys. You had been in the study before, you used to brag about it. Used to pretend you saw the portrait."

"How do you know I didn't?"

"Because you're still afraid. Not the way James and Philip are, but like a child. You want to know, and you don't want to. That's why you made your brother look at it first."

Audrey ran at her, and Teresa knew standing her ground would not work. She stumbled backward and fell on her ass just as the hammer swept by her face. Missing by inches. The swing threw Audrey off balance, and she slammed to the floor beside her cousin. To Teresa's surprise, she did not leap up again but lay there on her stomach. Eyes squeezed shut.

"He wanted to see," Audrey cried. "He begged me to show him."

"I know," Teresa said, surprised she could form words. Her heart was beating so hard that her entire chest hurt. Not to mention her tailbone. "I know he did."

They lay on the cement floor, barely a foot apart. As if the same invisible blow had flattened them both.

"I woke up and he was gone," Audrey said. "I freaked out until I found him there, by the door." She rolled slowly onto her back. "I was so pissed off that I thought, we're going to end this curiosity thing right now. Yeah, I had the key. I let us in. Then I teased him for being too scared to look, but I never believed that he..."

"You had your back to the painting?"

"There was a cloth over it. It was always covered when Grandpa was gone, just in case. I turned my head for one second, and James yanked it off. He had a letter opener, that sharp one Grandpa owned?"

"The mini Toledo blade." Teresa saw the cloth, old and discolored. Saw a hand upon it, ready to pull it free. Her mind swerved away. "Dad gave him that."

"He slashed the canvas right across the middle. Then he screamed and fell down, like it was him who was cut open. Worst sound I ever heard anyone make. I didn't know what to do. I couldn't do anything at first, couldn't even believe it happened. It was a nightmare. One you never wake up from."

"Then Ilsa showed."

"I didn't know who it was. Didn't care. Just someone coming down the back stairs, and all I could think, Tay. All I could think was my life is over. Cause either my dad was going to kill me, and I mean literally kill me. That's what I believed. Or he was going to beat me blind and send me to one of those teenage lockups. That's what my stepmother wanted. I would have hung myself if I had to go there. My life was over."

"Unless you found a way to save it."

"Yes," Audrey exclaimed. With a profound grateful-ness at being understood. "I grabbed that fire iron and ran behind the door. And when she came in I swung like my life depended on it, because that's how it felt. Poor Ilsa."

"Then you had to hide the painting. Make it look like a robbery. How did you do that without seeing it?"

"Threw the cloth over it again. Maybe I saw something, but I was too scared of being punished to worry about a picture. I remembered the crawl space, and the stairs were right there. So I came down and slid it in as far as it would go. Then ran back upstairs to get Jenny."

He didn't do it, Teresa thought. Tears pooling in her stinging eyes and running down her face. You didn't take it, Dad. I'm so sorry I almost believed it.

"Afterward," Teresa said, "when everyone was blaming everyone, and the family was falling apart. How could you keep silent?"

Audrey sat up beside her. For all the grief in her voice, her eyes were dry.

"The family was never together, Teresa. Everyone was always at everyone's throats. You were too young to see, thought this was some kind of fairyland. Grandpa up there banging the maids while Grandma walked around humming to herself. The wives hissing at their useless husbands. Pete and Philip putting their hands all over me and my parents too drunk to notice. I didn't owe these fucking people anything."

"You were just going to leave it hidden forever?"

"I only came back a couple of times. I had this idea to hide it in the woods where someone could find it. But when I reached into the space I couldn't feel it. I couldn't tell if it was gone or just out of reach, and I was too big to climb in and look. Then they sealed the damn thing up."

"Where would it have gone?" Teresa asked in confusion. Audrey leaned over and looked into her eyes with those mad blues.

"Good question. Because there were only two people small enough to fit."

"Come on, you don't think I took it. And faked not knowing all these years? While people were accusing my father?"

"It seems unlikely. But facts are facts. That's why I was following you and James around last week."

"In the woods," Teresa said angrily. "That was you."

"Figured I could save myself knocking down a wall if one of you could lead me to where you had stowed it."

"Why was your head covered?"

"What the hell are you talking about?" She looked genuinely puzzled.

"Never mind. If either of us took it, why would we have left it here?"

"Because you were children. How would you have taken it away?" Audrey stood and dragged the sledgehammer behind her, back over to the cratered corner. "But since I've started and there's no going back, let's stop guessing. Come here and show me exactly where that opening was. Now."

Like a sleepwalker, Teresa rose and went to her. She knelt by the cool, damp wall and felt around. Keeping Audrey and the hammer in her peripheral vision at all times.

"I already tried tapping. There's no hollow sound anywhere."

Teresa tried it anyway, and found an area where the acoustics seemed slightly different. All of Audrey's blows were too high, even if she had found the right spot.

"Here," Teresa said. "But lower. It wasn't more than about two feet high."

"Christ, how am I supposed to..." Audrey dropped to her knees, facing sideways to the wall. Then she took a high grip on the shaft and swung. The first two blows barely chipped the surface, but she found her stroke, and the next few dug deep. On the fifth blow, a dark hole appeared. The women froze and looked at each other. Then Audrey seized Teresa and kissed her furiously on the forehead.

"Nice work, Tay," she said, switching to a punching motion with the hammer, opening the hole wider. "Cut you in for twenty-five percent, how does that sound?"

"Who are you planning to sell it to?"

"I got a guy lined up, don't worry. We're talking millions. You understand? Screw Ilsa and all of them. They can squabble over this mausoleum."

In a few minutes the hole was big enough for one of them to squeeze through, and that one was not Audrey. Teresa figured she could crawl in voluntarily, or be stuffed in after her cousin hammered her to death. Which she might do anyway, but with life there was hope. Unless something really bad had happened to Dave.

"Flashlight," Teresa said.

"It's here, somewhere." Audrey's voice had grown shaky, and there was a fresh film on her face that was not about exertion. If the portrait was in there, could she even face it? Or might Teresa be able to rush it out of the cellar without interference? They found the flashlight and examined what they could of the small chamber beyond the wall.

"Nothing," Audrey said anxiously. "I don't see it."

"It's bigger inside," Teresa replied, her own voice becoming constricted. Now, she told herself. The longer you wait, the more afraid you'll be. The danger is here next to you, not in there. But it was hard to make herself believe it. She lay carefully on her stomach, pushed the bright beam ahead of her, and wriggled in.

And there it was. Sitting inside the dark alcove that she and James had shared so many times, in some faraway life. Not a painting, but an old and empty wooden frame. The canvas that had once been stretched upon it was gone, though there were paint chips scattered about. And very small nails of a type that might have been popular in Madrid a hundred and fifty years earlier. Teresa held the nails in her palm and understood everything. She saw him huddled here in voiceless terror. Saw him work his fingers bloody to remove the nails. Her tears came again, in a hot torrent this time. Not for herself, or her father, but for the little boy whose soul had died here fifteen years ago.

"What's going on? Tay, is it there?"

"Pull me out."

She had the paint chips and nails in one fist and the frame

in the other, and could not use her hands. Audrey grabbed her ankles and dragged her from the hole, not gently. Teresa's jeans and sweatshirt were smeared in filth, but she kept hold of her discoveries. Audrey stared at the empty frame in incomprehension, then looked at her cousin. Teresa only sat there wiping her grimy face.

"James?" Audrey said faintly. As if testing the word before shouting it aloud. "How? How could he do that? He was afraid of it."

"Where is he?"

"Now? I don't know. You think he has it with him?"

"Maybe," Teresa said. "It was in the attic for a while. Maybe for a long time. I saw nails and paint chips like these. I just didn't put it together."

"Could it be there now?"

"He might have put it back since I've been gone. I'm guessing he has other places."

"Where?" Audrey demanded. She sat down hard, exhausted. Defeated even, which was how Teresa felt. Yet neither of them could afford that. It was no longer about Audrey's crazy scheme. It was about helping the cousin and brother they both loved.

"I don't know," Teresa sighed, her mind racing through the house ahead of her. Every room and corridor, every secret place they had ever found and forgotten. Then out the door and across the lawn and into the trees and...

"Wait. I do."

27

Audrey left the sledgehammer but took the shotgun. Teresa's insistence that they didn't need it went ignored, and she could not even swear it was true. Because clearly something bad had happened to Dave. No distraction, however serious, would have kept him this long.

"Unless *he* found it, and took off with it," Audrey posited. Having decided to believe in his presence just in time to make a thief of him. The idea incensed her. "The shifty bastard, I'll murder him."

"Dave did not take the painting," Teresa said, as they marched across the darkening lawn.

"How do you know?" Audrey's eyes were everywhere, expecting a trap. She handled the shotgun too casually, shifting it from hand to shoulder to elbow crook. "What does either of us really know about the guy? He's stolen paintings before. Maybe he's been playing all of us the whole time."

Teresa was anxious enough for such a foolish idea to get a foothold in her imagination. Yet she almost wished it were true. It would mean that Dave was safe, and the painting was out of their lives. Her gut told her there was no way it would be that simple.

"I'm sorry about what happened to you," she said.

"What?" Audrey asked irritably.

"With Philip, and I guess Pete, too. I didn't know."

"Hey, don't go inducting me into your cult of victim-hood. Nothing happens to me without my say-so, okay?"

"I'm sure it's important for you to feel that way."

"Shut up." She swung the shotgun in Teresa's direction. "Philip is my bitch, always has been. Pete was crazy, but nothing serious happened. He's the only one I feel bad about. I mean okay, he's a thief, but they were harder on him than they had to be. Ten years, hell."

"Five," Teresa corrected. "He earned the rest while he was inside. So that's why you made Philip testify for him, because you felt guilty."

"Phil *hated* doing that," Audrey jeered. "I didn't give him a choice. Yanked that chain and he did what he was told. I own him."

"Do you own Kenny, too?"

"Nah, that was only one time. Before he figured out he liked boys."

Teresa stopped short. She could not even speak before Audrey was laughing at her.

"Of course. You would be the only woman in the family who doesn't know that."

"But all those girls…"

"Yeah, different one every month, right? Maybe he

sleeps with some, I don't know. Look, he's a handsome guy. Smart, fun to hang out with."

"Are you saying that's his secret? That's what was in the letter?"

"You know another one?"

"Mother of God," Teresa nearly screamed. "It's the twenty-first century. It's cool to be gay now."

"Not everywhere. Not in the tiny mind of Philip Morse anyway. Or Alfred."

"So Grandpa knew."

"Yeah. Probably Ilsa told him. She's tattled on all of us. For two generations. I think the deal was he had to get married and produce a child within a certain time."

"That's ridiculous."

"Right? For two-fifty? Now for a million, maybe."

"But Philip doesn't know."

"No, and Kenny's afraid of him finding out." Audrey shook her head. "It's pathetic. Gives me leverage with him, though, so it's all good."

"Is there anyone in this family you don't have leverage on?"

"You," Audrey spat, looking unhappy about it. "Now where are we going?"

"Haven't you figured it out?" Teresa started forward again. Stopping had been a mistake, it let fatigue catch up. She was tired enough to fall down on the grass and sleep, but not yet. The pines were ahead. Another chance to make a break for it. Rush in among them, get low and switch directions. But she was too curious, she had to know if it was there. In a minute or so of thrusting branches aside they were in front of the old oak.

"The tree house?" Audrey said.

"Close." Even if Pete had not broken one of the rungs, it would be too far for Teresa to reach the hollow spot. "You'll have to give me a boost."

She expected some complaint, but Audrey only examined the trunk until understanding transformed her face.

"The hellhole," she exclaimed, leaning the gun against the tree. "Damn, I should have thought of that."

"Hellhole?"

"That's what we always called it. It was, like, the door to hell."

"I didn't remember," Teresa said.

"You were afraid of everything. Maybe we weren't allowed to say it in front of you."

It seemed depressingly likely. How could such harmless exclusions mean anything to her now, yet they still stung.

Before Teresa was ready, Audrey seized her around the thighs and lifted. Teresa clawed at the thick bark, ascending until she had a hand on the opening of the hole. Audrey shifted her grip down around the knees to boost her higher. To where Teresa could look straight into the dim cavity. The hellhole. It was deep. Deep enough to hide a serving platter, she knew that. Not quite wide enough for the portrait still on its frame, but surely for the loose canvas. It was too dark to see inside, but she sensed a presence. Not malevolent, as Dave had described it, but dismal. Forsaken. Full of a misery that had soaked into its every fiber, and now emanated from it. Just an arm's length away, if she was right. Nothing to do but put her hand in. She hesitated until she felt Audrey's grip weakening, then lunged.

"Anything?"

Leaves, mulch and something else. Not heavy enough. Paper, not canvas. Teresa drew it into the waning light and recognized the sketch of James she had done last week. Crumpled and stained despite being carefully folded. He had been here, he was using this place. But no Goya. Did he no longer have it? Had he ever?

"Would you look at this," said a voice close by. An insinuating male voice that Teresa had not heard in years. "Hello, beautiful girls."

"Pete," Audrey said coldly, letting go of her cousin's legs. Teresa thrust her arm back into the hole to catch herself while her feet swung four feet above the ground.

"Here we all are again," said Pete. "Like a family reunion."

There was something wrong with his voice, and Teresa twisted her head to look. The same green army jacket, stained brown in front with the blood from Fred's beating. His face was so bruised that Teresa would not have known him. One eye was red with broken vessels, and there were scabs on his split lips, impeding speech. He looked dazed, but not dazed enough to miss Audrey leaning for the shotgun. His right arm swung up, pointing at her.

"Now, now, missy. That ain't friendly."

He was not pointing, Teresa realized. There was a small black pistol in his hand. She did not believe he would shoot, but evidently Audrey did. She straightened up.

"What are you doing, Pete? Haven't you been in enough trouble?"

"Trouble, yeah." He dropped the arm to his side again. "It's a troubled world. I didn't make it. What are you two up to here?"

"Right now I'm hanging on for life," Teresa said, her arm growing sore.

"You hear?" Pete grunted with a little smile. "Better help her down."

"She's fine," Audrey said, not moving. Teresa realized no assistance was coming, and the drop was not far, just awkward. She pulled her arm free and fell. Her left foot hit a big root, and she felt a twinge in the ankle. Audrey caught her hand and tugged her to standing. The two of them faced Pete, about eight feet away. The shotgun was between and just behind them, leaning on the oak.

"What's that?" Pete asked, pointing at the folded paper Teresa still clutched.

"A sketch I did."

"Must be an important sketch to hide it. That's my spot, you realize. I feel a kind of ownership of anything that ends up there, know what I'm saying?"

"Audrey's right. You don't need any more trouble, and there are other people around."

"Sure are. Two of them are laid out in the woods right now. Couple of your playthings, I do believe," he said, leering at Audrey.

"They dead?" she asked, seeming only mildly curious.

"Hard to say with head wounds. The seriousness. One's in bad shape, for sure."

"Either of them dies, and I'll kill you," she promised. She, who was unarmed, speaking to the crazy man with the pistol. Yet it was Pete who seemed discomfited. Un-nerved in a way that his flickering grin could not hide.

"You used to like me," he said morosely.

"I like you fine. I'll like you better if you help us out, instead of messing with us."

Teresa would never find out what sort of help Audrey meant. Pete's gaze drifted past Teresa's left shoulder and fixed on something. The lost and bloody eyes sprang open in wonder. Shifting quickly to fear.

"What the hell is that?"

Teresa and Audrey turned together. Twenty or thirty yards off through the trees, a figure approached. Its clothes were all gray. Its head and shoulders were covered. Its footfalls were inaudible. Tree trunks intervened and it was gone. Then suddenly there again, much closer. Maybe ten yards away. None of them spoke. All three held their breath, unmoving, as if bound by a spell. Until Pete swung the pistol up.

"Stay where you are." The ghost came on, neither hurrying nor pausing. "Stay back, damn it. What *is* it?" Pete demanded, just before he pulled the trigger twice.

Small as the gun was, the shots were stunningly loud, and Teresa felt physically propelled against the tree trunk, hands over her ears.

"No," Audrey screamed, stepping directly in front of Pete, where the next shot would strike her. And Teresa was certain Pete meant to shoot again. Terror had full possession of him. He would empty the weapon into Audrey, the ghost, the trees, whatever target presented itself. Not assessing damage until the fever broke.

The gun discharged a final time, but Pete was already pitching sideways. A man in a dark jacket had barreled out of the pines and caught the shooter low, bringing them both to the ground with a dull thud and the groan of expelled breath. The second man was Dave, Teresa realized, though the blood on his face had disguised him. There was a gash on his forehead and one eye sagged, but he was pummeling Pete as best he could.

Audrey's eyes flared in shock and rage, and she looked down at herself. Prepared for whatever she found, but there was nothing. The bullet had missed. Blinking once, she went for the shotgun, swinging it up and aiming at the two wrestling men. Teresa saw that Pete was now on top, but more than that she saw that Audrey did not care whom she hit. She meant to hurt someone. Teresa ran at her, knocking her shoulder as Audrey squeezed the trigger. There was a loud click, no more.

"It's not loaded?" Audrey shouted at Teresa. Looking as if she might beat the smaller woman with the empty gun.

"Don't ask me. You're the one hauling it around."

"I thought my dad… Never mind, go after him. Okay? You go after him. Go," she shouted a last time before rushing toward the struggling men.

Teresa stood motionless. As if bumping Audrey had taken all her strength. She knew that she should help Dave, yet her instinct and her cousin's words pushed her the other way. The twin impulses froze her in place. *You go after him.* She saw a vision of her father, his face twisted in pain, ready to fall forward into a dark abyss. *It is all surface, my girl. Do not trust it. Look deeper, look beneath.* She glanced again at the pile of writhing bodies to see Audrey with her arm around Pete's neck, dragging him off of Dave. That was enough. She turned to the spot where the ghost had vanished and ran that way.

The ankle was hurt worse than she had realized. She

ran with a limp, slowing with every stride. It did not matter. The figure had not gone far. It rested upon its knees
in a small clearing of ferns and maple saplings. Swaying
slightly. The sun was behind the trees, and the canvas over
the figure's head seemed to glow in the twilight. Teresa
approached cautiously. More concerned about startling the
ghost, or of waking from the dream in which she had conjured it, than of any harm it might do her. She dropped
to her knees, reached out a shaking hand and took hold of
the rough cloth. Her heart rose within her, and she longed
to speak the precious word aloud: *Dad*. But she knew, she
knew before she dragged the canvas from the sweaty, tou-
sled hair that it was not so. Only a fantasy she had let herself believe for a few brief days. The deeper part of her,
where her father still lived and instructed her, where so
many things were understood that Teresa would not let
herself see—that part had known all along, or at least since
the day she and Fred stood together by the oak, whom she
would find under the painted mask.

"Tay," James said, his face deathly pale, his eyes wide
with puzzlement. Then concern. "Don't look."

The canvas lay in a heap between them, Teresa's hand
still clutching the edge. Despite the warning, she smoothed
it out flat, and gazed upon the family demon. There had
surely been paint loss before Alfred Morse took possession
of the work, and much more since it was pulled from the
frame. Its strength dispersed in paint chips strewn around
the house and property. Yet great power remained. The
background was all brown murk. Only a shadow of the
face that had caused death and madness remained, but that
shadow carried more horror and desolation than any Te-

resa had seen, flesh or pigment. Details suggested Goya's countenance, the curly gray hair and broad nose, but these shrank to insignificance beside the overall effect. Of the intelligent black eyes from other portraits there was no trace, only yellow-white orbs. The skin was jaundiced and blotched, and the mouth hung open in an endless scream, revealing brown and broken teeth. It was not simply an image capable of shocking a fearful and diseased heart into inaction. It was a profound vision of despair. An emotional black hole leeching hope from the very air around it. A spirit in mourning would find no help here, only the knowledge that its grief would be endless and without respite. Death, or the headlong flight from sanity, would seem a wise decision.

Teresa did not see how a soul in this state of collapse could manage to create such a brilliant and devastating work. Sadness and compassion welled up in her, drowning out all other feeling. She was not afraid. Perhaps because the blood that protected her father protected her also. Or possibly because she had been immunized by her previous viewing. Fifteen years ago, the night before her grandmother's funeral. When her father Ramón had taken her into the study and shown her the painting. She ran her hand across the slash mark her cousin had made hours later, trying valiantly to heal her. Teresa's eyes filled again. She grasped his cold hand and looked up at him. His gaze had not moved from her face for an instant.

"Thank you, James. Thank you for saving me."

His face showed confusion, then transformed into an expression of astonishment Teresa had never seen there.

"Did we do it?" he asked thickly, his throat full. "Is it gone?"

"Yes," she assured him. "Yes, it's gone."

He smiled. There was blood on his teeth. It dribbled over his lower lip, and then he pitched forward. Teresa caught him, but his weight pressed them both to the cold bed of leaves. She extracted herself from under him and, with great effort, rolled him onto his back. His eyes looked vacantly skyward. The bubbling blood at his mouth told her he was still breathing. It was only then she noticed the dark patch on his coat. She pulled it open gently to see the large red stain on the T-shirt underneath. One of Pete's bullets had found its mark. Teresa tugged her phone out and dialed 911, squeezing James' hand as she calmly reported shots fired, one victim and possibly more, and the address. Then she pulled her sweatshirt over her head and looked for a clean patch.

"I'm not sorry," James said weakly. "Some people never do anything important with their lives."

"This is going to hurt," said Teresa, "but it's necessary."

He grabbed her wrists before she could press the balled shirt to his wound. His hands were still remarkably strong.

"I am sorry about Grandma."

"You didn't hurt her."

"I did," he gasped, the pain finally hitting. "I pushed her down the steps on the terrace. I didn't mean to. I was misbehaving, and she said I had a devil in me. It made me so mad. I was fighting off the demon every day, like you were. He wanted us, but we were fighting him, and then she said that."

"It's okay, let me stop the bleeding now."

"I didn't know. I didn't know children could hurt grown-ups. Grandpa saw."

"I'm sure he knew it was an accident."

"He never told, but he never forgave me. All those years, writing down my mistakes. He wanted me locked away."

A spasm of pain made him grab at the wound and kick his feet. When it backed off he no longer had strength to resist, and Teresa pressed the shirt to the wound.

"It hurts," James whimpered.

"I'm sorry," she said, not relieving the pressure. "I have to."

"I know. I know you would never hurt me for no reason. You've always tried to help, I know that."

"I've done nothing," she cried, choking on the words. "I've been useless."

"You understood," he whispered, closing his eyes. "You always understood me. That meant so much."

"Open your eyes, James. Talk to me."

"I'm not sorry about Grandpa," he said defiantly. "I'm not sorry about him."

"He said that he wanted you locked up? Like, an institution?"

"He was the one who needed locking up. *Him*. He said I would have to be there a long time. And Audrey. Audrey would have to be my guardian."

"To get the money," Teresa said.

"I was so proud of her when she burned the letter. So proud of us all."

"Me, too."

"I told him it was his fault. What I am, he made me. I tried to destroy it, but it went inside of me instead. Then when I tried to hide, when I tried to hide from what it had done to me, it was there. In our secret place, Tay. I climbed in and it was *there*, waiting for me."

"I know." She could not tell him it was Audrey. That would be too cruel.

"He didn't believe. Grandpa. He waved his hand like I was…"

A coughing fit took the rest, and he turned his face to spit a red wad. A gunshot sounded in the faraway woods. Then another. The fight had moved. God help them all. Teresa hoisted James' head onto her leg so he could breathe, while keeping what pressure she could on the wound. The sweatshirt was nearly soaked. Too fast. Too much blood. Such a small gun and so much blood.

"Okay," she said, "don't think about that. Just breathe."

"I had to show him," James gasped, sounding exhausted. "I had to show him what he made. I let the demon appear."

"You got the canvas from the attic and put it on."

"I let it appear," he repeated stubbornly. "Unlocked the window. Ilsa drove me to the train but I didn't get on. I came back. I let the demon appear in the study. Grandpa would come there at night, when he couldn't sleep. He walked in and saw it in his chair and…he believed then. Just for a minute, or half a minute, before it took his soul. But he believed it all then."

He clenched up again, but only briefly before he seemed to relax completely. Teresa thought she had lost him, but he was still there.

"I shouldn't have let it appear," James said. "It's had me ever since. I thought we might put it back inside, you

know? Like Goya did, we might do it again. I don't know
how you… How did you defeat it?"

"We did it together."

"Don't let them lock me up, please."

"I won't," she promised. "I won't let that happen."

"I'm tired. I'm going to stop now. You keep talking."

"What should I say?"

"Anything. Say anything, I like your voice. Tell me a
story."

So Teresa did. She told a long and rambling tale she
would not remember later. About a boy who fought a
demon and won. She spoke forcefully and without cease
while pressing the shirt to his chest, until she heard the
approaching wail of the ambulance. She went on talking,
went on weaving the myth long after James had gone still.

28

It had struck Dave before that personal insights came during times of duress, and were usually fleeting. The night he found Ray Castro—or whatever his real name was—murdered in North Miami, the adrenal surge of fear and the relief at escaping alive rearranged his perspective. Driving away, he wanted desperately to call Luisa. Not to harangue her for being an emotional coward, nor to beg her to come back. But to thank her for sticking with him as long as she did, and apologize for everything he had put her through. He never made the call. Struggling now with a frantic Pete Mulhane, head screaming and blind in one eye, Dave remembered that old impulse, and wondered if he would live long enough to make good on it this time.

Pete had punched him twice and was going for three when he inexplicably paused. Only then did Dave see Audrey's arm on Pete's throat, pulling him backward. Dave assisted with a kick in the stomach that sent the other two reeling, then looked around for the pistol. A little black nine-millimeter, Glock maybe. Dave didn't know guns that well. There it was, near the base of the oak. No sooner did he start toward it than a foot struck his face. He could not say if it was Pete or Audrey, nor even what day of the week it was for a couple of seconds. Someone kicked the gun, which sailed past him into the weeds. He heard a few more thumps and grunts before his senses returned. As he sat up, Audrey was rushing away into the trees. Pete was nowhere in sight. Nor was Teresa, whom Dave had not seen since he tackled Pete. He crawled over to the crushed and fragrant weeds, but it was too much to hope the gun was still there. One of them had it, no knowing which.

He rose slowly, glad that he had vomited already and did not need to again. Then he lumbered in the direction that Audrey had disappeared. Trees continually leaped in front of him, and Dave careened off these without falling. Stealth was not possible, and probably pointless. Pete, he guessed, had moved from fight to flight, and Audrey was pursuing, armed or not. He didn't like any of their chances, but someone was bound to survive, and it could as easily be Dave as anyone else. He began to succumb to morbid laughter, but it hurt and he stopped. The woods. Oh, man, he hated the woods.

Back in the sightless pines, a gunshot made him stop and crouch. Another followed it quickly, but there was no whirr of bullets passing. He was near the lawn, and pulled branches aside for a better look. Within moments, he spied two figures racing across the green. Dave stood warily, then bulled his way through to the grass.

He saw Audrey first, in the dust-caked jeans and tank

top, the pistol held out before her in both hands. Pete was thirty feet beyond, backing up slowly toward the sea ledge and talking fast. Dave shouted something a dog might understand; he sure as hell did not. But it got Audrey's attention, and a moment later the pistol was pointed at him.

"Jus, jus hoedon," he heaved. "Youdawanna."

"What the fuck are you saying?" she demanded. The mad look was in her eyes. She did not know him right now, or knowing him would not matter.

"You don't want to shoot anyone today," Dave translated for himself.

"Oh yeah," she said, eyeing him along the top of the black pistol. She had a bloody nose and brightly flushed cheeks. "I do." She swung ninety degrees back toward Pete. "This son of a bitch right here."

"I was protecting all of us," Pete insisted. "You saw that, that…"

"All I see is some psycho ex-con, who beats up and shoots everyone he runs into. You don't deserve to live."

"Nobody deserves to live," Pete said savagely. "You can't judge me. No one in your twisted family can judge me."

"Stay still."

"I ain't moving. Shoot if you've got the nerve, little girl."

"Audrey," Dave said sharply, approaching within a dozen feet. "You can't do that."

"Watch me."

"You can't take it back when you stop being angry. It's permanent."

"Shut up," she snarled. "You're next."

"What do you got against him?" Pete asked.

"He's a thief."

"Oh yeah? Well, good for you, man. Steal everything you can from these cheap pricks. They don't pay their debts."

"Pete," Dave said, seeing the man was a yard from the ledge. "Don't take another step."

Dave was now six feet from Audrey. Close enough to rush her. She noticed the same thing from the corner of her eye and took two quick steps forward. Dave saw her close one eye, saw her fingers go white and the muscles in her forearm clench. All the signs of someone a split second from pulling the trigger, and yet he knew she would not.

"Stop," Audrey commanded. Whether she was telling Pete to stand still, or warning him, or speaking to someone or something else entirely, Dave did not know. Pete only registered her quick advance and instinctively retreated. To where no ground supported him. He plunged backward over the ledge and was gone.

Audrey made a confused noise as her arms fell to her sides. Dave's gut dropped with the ex-Marine, ex-handyman, ex-con who had gotten the better of him three times. He pulled a quick breath and rushed to the edge. It was not so far a fall, thirty feet at most. But it was steep and rocky and Pete had landed badly. The water surging around him obscured any sign of blood, but he was completely still. A piece of ragged flotsam in the white surf.

"How do we get down there?" Dave asked, turning back to Audrey. Only to find the pistol pointed at him again. Her expression had changed. She looked hurt and fragile, and sorry about what she had to do next.

"You were supposed to protect us," she said, her voice breaking. Dave felt the rebuke deep within his sore chest.

God knew he had tried. There were so many lies and agendas. But he hated excuses and explanations himself, and could see Audrey wanted none. She intended to act this time, and he guessed he knew what she would do.

"I failed, Audrey. We fail sometimes."

"Yeah," she said. "I let my brother die."

That took him a moment, but only a moment. The ghostly figure in the trees that Pete had shot at.

"We don't know. He may be all right."

"No. He died years ago. Everything since. Trying to protect him all this time, it was pointless."

Dave started toward her, slow and steady. She raised the weapon higher.

"Just because I didn't shoot Pete doesn't mean I won't shoot you."

"It's not me you want to hurt."

Four steps, three steps, two. She turned the gun on herself as he reached her. He caught her wrist with his left hand and seized the top of the pistol with his right. She hit his shoulder with her free hand and the barrel swung back and forth, pointing briefly at each of them. But her finger never squeezed, and a moment later he had the gun away from her. She punched his chest a few more times, but there was no screaming or crying. Her face looked like someone who had just woken up.

After a time, Audrey dropped her arms and stared past him to the water. The breeze off the Sound was cold. Dave waited half a minute longer and put his arms around her. She was stiff as a corpse at first, but eventually relaxed into his embrace. Not returning it.

"Everything is so messed up."

"Yes," he agreed.

"What am I going to do, Davie?"

"I don't know. What would your brother want you to do?"

She had no answer for that, but it occupied her mind as he walked her back toward the house.

29

In 1824 Francisco de Goya traded his internal exile for the truer kind, moving to Bordeaux, where he died four years later. Medical treatment was the official reason, but disaffection with the reactionary regime in Spain was the more likely cause. Or maybe, Teresa considered, he just needed to escape the house he had defaced with his misery. He never recorded his feelings about the Black Paintings. He never spoke of them. Leading many to assume that he had not made them, for how could work of such terrifying magnificence go unmentioned? Goya suffered the usual illnesses and regrets of old men, but as far as history could report, no demon haunted his last days.

"You think it was all invented?" Dave asked, hunched over his coffee. He had a small reddish dent on his forehead that was likely permanent, but otherwise he was unbruised and unhampered by pain for the first time since Teresa had met him.

"All what? There was a painting. We saw it."

"You know what I mean. The power to unhinge the mind. To kill."

"Art has power," Teresa said, clutching her own coffee mug. The November chill on Amsterdam Avenue had gotten to her. "We're moved to tears by poetry, or by music."

"It's not the same thing."

"It is," she insisted. "It's a matter of degree. People walk out of disturbing plays, or have heart attacks during movies. There's this bad boy author whose stuff is so provocative that audience members pass out at his readings."

"That's, like, power of suggestion or something."

"Exactly. That's exactly what it is. Grandpa Morse invites a nervous, overweight expert to see the portrait. The guy has already heard and read everything. He's strung tight as a bow. The scene is set, the lights are dim, he's left alone to pull off the cloth and…"

"Kapow goes his heart," said Dave, nodding. "You think Alfred meant to kill him?"

"He couldn't have planned on it, but I don't think he was sorry."

"That's what DeGross said." Dave leaned back and glanced around the cramped Hungarian Pastry Shop. Students, visitors to Saint John the Divine Cathedral across the street, artists, the lost and lonely, all crowded in on this gray day to load up on caffeine and oversweet strudel. Despite being rested and healed, Dave was missing something vital, Teresa thought. He was like one of those working dogs—a border collie, maybe—when it did not have a job to do. Anxious and blue. "What about James?"

"What about him?"

"That wasn't just fear. It sounds like he became some-one else."

"You never knew him," Teresa said sadly. "You relied on my portrayal, and I've come to understand that I didn't know him either. Not everything. I heard more from Lau-rena about the incidents at school, going at Audrey with the knife. Apparently he could be violent, on small prov-ocation. Look, he shoved my grandmother down the ter-race steps before he had even seen the portrait. The sweet part of him, which was real, which is who he mostly was, couldn't reconcile his own behavior. He needed an explana-tion. It was the painting making him do it. He fought and lost, and then it owned him. He was sweet, gentle James ninety percent of the time. And the demon when he was angry, when he wanted to harm. I don't think it was put on. I think he believed it completely."

"That's pretty extraordinary," he said. Sounding either skeptical or disappointed, she could not tell which.

"I'm sorry, Dave. Did you want it to be magic?"

He looked briefly irritated, but then smiled.

"Sure. Didn't you?"

"Once upon a time."

"We'll have to settle for bringing it back into the world. That's all I wanted to do when I started out. Recover lost great art."

"I guess we did that."

"I wasn't gloating," he said quickly. "I know the cost was too high, Teresa."

So it was. She had spent the last month meditating on the losses the discovery had incurred. Pete had been court-ing destruction since he got out of prison. She did not celebrate his death, but she wondered who else he might have taken with him had he hung around longer. James would haunt her for the rest of her life. She had so desperately wanted to save him. Yet the fate he most feared had surely awaited. Institutionalization. Mind-scrubbing medication. Was it craven of her to squeeze solace from the knowledge that he had escaped all that? The worst damage may have been to the living.

"Audrey sends regards," Teresa said.

"Huh." Dave looked uneasy. "How is she?"

"No idea, honestly. She left the country as soon as they decided not to charge her."

"They didn't have anything. Shotgun wasn't loaded. She didn't shoot Pete, and that could have been self-defense. It would have taken Ilsa pursuing the vandalism, or you reporting the hammer attack."

"You're the only one I told about that," Teresa replied, trying to sound casual. "It wasn't much of an attack."

"She could easily have killed you," he said, seeing her discomfort. If Audrey did harm in the years to come, it would be on Teresa's head. For not exposing the dangerous creature she had glimpsed behind that cool-girl exterior. No one else would agree, but Teresa understood that she had taken responsibility for her cousin. They were bound.

"If she shot Pete, would you have covered for her?"

"I don't know," Dave answered after a pause. "Maybe. Where is she, anyway?"

"Croatia. The Dalmatian Coast."

"I hear it's quite the place," Dave said with a wistful smile.

"She sounded okay, better than I expected. It was the

first time I'd heard from her since, you know." She paused for a sip of coffee, trying not to say more, and failing. "You should go over there and find her."

Dave gave her a long and poignant look.

"No," he said with quiet finality. "That's not happening. How is Philip?"

"Still in rehab. Speaking normally now, but he's not right. Head trauma. There could be lasting personality change."

"Sorry if I'm not broken up," said Dave. "He's more or less responsible for all of this. If he didn't have the decency to die, the least he can do is change his rotten personality."

"You cash that check?" she asked, which was unkind of her.

"I did," he answered without apology. "It got me through the last month, but something needs to break soon."

"They suspended your license."

"Only in Connecticut. Oh, and Florida, but that's old. I'm still good in New York, for now. Did Fred ever show up?"

"Last week, motel room in Nevada. Alcohol poisoning. Laurena has him in a clinic now. This will be his third try, and after what happened to his son…"

"You think he knew it was James? That day in the woods?"

"Maybe not consciously. But any parent knows his child, even at a distance. The way they hold themselves, the way they move. Something registered."

"With you, too?"

"Faintly. I was still trying to make him into my father at that point."

"Yeah. How is your mother?"

"Doing better than anyone. She told Ilsa the family won't contest. Ilsa's selling the house and there's been talk of setting up a fund. Medical expenses for Philip and Fred, maybe a trust that ends up with the remaining grandchildren. Eventually."

"How about that? They should have left it to the women in the first place."

"The only thing is Audrey put a curse on any of us who touched that money. So I don't know. I may have to work for a living."

"Take it from me, it sucks."

"No, you love it. It's what you do. Hunt clues, get people to reveal themselves. You're good at it."

"You're generous. That was the most screwed-up, unsystematic investigation of my life. Kind of hard when your employer is your biggest obstacle, but still. You're pretty good at it yourself. We should go into business."

She was so tempted to take him seriously that she did not let herself answer.

"Is the art collection all settled?" Dave asked.

"My work is done. At least until the will clears probate. I've been painting. I quit for a long time, but I'm feeling the urge again."

"That's great. Can I ask what?"

"A portrait. It was a request, though at this point it's really just for me. Hey," she said, before he could ask her any more on the topic. "Did you call your wife?"

"Oh." He was surprised she remembered, or maybe surprised that he had mentioned it. "Ex-wife. Yes, I did."

"How did that go?"

"Pretty well, I guess. She wasn't thrilled to hear from me, but she did listen patiently."

"You needed to hear yourself say it," Teresa replied. "So? Is a reconciliation possible?"

"Reconciliation?" He looked puzzled, then amused. "Is that what you thought? No, she remarried years ago. They have two kids. Like you said, I just needed to do it, for me."

"Oh. Okay."

"Are there any more women you want to throw me at, or are we done?"

She covered her face and laughed. It felt good, even with her embarrassment.

"Um, I'll let you know. Thanks for doing this, Dave. Coming up here."

"My pleasure. I've thought about you pretty often this last month."

"Yeah? You had my phone number."

"I wanted to give you space. You went through a lot. Would have been understandable if you wanted to forget everyone and everything associated with the whole business."

"I'm not a forgetter."

"Well, don't be a dweller in the past either. Also, you know. I'm a little old to be hanging out with college girls."

"How old are you, anyway?"

"Forty last June. A very old forty."

"Big deal. I'll be twenty-seven in January. My father was twenty years older than my mother. Oh, God," she laughed again, "look at your face."

"What?"

"Don't worry, I'm not confused. You are not my father,

and I am not your wife. Just, next time you're going to the Jersey Shore, give me a call."

"Pretty bleak down there this time of year," he mused. "Then again, it's a long time until next summer."

Neither of them said any more until they had paid up and were standing on the sidewalk.

The face of the cathedral rose dramatically before them. There were no tall buildings around to challenge its scale. The soot-blackened statues above the doors were life-size, Teresa knew, yet from here looked tiny in the massive and richly ornamented face. The gray sky broke open in blue patches, and low clouds raced above the perpetually half-finished towers.

"Amazing, huh?" said Dave.

"I never get tired of looking at it," she replied.

"Teresa. It's not my business, but I can't get it out of my head. Why do you think your father showed you that portrait?"

She gazed at the sky a little longer before turning to face him. He had such a kind and curious way of looking at her. Men were always searching for their own reflection in women's faces. Not Dave.

"He was trying to heal me. Trying to calm my noisy mind. Call it shock therapy, if you want, but he meant it with love. I'm not angry with him, Dave. Don't you be."

"All right."

"Have you been inside," she asked, gesturing to the great church.

"Not for many years."

"Do you want to go in?"

"Don't you have class or something?"

"Yes or no?"

"Yes," he said. "I would like that."

They crossed the avenue together, and started up the wide stone steps.

★ ★ ★ ★ ★

Acknowledgements

My editor Peter Joseph saw instantly what this book could be, and expertly shaped it into the package you hold. It's an honor to play a part in launching Hanover Square Press. Thanks to Meredith Barnes, Kayla King, Margaret Marbury, and everyone at HSP/Harlequin in the US. In the UK, thanks to Charlotte Mursell and Lucy Richardson at HQ. A more caring and energetic group is hard to imagine.

Thanks to Judy Sternlight and Jake Morrissey for bucking me up when I was ready to quit.

Thanks to the Olsons: Brad, and Brad, Cameron, Elizabeth, Laura, Marcia, and my father, Neil, all of whom have inspired and supported me beyond measure. My mother, Rose, artist and teacher, instilled in me a love of painters and painting practically before I could speak, and first turned me on to Goya.

Thanks to Caroline for sharing the joy, and the pain, and for more things than I can possibly say.

ONE PLACE. MANY STORIES

Bold, innovative and
empowering publishing.

FOLLOW US ON:

@HQStories